THE HEART OF IT ALL

BOOK 1

Pillar's Fire

Michelle Heisel

Published by Michelle Heisel

ISBN: 978-0-9986935-0-7
Ebook ISBN: 978-0-9986935-4-5

Cover art by Extended Imagery
Cover design by Extended Imagery and Cody Heisel

Printed in the United States of America

www.michelleheisel.com

Praise for Michelle Heisel's
Pillar's Fire

"If you are a fan of Dystopian Fiction, like the Divergent Series, you will enjoy this book!...The author does an amazing job describing this emotional change in the characters...This book will keep you guessing about which characters are trustworthy or deceitful."

- Rachael L. (Librarian, MLS)

"The suspense pulled me in! This thriller has action, heart, and hope!"

- Debbie W. (Coordinator for local writer's group)

"This book had me hooked from the very beginning! Michelle created relatable characters who easily draw you into their world. This is one of those books that make you look at life around you a little differently than you have before. If you like stories that you can't put down and after the last page leave you wanting to know what's next for main character Miracle....then Pillar's Fire is perfect for you!"

- Nancy V.

Look for the next book in

THE HEART OF IT ALL

Wormwood's Water

Mira had thought that by finding the powerful book – the Enchiridion of Emmanuel – that she'd be satisfied in the colorful world it had unleashed. But she's not. When a friend is tragically murdered, and Nash, the guy she'd thought she'd be with forever, leaves her to go on tour, Mira's hopelessness spikes to an all-time high. She connects with a group that shows her how she can create the life she wants and make destiny work for her. At first the path she takes refreshes her soul and quenches her thirst for significance, but then she discovers the bitter truth that lurks beneath the surface. Join Mira and Nash in Wormwood's Water as their journeys collide and reveal the truth even as they threaten to destroy everything they truly hold dear.

*Our hearts are the core of who we are — the deep-down real "us", the part that urges us to keep going when we need to…the part that connects us with something bigger than ourselves…the part that weaves our inner selves with our purpose and perspective. Sometimes we lose heart and we wonder, "Why am I even living this life? Where does my story fit in? Why do I feel like my heart is aching for more…of something?" In **Pillar's Fire**, the first in* The Heart of It All *series, Mira's heart burns for more than the colorless world she finds herself in. Along her journey she discovers a powerful enemy, a deep and fierce love, and unexpected answers to the yearning of her heart.*

Do you ever feel like you don't fit in, no matter how hard you try? When I was young, I often felt this way. Then I asked, "What if I had the power to change the world around me so that I did fit in?" This mindset led me to start many "groups" over the years, all of which created a place to belong. In Pillar's Fire, the first novel in The Heart of It All *series, Mira's journey, like my own, begins with an inner longing to change her emotionless world to one filled with color and passion, a world where she can fit in and thrive.*

Chapter 1

Miracle pressed her forehead against the glass of the dining room window. She could see Pillar's city park clearly. It was a cold and lonely place, just like her home…her family. It didn't feel right anymore, not since the episodes started.

"Still working on that history assignment?"

Mira didn't turn at the sound of her mom's voice. "Almost done," she said, prying herself away from the window to go sit at the table. The stiff metal chair she settled into seemed like ice against her skin. She didn't react, though. She couldn't let herself. Squinting down at the Newscreen, her city-issued computer tablet used for homework, Mira asked, "Where's Dad?"

"Too busy to shadow me for once in his life."

A shadow…good name for him, Mira thought. "Can I ask you a question?"

"Of course," her mom said, walking toward the table.

"What was it like…before the war?"

Her mom paused before sitting down beside her. "Isn't it in your history book?"

"I guess." Mira swiped a finger across the screen to turn the page. "I just wanted to hear it from you. You were there, right?"

"I was only seven when the war ended, so I don't remember much."

"What *do* you remember?"

Her mom looked toward the hallway. "I remember hiding in the bathtub when the bombs went off," she said softly. "I remember seeing my teacher being beaten and then killed for what she taught." She looked down at her hands. "I saw someone thrown off a roof once, too." She shook her head. "But all that was thirty years ago." She took a deep breath. "And now we have LifeChips to make sure our world isn't destroyed by passions ever again."

Mira looked down at her tablet, which showed the city of Pillar in shambles with dead bodies lying everywhere while other people roamed around crying. "Do you remember anything good?"

Her mom shifted in her chair. "Why so many questions?"

That she'd spoken with a soft urgency instead of the usual monotonous rote made Mira want to look up, but she didn't dare because the pressure behind her eyes suddenly surged. It felt like her brain was expanding and trying to make room by pushing her eyeballs out of their sockets. She shifted sideways so that her back was to her mom. "No reason." She squeezed her eyes shut, but couldn't stop their quivering. *Go away,* her mind begged.

"There has to be a reason." Her mom gently turned her around to face her and gasped. "What's wrong?"

"Nothing." Mira jumped up, and after a glance down the hallway that was thankfully still empty, she said, "I'm going to my room to finish my homework." As she fumbled for the Newscreen, her mom grabbed her arm.

"Let me go." Mira yanked her arm from her mom's grasp, but it was too late. Nothing could stop it now. The tablet fell from her hands and her eyes rolled back. "Please! Just give me…" she rasped, "a minute." She slumped back into her chair as the images flew at her – the deep dark cavity of groaning voices, the man who helped her, who showed her the flashes of color and light in a mysterious world so unlike her own. Slowly, the pressure disappeared, but the vision did not. Finally, she dared to look up. Her mom was *crying?*

"What…what…" Mira stammered, frowning. "Your LifeChip! It…it…it isn't working!" She'd never seen her mother like this.

Her mom smiled slightly as she shook her head. "No, it hasn't for a long time now. I'm one of the lucky .1%, and I'm guessing you are too." She wiped her tears onto her tan city-issued pants.

Something *was* wrong with Mira's LifeChip. For reasons she didn't understand, over the last four years her LifeChip's power, and its effect on her, had been dwindling. And obviously the required implanted chip that dulled and often neutralized their emotions wasn't working on her mom, either. Grabbing her Newscreen off the floor, Mira said, "You think visions of another world combined with feelings is lucky? Yeah, right. That's just what every seventeen-year-old wants."

Her mom took the tablet from her and laid it on the table. "Let me help you."

Mira stared at the stranger in front of her. These past four years, Mira had thought she was the only one who had managed to suppress her emotions. Oh, she'd heard about the .1%, but she'd assumed they'd all been sent to the Stint, the place that people from Pillar went to fix their faulty LifeChips. They had their memories eaten away by Amender bugs there, too. Her skin crawled at the thought. "There's no way to fix this, at least in a way that I'd want," she rasped.

"You have more options than you think."

A jittery warmth flooded her core as she visualized a new belief…one that told her that she wasn't stuck after all. "Really?"

Her mom nodded. "But we need to start with the truth." She knelt in front of Mira. "Tell me exactly what just happened to you."

The quiet assurance mixed with a look that said she understood was enough to trigger the tears Mira had worked very hard to hide. She'd wanted to tell someone for so long – someone who could comprehend how she felt. "Why didn't you tell me about yourself? Or somehow show me…" She brushed away her tears, helpless as the inner ache of aloneness that she'd hidden for years burst free.

Taking Mira's hands and crushing them between her own, she said, "I've been trying to protect you."

Mira wanted to believe her but didn't know if she could. "Protect me from what?"

After glancing into the hall that led to her father's office, her mom whispered, "I thought it was better…safer…that you didn't know about me. I'm so sorry!" The last came out as a sob as she bowed her head.

Mira stared at the top of it. Her mom's short blonde hair was styled like the rest of Pillar's citizens, but the woman she saw here wasn't like them. She had secrets, and it really *looked* as if she felt bad about it and in a much more intense way than anyone in Pillar. Mira pressed her hand against the soft flaxen strands. Her mom leaned into her hand and her entire body started to shake with stifled sobs.

"I have these images that come to me," Mira confessed faintly, "like they did a minute ago. Then they get stuck in my head."

Her mom slowly lifted her head. "How often do you have them?"

Mira shrugged. "On and off during the night for the past year, but now I'm having the episodes at various times during the day, too." Mira let her hand drop to her lap. "I don't know how much longer I can hide them – *or* how they make me feel."

"Okay." Her mom brushed at her tear-stained cheeks as she stood and wandered over to the window. "Then we'll go where you don't need to hide anything," she said with a loud sniff. She pointed to an area south of Pillar.

"You mean to where the Accordance live?"

She nodded. "A group of them has set up a camp not far from here."

Mira couldn't believe what she was hearing!

"I have some supplies stashed just in case I, we… It'll work. It has to," her mom said as she began to pace.

Mira's heart skipped a beat and her mouth suddenly felt like she hadn't had a drink in a year. "But Mom…the 'Cords…they're monsters!" Not only did the group of traitors live a lawless, chip-free life, but they were also constantly being hunted by the authorities.

After checking to see if the hallway was still clear, her mom said, "That's what the LAW wants you to believe."

The Life After War unit had been formed to rebuild the city of Pillar after passions had nearly destroyed the world. The unit was made up of various groups, but the Reformers were the main enforcers to watch out for. They kept the peace and made sure the city – and everyone's LifeChips - were in working order…which Mira's wasn't. "So what's the truth then?"

"I'm not entirely sure but…" She placed her hands on Mira's shoulders and squeezed. "I'll explain more on the way."

Mira shook her head. "What if it's not better out there?"

"If your father finds out about the episodes…" Her mom sat down again on the chair beside her, a deep frown on her face. "Look. I can't promise you that it will be easy, but I can guarantee that we were meant for more than," she paused to gaze across the room, "this."

"I just don't know." Mira's heart hammered in her chest as indecision forced its way through her veins.

"I think your visions will lead us to something better. You said you saw another world, right?"

Mira looked away from her mom's intense stare to swirl her finger over the tablet's screen. "I did." She *did* want a way out of the monotonous controlled routine of their city – and the controlling thumb of her father - yet she shuddered at the memory of that envisioned dark shadowed world even as her heart leapt at the thought of immersing herself in the colorful one. "But there's more."

"Tell me."

Could her mom know what it all meant? The visions weren't going away. They were only getting stronger and more frequent. She had to do *something*. "Okay." She paused to take a deep breath. "In the vision, I'm standing behind our gate, looking down the hill toward Pillar. Wisps of black smoke weave through the streets until I can barely make out the buildings." Mira clutched the edges of her seat. "North of the city, the ground groans and opens like a mouth. Pillar begins to shift off its foundation and inch toward it." She frowned, staring out the dining room window that gave her a view of one of the few cities that had survived the war. "I can't believe what I'm seeing! I step through the gate to get a closer look, only the hill is slick with mud and I lose my footing. I slide down, down, down toward the gaping hole. I'm trying to grab tree limbs or rocks, but I can't get a hold of anything." Her heart raced as if it were really happening. "I plunge into the deep, dark trench, but manage to latch onto a rock jutting out close to the edge."

"What happened then?" Her mom's quiet, encouraging tone prompted Mira to continue.

Closing her eyes, Mira shuddered, remembering the scene in vivid detail. "I look down into the steamy mist and it suddenly parts, giving me a clear view of a forever-long stretch of dreary road. There is no place to rest. The only sign of water is a dried-up bed of clay that looks like it had once been a stream. Everything surrounding me is dead, except I can hear all these voices crying out. I can't see anyone, though. Somehow, I feel this road is mine to travel alone. That loneliness squeezes my heart until I begin to cry." Mira rubbed her heart that was aching even now. "As I scramble to pull myself back up, I see images of things I have only begun to wish for – beauty…joy…love. I grab for them as if they could pull me out of the abyss, but they hover just out of my reach. Why had I gone outside? Why had I stepped closer?" Mira's lips trembled and her eyes filled with tears.

"I wonder…" Her mom's voice trailed off, and her hand pressed reassuringly against Mira's knee. "Is there more?"

Mira nodded. "I see this man on the other side of the chasm," she rasped. "He has something on his hands, and he wipes them on his overalls as he walks around the edge toward me. As he gets closer, I can make out the blood-red smear on the pin-striped fabric…his shark's grin…the strange look in his eyes. I somehow sense what he wants, and it isn't to rescue me." Her stomach churned and she swallowed hard. "I scream so loudly it hurts my ears, and I frantically pull myself upward, but my shaky arms are too weak. That's when I see a hand reach down. It's scarred and calloused. I look up to see a man with soft, yet determined eyes." The heaviness pressing the air from Mira's lungs eased a little. "After a glance at the never-ending dismal road below me and the man with the evil stare heading my way, I know in my heart that the hand held out to me is my only hope of rescue. I grab it and the man pulls me to the surface."

"Who is he?" her mom whispered.

"I don't know," Mira admitted. "His features were ordinary, but his smile was welcoming, and holding his hand made me feel safe and warm and unafraid." She got up and wandered to the window to where Pillar stood - dismal, yet solid - like it had since she could remember. "I could also see a different Pillar while I held this guy's hand."

"What was Pillar like?"

This part of the vision was much easier to talk about. Mira smiled. "The entrance to the city had pillars of ivory that reflected light in a brilliant way, weaving color throughout the entire city. Kids were swinging on a playset, people were eating, drinking, laughing, their voices blending perfectly. A group stood on the band shell stage, holding different objects in their hands, creating a sound so beautiful, I never wanted it to end. But then it stopped, leaving behind a stunned silence. I looked up at the man holding my hand and he said…" She paused.

Mira's mom leaned toward her. "What did he say? Tell me what he said!"

"He said, 'Find me and you'll find what you seek…it's where you are meant to be.'" Mira paused, allowing the words to really sink in. She knew, deep down, that she had to find him!

"Did he say anything else?"

Mira shook her head as she again sat down beside her mom. "He disappeared but he left a book, one with a pillar of fire on its cover."

Her mom clapped a hand over her own mouth, barely muffling her gasp.

Now Mira was starting to freak out. "What, mom?"

Slowly, her mom lowered her hand back to the table. "I thought it was gone forever." The tight lines in her face relaxed somewhat as she stood.

"You know about this book?"

Soft dark eyes crinkled as she looked at her daughter. "Oh yes. It's the Enchiridion of Emmanuel," she said, running her fingers along the chain around her neck. "And maybe, just maybe, if we find it, we can take Pillar back and rebuild it in the way it was meant to be. But we need to keep it a secret for now."

"What do you want her to keep secret, Addison?" Mira's dad loomed in the doorway.

Mira froze, but inside, she was screaming with a terror that begged to come out. Thankfully, her dad's attention had turned to her mom who was carefully straightening her beige button-down shirt. There was no sign of her tears, no hint of any emotion whatsoever.

"I don't want her to tell that I answered a homework question for her." She pulled Mira's tablet along the wooden tabletop. "It is against the school's rules."

Her dad stared from one to the other, his face expressionless. As always, he was dressed in the drab uniform the people of his station always wore. Even though it seemed harder to do this time, Mira swallowed the unpleasant emotion that made her think something bad was definitely going to happen. *He can't see into my mind*, she told herself. Yet she wasn't so sure that was true. His assessment skills had raised their family's status to one that afforded them a comfortable life – one her mom was asking her to give up…if they'd still have the opportunity.

"You'd better go to bed, Mira," he finally said.

She obeyed, looking at the floor as she escaped upstairs to her room. She paused, leaning back against her door, listening intently. But her parents were too far away to hear unless they shouted, and people in Pillar rarely raised their voices. After a few moments, she prodded herself to move - in case her dad came to see if she'd obeyed his orders.

As was her routine, she headed to the bathroom. The single bulb of the groom-bot – a small multi-armed unit mounted onto the wall – lit up as she entered. Like the rest of the house, this room was functional but colorless. A single shower stall stood opposite the steel toilet. And beside that was a matching sink. According to history, window-sized mirrors used to hang over bathroom sinks, a tool that had been used to spark vanity and competition. Right now, Mira wished she had one to determine if her face was as expressionless as she thought, but the only mirrors anyone in Pillar had were smaller than her palm and used only for identifying and caring for injuries. Pressing her palms against the edge of the cold sink, the groom-bot zipped into action. It used a measured amount of toothpaste to brush her teeth and a squirt of soap on a damp cloth to wash her face. Another of its arms combed through her short hair.

That done, she went into her bedroom and quickly changed into her sleep clothes. Jumping beneath the covers of her twin bed, she stared at the grey walls. A sick feeling curled inside her. How much had her dad heard? And what would he do to her mom, and to her? Then the pressure started behind her eyes again. "Already?" she whispered. She pressed her palms against her eyes, but she knew that pushing it back was as likely as convincing a butterfly to move back into his cocoon. All the scenes she'd ever imagined came, one after the other. "Leave me alone," she said more loudly than she'd intended. But the images didn't stop until the door to her room opened.

"It's time to go," her mom said, and threw her a jacket.

Mira put it on, then slipped on her shoes before following her mom outside. Stopping at the waist-high fence that surrounded their property, Mira whispered, "Wait. Will this be the last time I'm here?"

Her mom reached for the gate as she glanced back at the house. "Probably."

The ache in Mira's chest was growing, and she didn't know what to do about it. An arm came to rest across her shoulders, which felt strange, yet good.

"Good-byes are never easy, especially when you don't know what you'll be saying hello to. But it's now that you have to make the choice," her mom said softly. "You can go where this is leading you, or you will probably be forced to get a new LifeChip and in the least, have the memories of these visions extracted."

Mira didn't like either alternative. "Can't we just go on as we are?"

Her mom shook her head. "You aren't going to be able to hide this much longer. If your father overheard us earlier, it may already be too late to turn back."

Chapter 2

The robust moon cast a beam over their surroundings. Down the steep hill to the south was the city of Pillar, the place Mira had been born. According to a rusted sign made more than thirty years ago, its population was 512,689. She had no idea how many people lived in Pillar now, but it wasn't nearly that many. Mira didn't feel any strong attachment to the place or to anyone who lived there, but tonight, that bothered her, most especially when she thought of it being swallowed up by that dark shadowed world of despair. She couldn't let it happen! She glanced at the Center Of Operations, which was run by the LAW along with their two thousand Reformers. "So where do we start?"

"I'd like to shake up the COO's tree," her mom said with a broad smile as she stared at the large concrete building that loomed behind the park's band shell. The government structure was twenty stories high and took up an entire city block. Beneath the tree painted on the COO's west side was their motto: *We Are Looking Out For You!* "But I say we aim high and cut it down," her mom added with a lift of her chin.

"I'm in," Mira said, no longer buying their motto and warming to the idea of changing their world.

"Excellent! Then we need to remove your LifeChip before we go any further." Her mom grinned and patted her on the shoulder.

Mira wondered how it would feel without the nano-chip, if she'd eventually end up on the island of Enab with the crazy people who wouldn't or couldn't be reformed by the LifeChip. The alternative was to become a full-blown rebel. Neither option seemed to fit how she felt, and any way she looked at it, her chances of survival were slim. She glanced at her hand to where the chip was located right beneath her skin. Was she actually doing this?

As her mom dug into the bag she'd brought, Mira looked down the hill directly east of her. She could see the two-story boathouse that always housed a few guards who assured no one but government employees used the watercraft. Beyond the structure was the shark-infested ocean that separated them from the island of Enab. A bay sat to the north of the boathouse, rows of docks storing the Elite Reformers' powerful boats that transported people and goods to the island. At least that's what she'd been told. Mira shivered and hugged her arms around herself, suddenly not so certain of anything, her decision included.

"Hold out your hand," came her mom's hushed voice.

Mira did as asked and watched as her mom ran something the size of a wristwatch over the top of her hand. It beeped close to her wrist knob.

"This will only hurt a little." Her mom quickly sliced a scalpel across her skin. Mira winced, but kept her eyes trained on the bracelet-like beeping tool. As it swiped over the cut, the LifeChip was sucked up into the device. "It only takes a moment to destroy it, then it will send out false signals from the point of extraction."

"I didn't know that was possible."

"We are very lucky to have this gem," she said, "And you can thank the son of the one who created the LifeChip for this luxury." She tucked the device back into her bag.

Mira pressed a hand against her skin, which was bleeding a little. "I don't feel any different," she said.

Her mom swept through the gate, taking the hill that eventually would bring them to Pillar. "The LifeChip wasn't working on you, so you might not feel a whole lot of difference."

A little of Mira's jitteriness faded and she followed her mom in silence. They moved quickly and kept to the shadows as they made their way to the wide strip of woodland that flanked Pillar. "You really know your way around," Mira remarked, her voice barely louder than a gust of wind.

Her mom dodged a fallen tree, one Mira hadn't noticed. "Yep."

They walked south for several more minutes. This wasn't the mom she knew at all, but Mira *was* curious about her secrets. "Aren't you going to tell me why?" Mira asked.

"Not now," she said, and crouched behind a tree that stood across the road stretching along Pillar's west side.

Mira scrunched down beside her, glimpsing the edge of the COO building that seemed to loom even bigger at the moment. "Why not?"

"Because we can't get caught here, alright?" After adjusting the backpack on her shoulders, her mom took off again, heading south, keeping to the trees. "I'll explain more when we get there."

"Whatever," Mira growled at her mom's back. At least she didn't have to pretend that she didn't feel anything anymore. "So where *is* there?" she whispered.

Without turning her head, her mom said, "Freetown."

Having been warned in school about the extremely volatile Freetown - an Accordance camp - Mira was worried. Her teeth worked over her bottom lip. "But it's dangerous there, isn't it?"

"Just because they don't agree with the LAW doesn't mean they are dangerous." Her mom weaved between the trees, her figure lithe and nimble. "But they can be," she said, "so stick close to me and be quiet."

They stepped across a weed littered dirt path and continued their hurried escape in silence, although Mira's senses were on extreme alert. Everything seemed so vivid. After what seemed like an hour, the landscape turned rocky and uneven, the steep incline making it hard to breathe. "Are we almost there?" Mira asked over the sound of relentless waves crashing at the base of the cliff to her left. "I don't know how much further I can keep going." She hadn't slept well for months and the smell of brine and fish was starting to get to her, as was her attempt to balance the hodge-podge of emotions shuffling through her brain.

"It isn't much further." Her mom stopped at the edge of an outcropping. A crumbling lighthouse stood behind them. Salty spray shot into the air in front of them, misting their clothes.

Mira looked around, confused. Where was the camp?

After a sweeping look around, her mom dropped to her knees on the bluff's edge. Slowly, she lowered herself down the steep craggy bank. "You have to be careful with the footholds. They can get pretty slippery," she said, and disappeared from Mira's view.

Mira crawled to the edge and dared a peek. She didn't like edges much, nor thoughts of slippery things, but her mom was already at the bottom, maneuvering across the sharp black stones littering the shoreline. Mira's heart started beating harder and she could feel her limbs tremble as the cool air whipped across her clammy skin. "It's another reaction to being chipless," she told herself.

Knowing she had nowhere else to turn, Mira flipped over, and clenching her teeth together, grasped the base of a large shrub on the cliff's edge. She felt for a toehold and tucked her foot onto it. It held when she put her weight on it, so she did the same with the other foot. When she tried to reach the next foothold, though, she realized she had to let go of the shrub.

"You can do this," she whispered, and finally managed to let go. She wobbled, gasping, but thankfully her foot found another secure place to rest. She continued, step by step, until she planted both feet on the sand below. Her legs felt like they had no bones as she turned around, yet the air seemed to have changed, spiking a gush of feeling she couldn't explain. She grinned at the energy that thrummed through her. When she couldn't spot her mom, however, that feeling was replaced with something different – a feeling she didn't like. "Mom," she called out, her heart beating double-time as she squinted through the darkness for any glimpse of her.

"Over here," she said, peeking around the towering craggy point to the south of where Mira stood. "The tide is out so we can walk on the shore rather than through the water to get to Spirit Cavern. Lucky us!"

Mira had heard about the mysterious cavern that had been used to store alcohol before the war. Supposedly, many people had died in that cave as a result of addictions turning violent. And the lust for power and money had caused even more demise. "I thought the LAW filled this cavern with eastern diamondback rattle snakes to make sure it remained unusable after the war."

"It was cleared and opened again by the Accordance." Her mother smiled. "It's Freetown now. Come on."

That was Freetown? The spring air suddenly seemed like a front just before a snowstorm. Mira zipped her jacket up to her chin as she stumbled over the pointy rocks and made her way over to her mother. "Will this be our new…home?" she asked, looking halfway up the cliff side to the dark opening of the cave.

"Maybe for a while." Her mom kissed the pendant around her neck and climbed the metal track hanging by hinges against the rocky side. Before and during the war, the track's ends were hooked to ships' decks so they could move barrels of goods up into the cool cavern for storage.

Her mother slipped onto the cave's ledge and looked down at her daughter. "I've been praying a long time for this, Mira."

"That we'd live in Freetown?"

She shook her head. "No. For hope. And finding the Enchiridion of Emmanuel is key to that."

Mira followed her mother's route up the rungs, trying to ignore the jagged rocks on the shore below. "Now that we're free, maybe we don't actually need to find it," she said, her drive fading with the mix of emotions flooding her mind.

"But we *do* need to find it!" Her mom reached out a hand and pulled Mira up into the opening. "I've already experienced freedom," she said, "but it just seems like another prison I need to escape. Nothing has ever been enough to permanently fill the emptiness I have inside me." She tapped her left fist twice against her chest. "I always feel like I need something more – like I'm an adopted child searching for where I truly belong." Both hands dropped as she stepped beneath the brick archway that would take them deeper into the cave. "And after that vision you had, I am *sure* I will find the answers through the Enchiridion of Emmanuel. And not just for me, but for all of us."

Mira wanted to ask more, but there was something about the stifling quietness that made her hesitant to speak. It was as if the darkness hid evil and if it even heard her breathe, she'd be at its mercy. She peered into the gloom and could see a faint flickering light about halfway down one of the tunnels. Her mother nodded toward it and whispered, "Let's go."

They slipped into the tunnel, the dampness making Mira shiver. Her hand ran along a cart sitting on metal tracks as they walked past it. She wondered if the wooden barrel housed inside it contained any wine…what it would taste like. Not that it mattered. When they finally reached the dimly lit area, Mira saw that its light source was a fire deep inside another tunnel, a much wider one that branched out from the main tracks. As they approached, sounds came to life, like cicadas in the evening.

"You made it!"

Mira jumped at the booming voice.

A big man she hadn't noticed before he had spoken, laughed and stood up, tipping over his crate seat. His skin was eggplant dark, his teeth white. "Welcome to Freetown." He turned. "And welcome back, Addie. It's been a while."

"I didn't know if I'd ever be back," she said, and gave him a hug. "It's good to see you, Nick."

That her mom was familiar with the man – and was leading a double life - surprised Mira. She wondered what else she hadn't told her.

Nick looked at her mom fondly. "Care for a bite to eat? I think he's almost done." He leaned down to turn the critter over. The poor dead animal had a stick poking out both of its ends. Its tail curled a bit, its teeth protruding as if it was sneering as it breathed its last.

"None for me," Mira said, not able to take her eyes off it.

Nick chuckled. "It was tough to look at my first time, too." He turned the critter over again. "But I realized soon enough that a man's got to eat, and without a LifeChip to get rations, this was one of my few options. And a tasty one, too."

Mira's stomach flipped as she looked at the charred rat.

He turned it over one more time. Removing his tattered cap, Nick held it against his stomach. "Aren't you going to introduce me to your daughter? She is your daughter, right?"

"Yes," Addie answered. "Nick, Mira. Mira, Nick."

Mira stared at the deep gouge in the large man's right ear, wondering if a rat had been the cause. Was that something they had to deal with here – eat, or be eaten? She could picture Nick sound asleep, a rat gnawing on his ear. Maybe continuing revenge against the creatures was one reason the guy enjoyed vermin in his diet.

"She looks a lot like her father," he said.

Besides his dark hair, Mira didn't think she looked like her father at all. Of course, she'd never gotten the full effect with only the mini mirrors. Her mom didn't respond to the comment, but asked, "Did Pastor Ettreim get in touch with you?"

"He did." Nick removed his meal from the makeshift spit and used a tin can to pour a little liquid on his fire. It hissed as he stashed his dinner inside a metal box. Turning his back on the steamy, glowing coals, he said, "Come this way."

As they followed Nick further into the black velvet of the dark interior, lights flickered to life above them. They were single hanging bulbs, casting a pale gleam throughout. "How do you have lights in here?" Mira asked.

Nick looked up. "We have one hundred ninety-two LED bulbs, all of them connected to one battery bank, which is charged each day by human pedal power."

Mira stared at a man as they walked around him. His stooped posture looked uncomfortable, but he hummed as he weaved a fork into his tent, which was made entirely of silverware. Next to him stood a young woman wearing layers of robes. Her face was pretty, though it appeared to be tinted green and her hair puffed out like a thundercloud. And some sort of figurine stuck out of the nest of locks. She pursed her lips as if pointing at the passersby. "If you prick us do we not bleed? If you tickle us do we not laugh?" she said in an overly bright and accented voice. "If you poison us do we not die?" The woman turned to stare at Mira with eyes open way too wide as she continued her speech. "And if you wrong us shall we not revenge?"

A large bird swooped out of nowhere. Mira ducked, but she wasn't quick enough. A squeal burst from her lips as the fowl's wing clipped her nose and a big wet glob of guck dropped onto her shoe.

"Yuck," Mira said, scooting closer to her mom. She squinted back at the giant bird that was now squawking from the strange girl's shoulder. "Maybe you need more pedal power," Mira said, "Then I would've seen that coming."

Nick glanced at her, his broad smile easy to see in the dimness. "The generator that's connected to the stationary bike works surprisingly well, but because we each have to put in an hour a week on the thing, we tend to use our power sparingly."

Next they passed a couple, only partly clothed. They fit together like two tree trunks entwined, making grunting noises that made Mira want to look and not look at the same time. Her face grew red when her mom put herself between Mira and the pair.

"Or maybe even less light would be better," her mom said.

"Dim lights do have their benefits," he said with a chuckle. He picked up the pace, giving Mira almost no time to study the other people they'd passed.

When they got to a more brightly lit area, they stopped in front of a tent about the size of Mira's bedroom. The illumination from behind its fabric created silhouettes of what was inside. It was full of stuff, and someone bent over a square object, hands moving on its surface.

"You have what I need, Millie?" Nick asked.

A fast clicking ended with a single loud clack. "It was a lot of work gettin' this, Nick," answered a raspy voice. "Pastor wasn't even around."

"Understood. Word of warning though; you might not want to show yourself," he said. "We have a newbie here."

The woman cackled as she rummaged around for whatever *this* was. Mira wondered about the people in this makeshift town. What had brought them all here? Like the disheveled group right across from where she stood. There were five of them, all male, hanging around a sizeable fire in a bathtub. A couple of the guys looked to be around her age, seventeen. Two others were middle-aged and one was old, if his craggy face was any indication. All of them except for the old man were laughing at the story being told by one of the middle-aged guys – the one wearing a helmet of some sort and short pants with long socks.

She zoned in on one of the teens, curious about his obnoxious laugh. The guy was tall and broad, his bright orange shirt smudged with dirt, and torn – a small vertical slit from chest to waist. His purple pants fit perfectly, but had a precisely cut hole exposing his knee. His dark complexion was complemented by even darker hair, which looked like he'd only minutes before left his personal groom-bot back in Pillar. Maybe he had. As if he could feel her eyes on him, he looked over at her.

She couldn't tear her gaze away.

He winked at her…unless the fire's flickering shadows on his face were playing tricks on her. Her heart kicked up to full speed.

Lifting a bottle in her direction, he called out, "Care for a drink? It'll warm you up."

The words sounded unnatural, but for some reason she felt the need to smile at him. So she did. He smiled back…a half-hearted one, as if his lips didn't quite work right.

The guy next to him wiggled his dark brows at her, shifting up the stocking cap that was fringed by his blond hair. "I think she needs a real man to warm her up, Smudge. Someone like me who's got some passion. Watch how it's done." He ambled toward her, but "Smudge" grabbed him by the arm.

Mira's mom huddled in close to her. Nick stood up tall and alert on her other side.

"I'd be careful with those newfound emotions, Smudge," the guy said, his nose flaring as he stared at the hand on his arm.

Nick stepped toward the two guys, but stopped as Smudge twisted the aggressor's arm behind his back and hiked it up. "And you don't know who you're messing with, blondie."

The blond's fist clenched, but he held himself in check. "Classic newbie reaction. I think I feel a lesson coming on." The blond winced when his pinned arm was pushed higher up his back.

"I think it's you who needs the lesson."

"Relax, muscles," he said, "I was just having fun…another thing I'm sure you're new to."

"Ha, ha, ha, ha." Smudge's laugh seemed robotic as he twisted the blond back around and shoved a bottle against his chest. "Why don't *you* relax and have a drink," he spat.

The blond glanced at Mira and then at his captor. He mumbled something, then with his free hand grabbed the bottle. Smudge let him go with a shove.

"I'd watch your back," the blond guy said through gritted teeth before taking a long drink. With one final glare, he stumbled over to his earlier spot by the fire, bottle in hand.

Smudge stood off a ways, alone, giving her a long, measured look, one she couldn't begin to decipher. She had so many questions, and she had no clue how to act. There were no rules here that she knew of, but inside she felt warm, a pulling to do…something. She raised her hand. Would Smudge come to her, tell her his name? What would they talk about?

But the guy only nodded and went back to his buddies.

Mira's heart felt too heavy for her chest, a sensation she didn't understand.

"What's taking you so long, Millie?" Nick asked, tapping his long fingers against the tent. Mira noticed that his feet were fidgeting too, and he kept glancing over at the group that had now grown much quieter.

Finally, a gnarled hand snuck out of the opening of the tent, palm up. "I'm waitin' for my payment."

Nick looked at Addison, who had removed the backpack from her shoulders. Unzipping it, she pulled out a book. She squeezed it briefly against her chest and then pressed it into the old woman's hand. It disappeared inside the tent. Millie's cackle echoed wildly throughout the tunnel.

The group across from them was very quiet now and all were staring openly at the scene in front of the tent.

"I can't believe you had a book, dearie, especially this one. *An Artist's Love.*" Millie sighed. "Here I thought all the passion-inciting books were gone for good – except for the ones I write. Mmmm, mmm, mmm!"

Nick bent over to peek inside the tent. "Quit reading it and hand over the package from Pastor Ettreim, or his assistant, or whomever you ended up getting it from."

"So impatient," Millie said and tsked, but her hand shot out with a cylindrical package about a foot long, wrapped in material.

Her mom took it. "Thanks."

"No. Thank *you*." The sound of a book page turning was followed by a giggle. "Love this stuff," Millie added.

"We have to go," Nick said, ushering them ahead of him. "We'll talk later - at my site."

They hurried back the way they came, in silence. What would Freetown look like in the daytime? What would Smudge look like? When they turned the corner and moved into an area less peopled, Mira asked, "So why didn't you want me to see Millie? She seemed good-natured enough."

Nick glanced behind them and then in a hushed tone said, "Millie can only write when she's naked and drinking coffee." He cringed. "It's...startling, even when you know it's coming."

Mira chuckled. Now that they were close to Nick's camp, Freetown didn't seem nearly as overwhelming.

"Can we stay with you tonight?" her mom asked.

He stopped to whisper something in her ear. She nodded, casting a quick glance behind them. "We'll have to think of something else then."

Mira looked back. At first she saw nothing that hadn't been there on the way in. But then she saw him standing less than twenty feet away under a flickering bulb. It was the old, quiet man. His hair was grey, his hairline similar to that of a monkey's. He wore overalls tucked into worn boots. His skin tone was...dirty, and the way he looked at her made her feel...dirtier. He seemed familiar, somehow, yet not in a good way. Mira scooted closer to big Nick.

Thankfully, they were right by his camp. Nick picked up a stick and poked at the coals of his dying fire. Tiny flames started flaring back to life. He pulled the rat back out of the metal box and propped it over the fire. The scene was the same as when they'd arrived, but Nick seemed different, more solemn. "You need something to eat before you go?" he asked, not looking at them. He continued to poke at the coals.

"We're leaving?" Mira asked, surprised.

"It's not safe here," her mom said, stuffing the package from Millie into her backpack.

Mira didn't want to go back to trying to hide her episodes – or her feelings. And there was so much to learn – especially about Smudge. "Home isn't safe either," she said. "And Nick can protect us, right?"

Nick shook his head. "You saw that old guy back there?"

She nodded. "What about him?"

"His name is Burt Guyver. Once he sets his mind on something, he has ways of getting it." Nick looked at her, his dark eyes solemn. "That something is you, sweetheart. And all I can do right now is make sure he doesn't follow you," he said.

"But…"

"Thanks Nick. For everything." Her mom reached up and kissed Nick on the cheek. Then, grabbing Mira, pulled her back out into the night.

Her mom's abruptness wasn't sitting well with Mira. "Don't I get a say in this?"

"Not if you want to survive," her mom said.

Chapter 3

Mira's mom led her back the same way they'd come. This time, their clothes were damp from their escape out of Freetown and they were in no better a place than they had been when they'd left their home.

"Where are we going anyway?" Mira asked, rubbing her temples and trying to ignore the squishing of her wet shoes.

Her mom crossed over the moonlit path, her pant legs brushing against the overgrown weeds. "I have a friend - he has a place we can hide for the night," she said.

The dusty smell of pollen-disturbed weeds littered the air and stuffed up Mira's sinuses. The pressure didn't stop there. "How much...further is it?"

At her strained words, her mom slowed and glanced back. "Is it happening again?"

Mira's brows puckered. "Yes."

Her mom shifted the backpack and started to walk again. "It's not much further."

Mira had to keep her mind off the buzzing in her brain. Watching her feet, she plodded along unevenly. "What's in the package you got from Millie?"

"Paints."

"Why did you get paints?"

"I thought if you could paint what you see, we can figure out what to do next."

Mira had been told about paintings in school. Not only were they useless, but they often directed minds where they shouldn't go and inspired passions that ended up hurting people. Yet the idea of seeing colors as she brushed them onto paper…she smoothed a hand over her sweaty forehead. "But what if I can't paint what I see?"

Her mom shrugged. "Then we try something else."

Mira squinted, trying to ward off the images, but they were like wild bulls in a corral. They could no longer be contained. "I need to stop here," she said. "Now." She grabbed for the tree beside her and held on. Her eyes fluttered and rolled back. In her mind, Pillar was getting closer to the crater, but even as it moved, the colors behind it seemed to latch on as if they were trying to keep it in place. So many colors…and so many sounds – like birds only with human voices and words. When she finally managed to open her eyes again, she was sitting on the ground, the rough barked ridges of the tree digging into her back.

"You okay?" her mom asked.

She nodded as she braced against the trunk and got to her feet.

"I really want to know what you saw, but the longer we're out in the open, the riskier it is for us. How fast will you be able to move now?"

"Fast enough," she said.

Her mom took off, her athletic legs determined as they ate up the space between them and Pillar. Mira kept up, but barely. Questions that needed answering kept distracting her.

"What about the Renovatrons? Won't they see us?" she asked. Even though the entire city of Pillar was asleep, the crew of droids did nightly city-wide cleanup and maintenance.

"They're done for the night."

"And the Sweepers?" The four-inch egg-shaped flying robots had quill-like fibers tipped with tiny eyes. Their job was to hover on street corners so they could report disturbances or abnormalities. Mira and her mom running through town was definitely not normal.

"We'll stay close to the business fronts." She turned to look at Mira. "We've come this far. I won't let them take you now."

"Oh…okay."

Her mom smiled and without an ounce of hesitation, stepped into Pillar. Mira followed, concentrating on the warmth of the sidewalks through her damp shoes. Halfway down K Street, they turned down an alley. Again, her mom seemed to know exactly where she was going. She stopped at a newer-looking building with perfectly aligned grey shingles – Renovatron handiwork for sure.

"Which business is this?" Mira asked, following her to the back door.

Her mom punched in a code and the door swung open. "Welcome to Pillar Media," she said, and hurried inside.

Again, her mom had surprised her. Mira hurried down a steep set of steps after her and then across the empty basement toward a stone wall. Standing in the far corner, her mom grabbed the edge of the wall and pulled.

"It's a hidden room?" Mira asked, slipping past the faux wall that was actually a heavy curtain with stones painted onto the front of it.

"Before the war, reporters often slept here," her mom said, dumping the contents of her backpack onto the bed. "They'd tack ideas and stories to that board over there," she nodded toward the far wall as she unwrapped the package she'd gotten from Millie. Handing the scrolled paper to Mira, she said, "Now paint."

Mira wanted to paint, but she also really wanted to look into the mirror hanging over the small sink in the corner of the room. She started toward it, but her mom stopped her. "Save it for after you paint."

"Why?"

"Because we don't need distractions – our time here is limited."

"Are you saying I'm ugly?"

Her mom laughed – a sound which still surprised Mira – and urged her daughter back to the bed where the paints were. "No. You're beautiful. Very beautiful in fact. Let's just focus on painting what's inside you first so you can know firsthand that a person is truly more than what's on the surface."

Mira was too tired to argue. After ditching her wet shoes, she unrolled the scrolled papers and flattened them against the mattress. There were about thirty sheets of thick parchment, each smudged with soot and miscellaneous stains. Scattered on the quilt were many tubes of paint - all different colors - and a ruler-sized tray divided into twelve sections. Held together with a thick rubber band was a variety of brushes. Some fat, some very thin, large and small. Mira unwrapped them and slipped the rubber band around her wrist. Sitting down on the edge of the bed, she picked up a small flat brush, thinking that it felt right in her hands. She swept her fingertips across the bristles. They were soft, like hair.

"Here's a flat surface to paint on," her mom said, moving the lamp to the far edge of the nightstand.

Mira laid the paper next to the lamp. She dotted paint into each compartment of the paint tray. The first image she painted brought an ache to her throat. The greys and blacks smothered her with a feeling of impending doom, but still her brush stroked across the page as if it had a story that needed to be told. Handing it to her mother, she said nothing of it, but got to work on the next piece...the one she wanted to paint, the one she wanted to believe in. The brilliance of each color amazed her. The bright yellow with sparkling flecks was the first color she smeared onto the paper. She smiled, forgetting that she was afraid. She forgot about the roasting rat. She forgot about her dad and the man in the overalls. In fact, she thought of nothing but the image that was stuck in her mind. Something else - some force - directed each stroke as the page came to life. When Mira stopped, she was dazed by the playground filled with spirited colors and laughing people, and yet it still wasn't as awesome as her vision had been.

"Here. Put this somewhere to dry," Mira said and handed it to her mom who tacked it up on the board next to the other. The contrast was startling.

Mira started on the next picture, her strokes quick and sure. Within moments, a book appeared. Its cover sported a pillar with a glowing flame curling around it.

"It really is the Enchiridion of Emmanuel," her mom breathed. "We have to find it!"

Mira stared at the finished piece. "How do you know it still exists? In school they…"

"They told you they'd destroyed them all to prevent any further religious wars?" Her mom plugged in a fan she'd found on the shelf and aimed it at the artwork. "I know they want you to believe that – and I know they *tried* to destroy them all, but…" Taking Mira's shoes, she propped them on the edge of the sink so that they were in the line of the fan's air flow as well. She returned to the bed and sat down next to Mira. "Go ahead and paint your next picture and I'll tell you a story."

Mira did as she said, feeling so much freer now that she was painting. And it was so easy, like she didn't have to think about it at all. Something just seemed to guide her strokes.

"Before you were born," her mom said, "I actually had a copy of the Enchiridion."

Mira froze. "You did?"

Her mom nodded. "But my mother stole the book from me before I could even read it. You see, she'd been abused in a…" She closed her eyes a second and swallowed. "A horrible way because of some sick religion. Even though the religion wasn't based on the Enchiridion of Emmanuel's truths, she said she wasn't going to let *any* religion ruin my life."

Mira remembered very little of her grandmother, only that she seemed to get along better with her dad than her mom. "What happened?" Mira asked as she brushed a window frame onto the page and drew a beautiful garden filled with flowers beyond it.

Her mom clasped her hands in her lap. "Your grandma told me she'd hidden the book and then she used it to blackmail me into doing things I did NOT want to do." She took a deep breath. "Then one day, she had a heart attack. In the hospital, she admitted to me that the attack had happened right after she'd read a passage from the Enchiridion." She shook her head. "Tearfully, she told me that maybe she'd been wrong all along. My mom never, *ever* cried."

Mira stared down at the painting she'd just completed. It was like spying through a window at a man who sat on a bench overlooking a flower garden. He was holding something. Mira glanced at her mom, who'd just pulled out a key hanging from her necklace.

"She gave me this and said that it unlocked the Enchiridion, which I didn't at first believe." She tucked the key beneath her tan shirt again. "But then a nurse who was administering medication "accidentally" gave her the wrong one. She died before she could tell me where she'd hidden the book. Coincidence?"

Mira didn't know how to answer that.

"*I* don't think so," her mom said. "And I don't think these episodes and images are a coincidence either. And they have power. Take this one, for instance." She pointed to the man in the garden picture. "You can't see his face, but you can see that he's holding a guitar and you can almost feel his sadness, can't you?"

Mira felt more than that from the painting – and she heard from it too. "It's almost like he loves the flowers but doesn't know how to hold onto their beauty," she said softly. "In my vision, I could hear his somber voice blending with something else - a mellow sound."

"He was playing guitar, and singing a song. It's called music." Her mom stood up and took the picture from her. "You have been given a gift, Mira." She tacked it next to the others. "And I truly believe it will lead us to the Enchiridion and the one who promises life in that colorful world." Her mom ran a hand down her tired face. "But the other part of your vision...it worries me."

"Do you think it's a warning of some sort?"

With a nod, she answered. "I think we are on the edge - that we're almost out of time to save Pillar from total destruction." She looked hard at Mira. "Whatever happens, don't give up on finding the Enchiridion, okay?"

Maybe Pillar *was* headed for another catastrophic war. And maybe the coveted book and the man who had provided it *were* the answers to Mira's restlessness – the reason she was having all these visions about a vibrant world she craved. Her mom obviously believed it was. "I won't give up. I promise."

Her mom's relieved smile eased the pressure in Mira's chest. "Now get to painting, young lady."

Mira painted several more pictures, each one more quickly than the last. It wasn't until her eleventh piece of paper that she finally propped her brush on the tray. Rubbing her back as she stretched, she asked, "So is there a meaning to all these pictures, a clue as to what we should do next?"

"I'm not sure," her mom said, straightening the painting she'd just put up. As she stared at it, she asked, "When did you envision this one?"

Mira looked at the picture of the tent with a hand reaching out. The hand held onto a book, and scrolled across the front of it was the title "An Artist's Heart." Her mom's book. "That happened already, didn't it," she whispered, trying not to freak out.

Her mom nodded. "But when did you see it in your mind? Before it happened, or after?"

She clutched the brush tightly in her fist. "Before…maybe a week ago."

Her mom continued to study the paintings.

"Are these all things that will…" Mira swallowed as she grasped for meaning, "happen?"

"It looks that way." Sitting beside her on the bed again, her mom asked, "Do you have any more to paint?"

"One more." Mira dipped the brush into the brown paint. Plain, unremarkable brown. Shaking hands swiped the brush down the page and then she made another line parallel to it.

"Is it a box?" her mom asked, looking over her shoulder.

"No. It's a stand of some sort. Or maybe it's a coffin?" She continued to paint what she saw…and felt. There was a warm yellow haze surrounding the object, and on one of its panels was carved the words *I am the way, the truth, and the life.*

Her mom's eyes widened as she stared at the painting.

"Do you recognize it?"

She picked it up, her eyes never leaving it as she tacked it up in the spot closest to the fan. "Um, I just need to study these more carefully, to see if I can figure out how they all fit together."

Mira watched her mom look over the paintings. The last one was the one her eyes kept returning to, but she didn't say anything more about it.

"You'll tell me if you do figure something out, right?" Mira said, not sure if she would. After all, she'd hidden things from her for seventeen years. Important things. Many things.

"I don't want to jump to any conclusions, so just give me a little time to sort it all out." Her mom opened the doors of the vanity beneath the sink. She pulled something out. A clicking sound followed. "Since you're done painting for tonight, we should celebrate." As she turned, Mira could see her sprinkling a packet of powder into the water bottle she held. After putting the cap back onto it, she shook it. It turned horizon-blue. "This drink is called SeaCrest Dream. I think you'll like it." She held the bottle out to her.

Mira took it. Even though her eyes burned from lack of sleep and her body ached with tiredness, her mind was still running an unending race. Apparently she wasn't ready to give up the day. After giving the berry-scented liquid a quick sniff, she decided to try it. She tilted the bottle so that the sweet drink slid down her throat. She paused to wipe off a drop that had dribbled down her chin. "Yum," she said, and slugged down the rest.

"I had a feeling you'd like it." Her mom took the empty bottle from her and tossed it into the trash. It clattered loudly then settled into silence. "Now you get some sleep. I'm thinking we're going to have a really big day tomorrow."

Suddenly exhausted, Mira curled up on the bed. The pillow was soft and smelled like the fresh, flower-filled air of a new spring day. Her mom pulled up a chair and sat down beside her. "We're going to be okay, aren't we Mom?"

She brushed a hand over her daughter's head. "Yes."

Her mom was still looking at the row of paintings. Mira tried to study them, too, but her eyelids drooped until her lashes came to rest together in heavenly fusion.

"Sleep well, my little miracle."

Miracle was only too happy to oblige.

Chapter 4

When Mira woke up, the first thing she noticed was that her mouth was very dry and that her right hip throbbed, feeling like it had been scraped raw. She peeled down the edge of her waistband. A tiny pillar of fire was tattooed onto her skin. "What the heck?" She sat up so quickly, prickles of light dotted her vision.

Frowning, she glanced around the quiet room. The paintings were gone and so was her mom. That's when she noticed the curtain. Had it moved? Or was she just imagining it? She looked at the fan aimed at the storyboard. It was turned off. The curtain fluttered again.

Mira clutched the edge of the bed. "Mom?" There was no answer.

She stood up slowly, grabbing a paint spatula from the nightstand. The curtain moved once again, albeit it ever so slightly. "Who's there?" Her throat felt thick as she imagined Burt Guyver on the other side. But he didn't answer, and neither did anyone else.

Silently, she inched toward the curtain. Less than an arm's length away, she reached out. Her hand flexed by its edge, hesitating. Did she want to know? It was the only way out, so she didn't have a choice. She grabbed the curtain and slashed it aside. It revealed nothing but a stark, empty room. It must have been a draft.

Mira's held breath puffed out, but the panic didn't. She paced the little room, rubbing the back of her neck as she went over every detail of the evening before. Why would her mom take off with the paintings and leave her here? Or had someone kidnapped her mom and stolen the paintings? And why the tattoo of a fiery pillar if it came to her often in her visions – and was now on paper too? None of it made sense. What was she going to do?

Mira laid the spatula back down on the nightstand and sat on the bed. Clutching the pillow, she tried to ward off her shakiness. It didn't help, and it did nothing to relieve the knot of pressure in her throat. As she stared down at her bare feet, the prodding feeling behind her eyes built up again. For once she didn't mind. Maybe it would give her a clue, one she could understand.

She let the image come to her, and she relished it – even though it was almost the same as the last vision she'd had in the dining room at home. There were two distinct differences, however. The barren tree on the Center Of Operations building now had leaves on it. The other difference was that she was in this picture, and she was wrapped in a man's arms. She couldn't see his face, but she could feel some powerful emotion pouring from both of them. She pulled out the last piece of paper and grabbed a paintbrush.

This picture she painted more slowly than the others, as if the details were important to get perfectly right. It didn't take long however. Mira caressed the still wet scene with her eyes, drawn to the curves, the colors, the mystery. How did it fit in with the rest of her paintings? If only she had the rest of them – and her mom. A heavy weight settled on her chest. "Why me?" she whispered.

"A better question is, why me?"

Mira looked up. Her dad, who stood at the base of the stairs, started toward her. The shadow had found her.

"After all I've done for you," he said, now so close to her, her pant leg almost touched his. "And this is the thanks I get." He grabbed the edge of the painting, but she didn't let go. Neither did he. "I suppose your mother got you started with this painting nonsense."

"It isn't nonsense," Mira said quietly.

His steady gaze on her always made her insides squirm. Today it was worse. "Do you know where your mother is?"

A chill breezed over her skin. "No. I don't." Now she was glad she didn't.

He grunted as if he didn't believe her and ripped the painting out of her hands. "Tell me where you went last night. And don't say your room because I know better and so do you."

"I was here." She hoped he believed her lie.

He tore her painting in half. She cringed.

"Are there more paintings than this?" he asked.

"No." She was glad the paintings were gone.

He ripped her artwork again by halves until it was a pile of one inch by one-inch pieces. "Your mother thought the Enchiridion could save us all."

He knew about the book!

Tossing the pieces of art into the garbage, he asked, "But do you know what that book will really do – if there's actually a copy left?"

Mira only stared at him.

"It will start another war," he said softly as he wiped his paint-splotched hands on the faux stone curtain, smearing them with color. "Is that what you want, Mira? To start another war?"

"I don't believe you." She'd said the words softly, but she'd never said them before. She hadn't dared.

His eyes locked onto hers. "It seems to me your LifeChip isn't working properly. And we can't have that, now can we?"

The numbness that had hid her hate and fear for so long suddenly disappeared. She got to her feet. "I'm done having you control me," she snapped. "That goes for the LifeChip, too." Swiping the paint spatula off the nightstand, she brushed past him and marched over to the sink where her mom had put her shoes. As she grabbed them, she caught sight of herself in the mirror. She paused. Blue eyes blinked back at her, soft in color but curious with a determined glare. Her dark hair was the required short style, her lips full. As she reached up to touch them, she caught the reflection of her father not far behind her. His jaw ticked, and she knew in that instant she'd gone too far. She swung around.

"If we want to completely perfect Pillar, I need to make sure nothing gets in the way." He slipped his hands into the pockets of his uniform. "And that includes you."

She was sure he could see her heartbeat knocking against her chest, but she straightened her shoulders anyway. "Let me go, Father."

He stared at her a moment. "Where? To the Accordance – my lifelong enemies?" He stepped closer, a looming roadblock between her and freedom. "Don't cross me on this Miracle Kinneson," he said as he took another step closer.

"No!" Mira lunged ahead, the spatula swinging. The metal edge of it slashed his cheek and knocked him off balance. She bolted for the stairs, but halfway up them, he managed to snag her swinging wrist. He whipped her backwards. She landed in a heap on the cold tile floor, her father's palm smashing her cheek against it. His fingers wrapped over her mouth as he shoved a vial up to her nose. "I tried so hard to change you," he said. Mira tried not to breathe as she struggled to get him off her, but she couldn't hold it any longer. Air sucked in through her nostrils, and so did the substance. "But I failed," he said. "And now you leave me no choice."

And then everything went black.

Chapter 5

Nash Montgomery stood beside his desk and raised his right hand, his voice perfectly in sync with the other twenty-four people in his Elite Reformer class.

"We promise to uphold the law at all costs and to abolish anything that might lead to war," they recited. "And in order to keep our city safe, we vow to search out and destroy anything that will oppose our efforts."

After taking their seats, the instructor, Rand Montgomery, nodded approvingly at his students. "Before I dismiss you for the weekend, there are a few things I want to go over. First, I want to congratulate you on completing your special assignments. A ten page written overview on that experience is due at the end of the month."

Nash thought about the week-long exercise he'd just completed, how it hadn't been at all what he'd expected. He shifted in his chair as his uncle continued.

"I also want to remind you that you are only four months away from graduating with your Elite Reformer Certification." Professor Montgomery strode across the raised platform to pick up a stack of sealed envelopes, each with a student's name on it. As he handed them out, he said, "Inside these envelopes I have posted your marks for each of the fields of training. The one or ones I've circled are priority areas in which you need to log forty hours or more between now and graduation."

Nash looked down at the envelope his uncle had just placed in his hands. He flipped it over and carefully undid the seal. As he pulled out the papers, he remarked, "This isn't standard."

"But it is necessary, number eleven." Rand looked at him. "A passion-inciting book called the Enchiridion of Emmanuel has resurfaced, or at least talk of it has, and we are forming a specialty group to deal with it." His gaze swung across the classroom. "Each of you is a viable candidate for this group, and working on the areas I've suggested will increase your likelihood of being chosen."

"How important is this to Pillar's safety?" number ten asked from behind Nash.

Professor Montgomery sat on the edge of his desk. "Class - refer to the bottom of your report."

As papers shuffled, Nash looked at the bottom of his page. It described the Enchiridion of Emmanuel as being alive and powerful. "It is sharper than the sharpest two-edged sword, cutting between soul and spirit, between joint and marrow. It exposes our innermost thoughts and desires." Folding his hands, Rand rested them on his thigh. "As you can see, the book is powerful, dangerous, and it will divide us. We need to destroy it before the Accordance gets their hands on it and before it wrecks everything we've worked for in Pillar."

Nash agreed. And to eradicate the Accordance in the process would be an added benefit. They'd been a thorn in the LAW's side for more than twenty years. Nash briefly glanced at his marks. He scored high in *Weaponry*, *Accordance Psychology*, *Blending with the Accordance*, and *'Cord Recognition*. The one circled was *Loyalty Class*. Nash frowned.

Rand stood and clasped his hands behind his back. "On the other page in your packet you'll find your Compatimate card and the information about the person you are to marry within a year's time. Your lineage, your background, and your intelligence and skills were inputted into our mainframe computer last week. These are the results, and I'm certain you'll find them," he paused, "ideal."

Nash flipped to the last page where his Compatimate card was clipped to the top. Reba Knight. Five feet, five inches tall. Dark hair, hazel eyes. She matched him skill- and intelligence-wise, but held a higher title as the daughter of the King of the city of Ezilli. The community was one of a few remaining in the world, but its location across the ocean might make the match more complicated. Nash tucked the papers back inside the envelope just as the bell rang.

"Homeroom is dismissed," his uncle said.

Nash approached the podium as the last of the students vacated the room. "Professor Montgomery?"

"Yes?"

"I don't understand why you circled Loyalty Class as my weakness. I am entirely loyal to our cause."

"Are you?" Rand shoved a stack of papers into his top right drawer. "I know you probably didn't realize this, but we had things in place to oversee your special assignment." He shoved the drawer closed. "There was one choice of yours in particular that was flagged as questionable."

Nash knew what it was. "I can explain."

Rand raised his hand to cut him off. "Explain it in your report. And use this time between now and graduation to prove your loyalty."

Nash squared his shoulders. "I will, Professor Montgomery. I will."

Chapter 6

Mira didn't want to wake up, but the screaming was getting louder and she couldn't move her hands to get them up over her ears. She opened her eyes. The first thing she noticed was the panoramic image flickering across the walls of the eight by eight room. That explained the screams. *It's not real*, she told herself. *It's just a movie.* But the man strapped in the chair across from her *was* real. At least she thought he was. He was breathing, but other than that, he didn't move, nor did he open his eyes.

Mira yanked up hard on the thick bands that cuffed her ankles and wrists, but it only gouged at her tender skin. Her efforts didn't seem to do much at all, and after only a few minutes, she felt totally wiped out. She gulped for the air that didn't seem to reach her lungs.

"*Go ahead and do it, do it,*" the man sang softly, his voice deep but with a smile in it.

This was hardly the time for singing. "Do what?" she rasped. Her throat was so dry.

"Scream. They'll come for us then and finish what they started."

At first she didn't think she'd heard right. "You *want* them to come for us?" She certainly did not.

He opened his eyes and stared at her a moment. "Maybe."

What? Mira frowned at the perplexing man. He was about twice her age, but not old enough to be senile. Maybe he was just crazy. "I'm not going to scream," she said, although she had to admit it was hard keeping it inside, almost like a sneeze…right on the edge. "Where are we?"

"The Stint." The man grunted and closed his eyes again, the corner of his mouth curving up slightly. "Just got done with the memory cell extraction. Like I'd hoped, it didn't work on me so my next stop is Enab."

Enab? Mira tried frantically to grasp at each piece of memory floating around in her mind, but they were like wisps of fog that couldn't be caught. "I can't remember anything," she said, her mouth tight, her skin suddenly clammy.

The grey flecks in his dark eyebrows shifted when he looked up at her, his icy blue gaze making her shiver. "But you're scheduled to be taken to Enab, which doesn't make sense if the memory cell extraction worked on you. Wonder what you did."

She wondered, too, but couldn't speak past the lump in her throat. Why did he have to stare at her like that? Hoping for something to jog her memory as well as to avoid his stare, she turned and looked at the screen. A boat was tied up at a dock. Inside it were five people wearing torn and dirty clothes, a big difference from the accompanying officers in their city issued uniforms.

"That's Enab," the guy across from her said, his blue eyes crinkling in the corners.

Now she remembered more about the island. It wasn't much, but it was enough to make her squirm.

He grinned.

She could feel her cheeks flush and decided she didn't like this guy much. "And it's not funny, you jerk!"

"I agree, but it *is* human...what we were meant to be."

She bit down hard on her lip to keep it from trembling as she watched her upcoming fate play out on the screen. The officers had a dead-eyed look as they dumped their prisoners out onto the dock. One prisoner fell onto the weathered wooden planks face-first before getting to his hands and knees and staying there. Blood dripped freely from his nose. One woman curled into a ball, sobbing. The other two prisoners, a woman and a young girl, spat and shouted at the officers, their eyes narrowed with hate and determination. The last prisoner jumped onto the dock of his own free will, and as he did so, he turned to look at the camera. His stare was familiar somehow, and it was one that said *You're next...and I'll be waiting for you.*. Mira yanked on her wrists. "I can't go to Enab! You have to help me."

The guy's long, straight nose flared a bit. "Enab won't be that bad."

Without warning, tears spilled from her eyes, winding down her cheeks and into the crease of her mouth. And she couldn't even wipe them off! "Well with or without your help, I'm getting out of here." This time she tried twisting her hands, but nothing happened except for a sharp pain bolting up her arm.

He tilted his head to the side. "You remind me of someone I knew once. What's your name?"

She tugged hard on her arms again. The straps didn't give at all. She lashed out, "What's yours? Idiot...Fool...Good-for-nothing?"

He chuckled. "No. It's Vaughn. Do you even remember your name?"

She did. And she remembered a few other things now too, like the fiend on Enab. She'd seen him before – in Freetown. Her chest felt unbelievably tight and she wondered if she was having a heart attack.

"I told you my name. It's your turn," he said, not seeming to notice that she was struggling to breathe.

"Mira," she barked, "short for Miracle – something I could use right now." She pulled harder on her wrists.

Vaughn stopped smiling. Whatever. It didn't matter. She didn't need to figure *him* out. She only needed to figure *a way* out.

The screen suddenly exploded with color and transitioned into a scene where a book with a pillar of fire on its cover was being ripped apart, each of its pages tossed into an incinerator by a guard with stubbly grey hair. And she was the prisoner on the screen, forced to watch. "You can't win," said the guard.

"Don't believe it, Mira," Vaughn said in a deep, commanding voice.

She looked over at him. His tears matched her own. Then he yanked up hard on his own bindings. "I'm getting us out of here," he said. "We have a world to save."

Chapter 7

Vaughn's arm cuffs snapped like brittle rubber bands. He bent to undo his ankles.

"How'd you do that?" Mira asked, watching as he moved to unshackle her legs and then her arms. It was then that she noticed how muscular his arms were.

"Where there's a will, there's a way," he hummed.

Neither his little tune nor his super-strength did much to calm her, but her options were limited. She clutched her pounding heart to keep it from escaping without her as she followed Vaughn to the door.

Rubbing his forearm, he peeked into the hallway through the four-by-ten-inch window. "The thing to remember about the LAW is that they think simply and they aren't good at anticipating anything outside their standard."

"I'll keep that in mind," she said, glimpsing the single guard who stood sentry right outside their door. "But how are we getting out of here?"

"First thing we need to do is to be able to blend once we're out." He rubbed his chin. "Now I'm glad they shaved my beard."

"Where can we get city-issued clothes?" Mira asked, looking down at the bright white emblem on her shirt that marked her as a prisoner.

Vaughn grinned. "All we have to do is flip it inside out." He whipped his shirt over his head and put it back on, the emblem now hidden against his skin.

"Nice." She told him to turn around and flipped her own shirt around.

"Now you look the part, but we might run into some… complications, so you'll need to focus on controlling your emotions too. Can you do that?"

"I've done it before." Not under these circumstances, but at least she had a little experience.

"Good. Hand me that tray by the computer sitting right next to you."

She turned, her eyes zoning in on the bloody cotton ball and the tiny metal pick lying on it. Eew! Nudging the pieces off to the side with her fingertip, she handed the tray to Vaughn. "What next?"

"I open the door, clock the guard with the tray, and then we walk out and blend. You ready to spend a weekend in Necropolis?"

Necropolis was an area preserved by the LAW to serve as a reminder of the catastrophes of war. Mira had seen pictures of it in school – the mass graveyard of both machine and man. It was hardly ideal. "Do I have another choice?"

"Just Necropolis or this lovely palace," Vaughn said.

She didn't have to look around to answer. "Any place is better than here," she said, swiping at the sweat on her neck.

"Good." Vaughn reached for the knob and turned it slowly. "On the count of three. One, two, three."

Chapter 8

The Loyalty classroom was identical to Nash's homeroom. The only difference was the teacher. Ms. Smith stood on the platform facing her students.

"A few moments ago, LAW officials informed me of an escape." She stepped down one of the two steps. "And with this information came a request that I use it as a true-to-life example. I will give you the details about the case. You will write a paper on possible strategies for capturing the prisoners as well as how you would go about locating and destroying the Enchiridion of Emmanuel."

"This isn't standard," Nash said.

"I realize that, but the Accordance is getting bolder, and..." She picked up the remote control, which she aimed at the projector. "Well, after I show you this, you'll understand." She clicked the remote. A man's picture popped up onto the screen. "Here is one of the two prisoners who escaped yesterday. This one is thought to be the leader of the Accordance."

Nash studied the man's face. He should be easy to spot with his beard – unless they'd shaved it at the Stint.

Ms. Smith clicked to the next slide. "And this is the other escapee. She is reported to have visions that can lead the Accordance to the Enchiridion of Emmanuel."

The picture of the woman wasn't clear, and her hair and clothing were fitting for a citizen of Pillar, which would make her hard to pick out. And yet...there was something about her that made him unable to pull his eyes away.

The professor swung back around to face her class. "Seal these images in your mind and remember that they are our enemies."

At the nods from the rest of the class, she continued. Clicking to the next page, she showed a picture of the Enchiridion. It had a pillar surrounded with fire on the cover.

Nash made notes as the teacher went on to say, "This paper is due at the end of the week and will be scored by the School Council before the end of the summer."

"That isn't standard," Nash said.

"It's not. But building a special force is vital – or we'll be back to this." Ms. Smith clicked to the next slide, which pictured Pillar after it had been bombed. "Or this." The slide following showed a place they called Necropolis, an area littered with gravestones, crashed planes, tanks, and submarines along with rows of shipping containers that were no longer used due to lack of overseas trading.

"Any questions?"

No one spoke up, so she dismissed the class.

Nash left the room. This paper just might be the advantage he needed to get his name on the list for the specialty group tasked with finding the Enchiridion of Emmanuel. "Pillar…you are safe with me," he said.

Chapter 9

They'd made it to the southwestern edge of Pillar without incident, but Mira still couldn't get the image of the guard's crumpled body out of her head. "Did you have to clock that guard so hard? You could've killed him!"

Vaughn snorted. "It barely dented the tray." He continued his trek into an area dense with trees. "And I would do anything to keep you safe," he added quietly.

The admission confused her. "Why?"

He didn't answer, only asked her another question. "Does anything look familiar to you? Anything at all?"

Were they lost? She scanned the area, her emotions jumping to high alert. "I don't know where we are." She latched onto Vaughn's arm as the forest, swamped with the gray of dusk, seemed to come alive.

"You're all right," he said softly.

"No I'm not!" Shadows shifted around her like wild animals or pursuers or both. "Over there in the trees, something moved."

"It's just a swinging tree branch." Vaughn pressed his hand over hers instead of peeling it off his arm. "Take a deep breath and relax."

She closed her eyes and saw the face of her enemy, so she opened them right back up again. Would she never feel safe?

He started walking again, but at a slower pace this time, tugging her along with him. After a few moments, she dropped his arm and fell into step beside him.

He glanced down at her. "You okay now?"

"That depends."

"On what?"

"Why you said you'd do anything to keep me safe."

He looked at her for a long while then gazed toward the mountain that seemed to be their destination. "You're not ready to know the truth yet," he said, "but you'll learn soon enough." He picked up the pace. "Come on. We need to get there before it gets too dark."

Mira stared at his retreating back. What did he mean she wasn't ready to know the truth? She stomped after him. "Tell me the truth! I deserve to know."

He glanced her way. He wasn't angry, but his look was stern. "When we get there will be soon enough."

She growled, rather loudly. Her emotions were starting to seem like they had exclamation points after them rather than question marks. She wanted to shout at him, only she held back. Right now, it was vital to keep up with the man who had rescued her, and who had some answers she was itching to uncover.

For several miles, she stuck close to Vaughn, watching the beige heel of his boot as he took each quick, rhythmic step. She tried to come up with viable reasons for him wanting to keep her safe, but she couldn't think of anything anyone would know about her that would make it worth risking his life to save her. Maybe it would make sense when she recalled more of her past – if her memory after the Amender process ever completely returned.

"How much longer?" she asked, her feet throbbing even though they were walking on a soft carpet of pine needles.

"It's just up ahead."

"Why are we going to Necropolis anyway?"

"It's a perfect place to hide – and I have a meeting there tomorrow night," he admitted.

"What kind of meeting?"

He stopped to wipe his sweaty face with the bottom edge of his shirt. "An emergency meeting with the leaders of all the Accordance off-chutes."

At hearing that, her limbs seized up like rigor mortis had set in. Had she just gotten herself into bigger trouble? "What do you mean by off-chutes?" Her voice trembled without permission.

Vaughn looked at her strangely. "You don't remember much, do you?"

She grabbed her head and pressed in on her temples with her fingertips. Why couldn't she remember?

"It will come back to you," he said softly. He tucked his hands into his front pants pockets. "For right now, all you need to know is that you are important and so am I. I'm the leader of the 'Cords. I have a lot of power and a lot of connections." He looked off toward the thirty-year-old battleground where they were to spend the night. "And believe me when I say that I'll do anything to protect you, Mira. The reasons don't matter. Just know you are safe with me."

Maybe it was the sincerity of his voice or that he'd risked his life to save her. Whatever it was, she was too tired to come up with an alternative. "Okay, I believe you."

"Good." He smiled. "Now let's get you to Necropolis."

Within fifteen minutes, they were standing in front of a rust-colored shipping container, punching in a code. A door at the end opened and they went inside.

Vaughn took a lantern off the wall and lit it. As he moved through the boxy metal container, he said, "We've created a network inside this area. It's never occurred to the LAW that we could be holding our meetings here, or that it's our main place to hide fugitives."

"So that's what I am then? A fugitive?"

"Yeah. And it means you need to lay low for a while." They continued on through the maze of connected receptacles until they got to the end of one that had angled upward. Vaughn punched another code into a box on the wall. A door swung open, the moonlight streaming through it to reveal a ship in front of them. "Come on."

She followed Vaughn onto the weathered wooden deck. Frayed sails drooped from the mast, swinging slightly in the breeze. A hole gaped just beyond the ship's splintered wheel. Even though the craft had been grounded, Mira could still picture it floating on the ocean, its crew under attack. The fear and the death that might have occurred on this very vessel camped in her mind and made her sad all the way through. Frowning, she moved below deck behind Vaughn.

"Here you go…captain's quarters of the only schooner left on earth," Vaughn said as he entered a small room. "Just for you, my dear." He looked at her. "What? You don't like it?" He held the lantern high.

She tried to shake off the gloom and followed the sweep of light. The room had a full-sized bed on one side, a desk on the other. A wardrobe and large trunk sat smack against the wall opposite the door they'd entered. There was a tiny round window behind the desk. She guessed it would give her a view of the shipping containers, or maybe the graveyard.

"This is usually where I stay," he said, "but it's where you'll be safest, so it's all yours."

"It's quite nice," she said, amazed at how fresh it smelled.

"There are clothes in the wardrobe and a bathroom right next to it if you need them."

She hadn't noticed the bathroom door that blended in with the wood-paneled walls, but the wardrobe was a bold salmon color that couldn't be missed.

"And help yourself to the snacks in the trunk," Vaughn said, edging toward the desk. "I replenished my stash last time I was here."

Mira wondered when that had been, how often he came, what they talked about at their meetings…but her mouth felt like it was too tired to open and her brain suddenly felt overloaded. She walked to the bed and sat down.

"I'll be back in the morning with breakfast," he said, "unless you need anything else."

She needed answers, but needed rest more. "Right now, I just want to sleep."

He smiled in a kind sort of way. "That's what I thought." He lit a lantern that sat on the desk and brought it to her. "Make sure you blow this out before you go to sleep. If you need to relight it, there's a pack of matches in the top drawer of the desk."

"Okay."

"See you in the morning, then."

"Okay," she said with a yawn, thinking the puffy square pillow looked as good as anything she'd ever seen in her life.

As Vaughn ducked through the doorway, he paused and looked over his shoulder. "I'm glad you're here, Mira." And then he was gone.

Chapter 10

Thump!

Mira popped upright, clutching her covers up to her chin. She listened. The muffled pitter-patter of tiny feet racing sounded above her. A squirrel running on the upper deck maybe? Smiling, she wondered if squirrels made good pets. She stretched and took a good look around. The room was pleasant enough, and surprisingly clean, and the bright sunlight peeking through the lone window was an added bonus.

She slid off the bed and padded over to the desk. A plate of cheese and crackers and a pewter mug of water rested on the scarred wooden surface. Had Vaughn brought the food in while she'd been asleep? That gave her pause, but she wasn't going to worry about it right now.

Mira stacked three slices of cheese on a cracker and stuffed the entire thing in her mouth. As she chewed, she noticed a chunk of gold stone sitting atop a pile of papers. She picked up the cool, smooth rock and settled it into her hand. She liked the weight and feel of it. Tossing it up gently, she caught it again and again in her left hand as she flipped through the papers with her right. One of the pages had a sketch of Necropolis. The rows of shipping containers and abandoned war apparatuses created an interwoven maze of lodging rooms, a communications chamber, a meeting space, a docking area, and a medical care unit. One structure was different, though. It sat in a tree and was named the Lookout.

She laid the golden stone down and grabbed a few more cracker sandwiches. Turning to the next page, she saw it was a map of Pillar and its surrounding area. Red X's marked several houses throughout the town. Outside of city limits showed a farm with a greenhouse, a facility called the Pioneer Center, and a factory of some sort. There were also a few unmarked areas circled and the island of Enab was circled in purple ink, several times, as was Spirit Cavern.

Mira took a swig of the lukewarm water and set the map aside. A sudden uprush of pressure formed beneath her skull. She stared at the cup in horror. Had it been poisoned? Legs no longer able to hold her up, she sank into the wooden captain's chair. Clutching the arms, she blinked at the picture lying on the desktop, wondering if it would be the last thing she'd see. Yet as it faded from her mind's view and her eyes began to quiver and roll back into her head, something else took its place.

A young man appeared, looking over his shoulder at her, his hair as black as his eyes. He wore tan pants like the citizens of Pillar, but his back was bare because his sweaty shirt was tucked into his pocket. The only flaw she noticed was an inch-long jagged scar on the bronzed skin just above his waistband. As she gazed directly into his eyes, the air seemed too heavy for her to breathe. She'd never been looked at like that before! Even though the throbbing in her head continued, she wanted to go to him, to touch him, to get to know who he was. She reached out, half expecting to feel his warm skin beneath her fingertips. Instead, her hand sliced through the air. The image dimmed.

"No," she rasped. Yet even though she tried to stay inside her dream, a fog drifted in and clouded her view until the guy disappeared completely. She frowned, feeling empty and frustrated. Slowly, Mira opened her eyes. Without thinking, she dug in the desk drawer and pulled out a notebook and a pencil. Then as if something was nudging her hand, she drew an exact replica of the guy she'd seen in her vision.

She stared at him. Who was he? Why had she drawn him? Was it just an overactive imagination due to her being chipless? She didn't know how long she stayed there studying her drawing of him, but the knock on her door was the first thing that pulled her gaze away.

"Yeah?"

"Can I come in? I have some supper for you," Vaughn said.

Supper? "Yeah, sure," she said, grabbing the picture, torn between wanting to show Vaughn and wanting to keep it a secret. She settled for holding it against her chest until she decided.

"Glad to see you're finally awake. I was starting to worry." Vaughn set the food tray down in front of her.

"I'm fine," she said. She must have been totally exhausted to sleep so soundly for so long.

"So what do you have there?" He pointed at the notebook in her hands.

"I had a dream – and I drew it." She watched his face closely to see how he'd react to her admission.

He didn't seem surprised...at all. "What did you draw?"

"Just a guy."

"Is it someone you know?"

She shook her head. "Do you?" She felt like she *had* to take a chance. She tilted the sketch toward Vaughn, but didn't let go.

Vaughn squinted at the picture. "His name is Gabe," he said. "He is a chef and occasionally delivers food here."

She couldn't believe it! Vaughn knew him! She snatched the picture back and hugged it against her again. Then something dawned on her. "Why aren't you surprised that I'd had a dream that I'd drawn? Is that a normal thing around here?"

Vaughn went to the window and looked out. "No, Mira, you're one of a kind and not just because you have visions that you draw."

Did he say visions? "Go on," she said, clutching the notebook until the metal ringed edge dug into her skin.

"Word on the street is that your visions – ones like you had today - are prophetic and that you've even had visions about the Enchiridion of Emmanuel."

Prophetic visions? No wonder they wanted her out of the LAW's hands!

"Any chance you remember your visions about the Enchiridion?" His voice dropped to a passionate whisper. "We need to find it before the LAW does."

As she rubbed her temples, she managed to recall pieces and portions of her past, but couldn't get much to come together or to make sense of it. "The only thing I remember clearly about the Enchiridion is that I made a vow to my mom that I would find it."

"That's a good start." Vaughn smiled, but it didn't quite reach his eyes. "And you need to stay healthy, so eat up. Gabe made that sandwich, by the way."

She picked up the ham sandwich layered with some smooth cheese sauce and something green. "Do you think I could meet him soon?"

Vaughn walked toward the door. "Since your vision was of Gabe and we don't know what that means exactly, I think it's best that you stay put for now."

"It could mean nothing…and maybe the only way to know what it means is to meet him."

He paused a moment, seemingly thinking it over. "Or it could be putting you in more danger than necessary. Just give us some time to formulate a strategy. Then we'll talk about setting up a meeting with Gabe."

She had to agree that he made some sense. "How much time are we talking here?"

He chuckled. "We have a meeting tonight to discuss strategy. We'll go from there."

A meeting might be fun. At least she'd be doing something! "So what time are we getting together to discuss all this?"

"*We* are not. You're not invited."

She stood up and leaned forward on the desk. "You're kidding."

"No. I'm not kidding. This is serious business, and like I said before, your security is of utmost importance."

She snagged the sandwich and popped a hunk of it into her mouth. The sauce was a little spicy, the green thing crunchy with a twist of sour and sweet flavoring. "I can take care of myself," she growled.

"And yet when I checked on you several times today, you didn't even stir."
He shook his head. "You'll have to trust me on this." Vaughn didn't wait to
listen to her side. He strode out the door, humming as he shut it behind him.

"I don't *have* to trust anyone," she yelled, flinging the sandwich at the door.
Splat! The shot made her feel better…until she heard a click.

No way! This can't be happening, she thought, scrambling across the room. She
grabbed the knob and twisted. Sure enough - it was locked.

Pursing her lips, she picked the sandwich off the floor. After putting it back
together, she bit off a piece and stomped over to the trunk. Opening it, she
muttered, "I was a prisoner in my own house…" She chewed and swallowed,
then shoved the remainder of the sandwich into her mouth. "I was a prisoner of
the LifeChip and the LAW…" She dug into the trunk's contents and picked out
a cap. "I refuse to be a prisoner now." Mira slammed the cap onto her head and
strode to the desk to look for something to pick the lock.

Chapter 11

After studying the map of Necropolis and jotting down a plan to eavesdrop on the meeting, Mira grabbed the bobby pins she'd found in one of the wardrobe's drawers. Propping the lantern on a chair she'd placed next to the door, she knelt in front of the lock. She straightened one of the bobby pins and shoved it into the key hole. She thought she felt the lock give, so she tried the knob. It didn't turn.

"How many people have you imprisoned here, Vaughn?" she muttered. What other explanation could there be for the knob locking from the outside? Well, she wasn't going to let it beat her – let *anyone* beat her. She was tired of being kept in the dark, tired of being controlled.

"Come on, now…unlock for me." Carefully, so carefully, she tried again. But again, the hairpin bent. She growled and inserted another one, jiggling the knob as she did so. Yet when she tried to turn the doorknob, it remained stubbornly immobile. She groaned and yelled, and jumping to her feet, kicked the knob hard.

"Ouch!" she wailed, hopping on one foot around the room. "Stupid door, stupid Vaughn, stupid dream!" After several aching hops, she slowly rested her throbbing foot back onto the floor. Gritting her teeth, she hobbled back to the door. She gave the knob a quick twist just in case her kick had worked to unlock it, but it held firm. Shoving back her frustration, she swung the lantern up to the brass knob and leaned in to get a closer look. It appeared as though there was a little pin that stuck up like a tooth on the edge of the key hole.

"If I can push that down…" she whispered, grabbing another hairpin. She bent the curved end over so it looked a bit like a boot for a stick person. Inserting the rounded tip into the lock, she hooked it over the tooth and pulled it downward. Sweat beaded on her upper lip as she took a second bobby pin, a straightened one, and shoved it across the first pin and into the lock. Gingerly, she used the tip of the straight one to press up against the downward-facing teeth. One by one, she maneuvered the hairpin ahead. *Click.*

She paused a moment, half-disbelieving, half-giddy. She tried the lock. It opened? It really opened! She sprang to her feet and twirled around and around, the ache in her foot gone. "Yes!" she said, and flung the door wide. The gust of fresh air was almost as exhilarating as her hard-won freedom. She would waste neither. Inhaling deeply, she bounded up the stairs to the upper deck. When she got to the rail, she paused. For a moment, she was caught up in imagining what it would have been like to be part of the crew of this ship. What would it be like to climb to the top of the mast, to look out across the sea, to the feel the salty spray on her face? Maybe she would find out someday. But someday wasn't today.

With the layout of Necropolis memorized and the moon shining brightly, she left the lantern on the deck and jumped over the side of the boat to the ground in which it was partially buried. After a quick look around and seeing no one, she started to move. Her fingertips grazed each groove of cool metal as she jogged alongside the shipping containers. Staying close to them was her best bet, and they would lead her right to the one at the edge of the property where she suspected the meeting was being held.

She slowed down to adjust for the uneven clumps of weeds sprouting up all around the containers, but she was still winded by the time she stopped. She'd counted twenty-four containers, which should put her right around the corner from the meeting. As she took a minute to catch her breath, she listened. Muffled voices drifted through the cool evening air, but she couldn't make out what they were saying. She had to get closer.

Crouching, she dashed between the half-crushed fighter jet and a rusted tank that sat only four yards in front of the place they were meeting. They'd left the door ajar, probably for the fresh air. Pausing beside the tank's enormous treads, Mira listened.

"First, I'd like to hear all your proposals on what we should do about Mira."

Mira held her breath as she waited to hear how the group would answer Vaughn. For several moments, no one said a word. Then someone spoke up – a female voice.

"I say we take her to the Innovation Station and analyze her dreams."

"How about we use her to make a deal with the LAW? A barter of some sort," another said. "She – and her visions - are worth a lot to them."

Mira's stomach cinched up. She couldn't just let them decide her fate. But should she run – or try to negotiate with the group? She didn't know what to do! She inhaled deeply, trying to think, and caught a whiff of something that made her stomach growl. The scent preceded its source. A van, marked with the words, "Deli Delivery", pulled up beside the container where the group was meeting.

Grasping the tank's stiff, thick tread, she peeked around it. The guy delivering the food got out of his vehicle. Mira gasped. It was Gabe! Eyes wide open, she drank in the sight of him. He was exactly as she'd envisioned, only instead of being bare-backed, he wore the typical Pillar-style shirt. Whistling softly, he went to the back of his van. After a few moments, he reappeared carrying a stack of twelve one-inch high cardboard boxes. When he was almost to the steps that would lead him to his hungry customers, she made a decision.

Darting to the back of the van, she jumped inside. She slipped over the single bench that sat about midway between the front seats and the cargo area. Crouching between the bench and the driver's seat, she waited. Finally, Gabe returned. He shut the back doors and slid behind the wheel.

As he drove off-site, she heard a soft click. A mournful sound filtered through the speakers of the van. She closed her eyes, listening to Gabe's voice as it drew her in. *"I see fire in the distance…will it bring warmth and light…or will it destroy our souls…"*. The van bumped along as she watched the street lights flash by, their rhythmic pattern blending with the solemn tune. Suddenly, the van screeched to a stop. Mira squealed louder than the tires did.

Gabe swung around and grabbed her wrists. "What are you doing here?" he shouted into her face.

This wasn't how she'd anticipated their meeting and she was trying not to freak out. He had to be a good guy, right? "I…I'm escaping."

His dark eyes narrowed. "I saw you by the tank. Are you a spy?"

"No, I'm ah…I really don't know who I am exactly."

His eyes softened. "Amender bug?"

She shivered.

It must have been enough of an answer for him because he let go. "Do you want me to bring you somewhere?"

Her bottom lip trembled in delayed reaction as she moved up onto the bench seat. "I don't have anywhere to go."

"Hmm." Shifting the van into drive, he looked at her for several seconds through the rearview mirror. "Want to see my restaurant?"

She managed a shaky smile. "I'd like that."

Gabe said nothing else, but kept glancing in the mirror and over his shoulder at her. She wondered what he thought. And then it hit her.

"I must look horrible." She swiped at her face, knowing there had to be dirt all over it.

"A little grimy, but not horrible." He smiled and her heart flipped. "Definitely not horrible," he said as he pulled into an alleyway behind a restaurant called Joe's Deli.

"Do you own this place or just work here?" she asked as he cut the engine.

"My family has owned it for generations. My brother and I are the only ones left, though." He got out of the van and opened the side door for her. "I don't suppose you remember much about your family." His eyes were questioning.

"Not much," she said, which was true.

"Well, come on then. I'll show you around the place. Then we can figure out what to do with you."

Chapter 12

The cleverly designed restaurant had two work areas. Gabe's brother ran the one located at the front of the building. It was set up with the basics used for cooking bland food for the citizens of Pillar. The other area was hidden behind a false wall and it was where Gabe created food for the Accordance. This secret area had shelves of spices and varieties of foods Mira hadn't even heard of. On the north end of the kitchen was a set of steps and Gabe led her up this skinny staircase to a rooftop garden.

They walked through a row of dwarf orange trees, the aroma sweet and citrusy. Stopping beside a planter, Gabe dug into its tangle of green leaves. "So this is pretty much my life in a nutshell," he said. "Grow a little food, create some interesting dishes, and deliver them under the cover of night." He picked a strawberry and handed it to her. "Taste it."

She gazed into his ebony eyes and felt warm and hungry. And as she bit into the strawberry, the gush of flavor was almost too much for her senses. She'd had practice with many of her emotions, but the one she was feeling now was new to her, or at least she didn't remember ever feeling this way.

"Gabe, I…" She swallowed the sweet fruit. Unable to help herself, she reached out to touch his shoulder. "I might be dangerous…I mean dangerous to be around."

"All 'Cords are dangerous to be around," he said with a slight smile. He covered her hand with his own. "Mmmm. That feels nice." His quiet acceptance emboldened her.

"But I'm different."

He looked at her just as he had in her vision. "I can believe that." Taking her hand, he led her to a bench. He sat down and patted the spot beside him.

She sat. When he didn't say anything for several long moments, she uttered, "I feel like I want to know you better." It was more than that, actually. It was a feeling that seemed to seize every one of her senses even as it inspired fantastical imaginings in her mind. She wanted more…more of him, more of this feeling rushing through her veins.

He grinned. "What would you like to know, beside the fact that I can cook better than anyone in Pillar?"

His perfect teeth dazzled her for a moment. Then she blurted the first thing that came into her head. "Where did you get the scar on your back?"

His smile faded. "How did you know about my scar? My shirt covers it up."

She realized her mistake, but he didn't look angry. "I had a vision. That vision was you," she admitted.

"Visions, huh?" He looked down at his scuffed shoes. "That meeting was about you, wasn't it?"

"Yes."

He laughed softly. "Now I get why you didn't want to stick around Necropolis." He paused to squeeze her hand. "I also know you can trust Vaughn."

"How do you know that?"

"Because he has a strong sense of justice *and* compassion." He looked out across the rooftops of Pillar's businesses. "Vaughn made sure I got the medical help I needed. He also helped my brother and me move to Pillar and assume new identities so we could continue the business that's been in my family for generations."

She felt better hearing that. "That's good to know." She stared at their clasped hands, which felt strange, but nice. "I just don't know how I fit in to all this."

He looked at her in a way she didn't understand. Then he said, "You know, I felt that way right after my surgery." Gabe told her his story, how he'd been very sick and, due to the medical system in their city of Ezilli being worthless, his brother Eli had gotten him to the Accordance's medical unit. Gabe had been diagnosed with a rare kidney disease and Eli had given him one of his. "So you see, I owe my brother big time and also the Accordance for saving my life," Gabe said, "and I also feel like a traitor because 'Cords were responsible for killing my parents."

"What happened to your parents?" she asked softly.

His jaw clenched and for a moment he said nothing. Then he whispered, "That story will have to wait for another time."

"I understand." She tightened her grip on his hand. "Even though I feel like I owe Vaughn for rescuing me from the Stint, I made a promise to my mom and I don't know if Vaughn and his group are going to be the ones to help me follow through on it." She paused, trying to think about how to best word it. "Supposedly, my prophetic visions include ones about the Enchiridion of Emmanuel. I promised to find it."

Gabe whistled. "So you're Mira."

She nodded.

"You are quite the celebrity, pretty lady. The Reformers, the Unified Church, *and* the Accordance – you're high on *all* their wanted lists."

Her heart dropped to her stomach, but she snorted and flicked her free hand as if to wave away a mosquito.

"I don't think you realize how much danger you are in," he said.

She didn't know the depth of the danger, but she'd felt it in a way that seemed to reach her soul. "I warned you I might be dangerous to be around."

"Yes. You did." He smiled. "But I don't care."

"You don't?"

"I have a feeling you're worth the risk."

I'm worth it? Although Gabe remained completely still beside her, it felt like he was closer, warmer. She leaned into that warmth, resting her head against his shoulder. She couldn't help herself.

After a few silent moments, he asked, "Have you ever thought about what it would be like to have someone to love, to start a family with, to grow old with in a free world?"

The vision she'd had of Gabe had filled her mind with all kinds of ideas. And Gabe in the flesh had sparked dreams she'd only begun to imagine, leaving behind a heart aching for more. Could love and family be the answer? She looked into his dark eyes, and felt hope flutter inside her chest. "Do you think it's possible?"

"I do." He looked away. "But not until we are free from the LifeChip and the LAW…not until we have the Enchiridion of Emmanuel."

"Wouldn't freedom be enough?"

"We've had freedom – a freedom that cost me my parents." Gabe got up, walked over to a cabinet, and grabbed a book called *Rooftop Gardening*. As he strode back to her, he pulled out a folded piece of paper and handed it to her. "I found this when we set up our business here."

Mira unfolded the tattered page and read the carefully written entries.

April 5, The War Has Begun

My city is crumbling before my eyes. I am afraid, but I will forever hold these words in my heart:

"My child, pay attention to what I say. Listen carefully to my words. Don't lose sight of them. Let them penetrate deep into your heart, for they bring life to those who find them, and healing to their whole body." *A Proverb from the Enchiridion of Emmanuel.*

September 23, War-torn and Weary

My friend died in my arms today. I am so tired, but my hope remains. When will the hate end and the healing begin?

"These things happened to them as examples for us. They were written down to warn us who live at the end of the age. If you think you are standing strong, be careful not to fall." *From Corinthians, the Enchiridion of Emmanuel.*

January 18, The LifeChip of Fools:

The war has ended, but I suspect another war of a different kind has just begun. The LAW has required us to implant something called a LifeChip beneath our skin. They tell us that it will "adjust" our emotions to help us cope, that it will lessen disease, and that it will prevent another war. Most are so tired and hopeless, they have voluntarily gone along with the idea. Those of us who oppose it are being rounded up for psychological assessment.

"When people are saying, "Everything is peaceful and secure," then disaster will fall on them as suddenly as a pregnant woman's labor pains begin. And there will be no escape." *From Thessalonians, the Enchiridion of Emmanuel.*

April 5

Peace? Destroying who we are isn't peace! Controlling us isn't peace! Peace comes from within our souls. But the LAW has hidden the truth…and they have found me. I pray someone finds these words, that they find the Enchiridion of Emmanuel. We are on the road to destruction, and there's only one way that we can be saved!

"He sent out his word and healed them, snatching them from the door of death." *A Psalm from the Enchiridion of Emmanuel*

"Do you know who wrote this?" Mira asked.

"No. It was here when we moved in." He looked around the small hidden rooftop area. "The more I see of our world, the more I read these words, the more I believe we're on the wrong path."

She felt the same. "But what is the right one?"

"I'm not sure. I know it's more than being shackled in mediocrity. It's more than stifled creativity. It's more than Compatimates and heartless relationships."

With a long drawn out sigh, he sat down beside her again. Taking the page from her, his eyes seemed to caress the words as he read. "I believe the answer is in the Enchiridion of Emmanuel." His eyes met hers. "And I believe that you and Vaughn working together is our best hope for finding the powerful book."

"I just don't know if I can trust Vaughn – or the leaders of the Accordance off-chutes. Did you hear what they were considering doing to me?"

He shook his head. "Vaughn is sensible and he has connections you'd never have on your own." He folded the paper and handed it to her. "Take this to Vaughn. Work with him to win our freedom. It's the best way to succeed."

Maybe Gabe was right. She tucked the folded paper into her pocket. "You wouldn't happen to have a spare knife and some more food to deliver to Necropolis, would you?"

"As a matter of fact…" He stood up and held out his hand to her. She took it. "I do," he said. Pulling her up into his arms, his eyes glittered with promise.

Part of her was inspired to take on the world, yet part of her just wanted to stay on this rooftop with Gabe. "What about us?" she dared to ask. "Will I ever see you again?"

"I swear I'll come back to you, Mira, if it's the last thing I do."

Chapter 13

Nash peered through the viewing room window at the interrogation of a man who'd been captured only moments ago.

"Are you taking notes?" his uncle Rand asked.

"I am," Nash said, jotting down the name *Gabe*.

"You do realize I'm giving you a big advantage here, right?" Rand shifted his feet. "This guy should give you enough information to write your final paper for Loyalty Class."

Nash watched the prisoner's white-knuckled grip on the arms of his chair. He jotted down the emotional term. *Scared.* "Why do you care about my paper?"

"No reason."

Nash grunted. His uncle's reasons didn't matter, but his own reasons did. He wanted to succeed as an Elite Reformer. Nash turned up the speaker's volume so he could better hear the exchange.

"I'm on your side," Gabe said. "I want the Enchiridion destroyed just as much as you do. My family has a history of trying to eradicate it from the face of the earth."

Nash made a note. *Gabe's look was in line with him telling the truth.*

The interrogator continued to pace in front of the prisoner, who was shackled to a metal chair. "That may be, but our records show that you are playing both sides."

"Records?" Gabe swallowed hard.

"Our sweeper picked up a disturbance in your van and followed you to your restaurant. There was a conversation you had on the roof with a woman. This conversation was recorded."

The guy visibly paled.

Very afraid, Nash wrote.

"Do you want us to play it back?" the interrogator questioned.

Gabe shook his head once. "What is it that you want from me?"

"We want you to lead us to where the Accordance is meeting and to where the prophetic woman is."

Nash watched the man carefully. He was struggling to decide.

"I'd die first," Gabe finally blurted.

The interrogator leaned toward his enemy. "I know how you 'Cords work. And I know what will break you."

The guy's eyes narrowed, his chin lifted as if he was daring him to try.

"If you don't cooperate, we will kill your brother Eli and burn down your business – all while you watch."

Gabe's eyes were hard, yet had a sheen of glassiness. Nash couldn't comprehend the combination. This emotion wasn't in any of the books he'd read.

"*If* I cooperate," he said, "will you guarantee that my brother and business will be safe?"

"We will."

Gabe closed his eyes. His chest rose and fell with his breathing. Then he rasped through a small gap in his lips, "I will bring you there."

As Nash watched them take the man outside, Rand said, "You know, this is a big deal. If we get to the hideout soon, we can capture the strategic leaders and disassemble the Accordance, too."

That would be beneficial, Nash thought. "What about the prophetess? Will she live?"

"For a while, I suppose." Rand moved toward the exit. "At least long enough for her to lead us to the Enchiridion."

Nash tucked his notes into his backpack and slipped it over his shoulders. "Are we riding with them, or alone?"

"You're not going," Professor Montgomery said. "This is highly classified."

Nash wanted to see how it played out. What strategy would they use? "I have a plan – one that uses their emotions against them."

"This is straightforward. Emotions would complicate things." Rand moved toward the door. "Besides, this is a capture reserved for the highest ranking officials."

Nash shrugged. "I guess I'll just have to look forward to being involved in this kind of stuff in the future – if there's an enemy left to destroy."

"One can only hope," his uncle said. "Go get that paper done…nephew."

Chapter 14

Mira still couldn't sleep. The time she'd spent with Gabe…each touch, each word, each glance…kept looping through her brain. When would she see him again?

She groaned as she flipped to her back. Staring at the ceiling above her bed in the ship's cabin, she replayed their goodbye. When Gabe had dropped her off at Necropolis, he'd given her what he'd called mementoes – so she wouldn't forget him. He'd gifted her with two slices of a food called pizza, a bag of strawberries, a square of chocolate-covered caramel, and a kiss. The food was the best she'd ever eaten, but the kiss… she could still taste the sweetness and the buzz of desire that had melted her will and had spiked her energy. But he'd pulled away, leaving her with a smile and a promise to return. She flipped onto her side and kicked off the covers that had tangled around her legs. The freedom, though, did nothing to assuage her. She wanted to see Gabe again - right now!

She got up and slipped her clothes back on. As she shoved her feet into her shoes, the door swung open. She half expected to see Gabe standing right in front of her, saying he couldn't stay away either. But it was Vaughn – and he was yelling at her!

"We have to get you out of here…now!" Vaughn grabbed her arm and yanked her out the door then shoved her toward the steps that would take her to the deck.

"What's going on?" she spat, clutching the rail until he explained.

"We've been discovered, and I think you know how," he said. "I told you to stay put," he shouted.

"I…" Her confused mind tried to put the pieces together.

"It's Gabe, Mira – he's on his way with a regiment of Elite Reformers."

Mira gasped. "It can't be!"

"It can and it is. We need to get you to the Lookout now…before they get here."

A heavy feeling squeezed her heart. "I need to get something first," Mira wailed, trying to push her way around him. She'd left the journal page with excerpts from the Enchiridion of Emmanuel on the desk.

"We don't have time!" Vaughn said, blocking her way. His look said he wasn't budging.

Telling herself that she'd come back for it, she turned to go up the steps. When she got to the deck, Vaughn bolted around her and jumped from the side of the ship to the ground. He took off running. Mira ran after him, half stunned, half filled with horror. The food she'd eaten balled up in her stomach, and as the tree house came into view, the ball transformed into a sharp stitch. Was this really happening? How could she have been so stupid?

As they approached the Lookout, she caught sight of six Clavicars riding bumper to bumper down the slope. It *was* really happening! And the small army of city-issued vehicles, all of which came supplied with government monitored and individualized routes, was only moments away. "Did everyone get to a safe place?" Mira asked as Vaughn shoved the rope ladder into her hands.

"I didn't have time to make sure of that. You are my first priority."

Her stomach squeezed painfully, shifting the food upward. "I'm sorry."

He didn't respond to her apology, but said, "Climb up into the tree house, pull up the ladder and lock the hatch. Don't come out until either I come back or until each and every one of the Reformers are gone."

"You're not staying with me?"

"No. Now get up there." He didn't wait to see if she would follow his orders but bolted toward the entrance where several Clavicars had begun to park.

Mira's legs trembled as she climbed the ladder, but it was nothing compared to what she felt in her heart. She still couldn't believe Gabe would turn them in. There had to be some mistake!

She crawled in through the opening in the Lookout's floor. As Vaughn had instructed, she pulled up the rope ladder and locked the hatch. Racing to the window, she grabbed the pair of binoculars from the sill and held them to her eyes. She focused on the Clavicars that had rolled up to the main meeting room. The first Elite Reformer to get out of her car was a woman who looked heartless and cold. Her gun raised, she strode toward the shipping container's doors.

Mira looked on in horror as the LAW unit methodically captured person after person and shoved them into the backs of the Clavicars. Every one of the Accordance put up a fight, but none of them succeeded in escaping. There were too many Reformers! Then she caught sight of Vaughn, a gun aimed right at his chest because he wasn't giving himself up.

"No!" Mira cried. Dropping the binoculars, she raced for the hatch. Her fingers shook so hard, it took three tries for her to get it open. She flung the ladder down and grasped the rope sides and slid to the ground. Hands ripped raw from the rope, she sprinted across the yard to the first row of shipping containers. Think, Mira, think. If she could get their attention and trade herself in for Vaughn, it just might save his life.

She crept up behind the container where she'd last seen Vaughn and the Reformers. She chanced a look. *No* her mind screamed. "Gabe!" *she* screamed. "Don't!"

Chapter 15

Nash exited the Reformer Training Center. As always, his parents were waiting for him in their Clavicar. He slipped into the backseat and tapped his wrist onto the Regimen Monitor, which was attached to the headrest of the passenger seat.

"So how was class?" his mom asked from the driver's seat.

"Class was fine," Nash said as the reader scanned his high-rank ID and his daily information. *Monday, August 1 Sleep: eight hours restful sleep…Breakfast: two scrambled eggs with spinach…Exercise: five mile run…*He didn't bother reading the rest. He already knew what he'd eaten and what exercise he'd done. Two point three minutes later, his stats had been sent to the Center of Operations for review.

"So one month from today is the big day?" his dad asked, looking out the passenger side window.

"Yes. I'll officially be an Elite Reformer."

"Did you make it on to the specialty locator team?" his mom asked.

"My paper outlining a strategic plan to infiltrate the Accordance assured me a position, yes." If they had followed that plan he'd suggested after the interrogation of Gabe three months ago, the Enchiridion would already found and destroyed and the leader of the 'Cords and his sidekick would be on Enab. But they had insisted on using their own plan…one that had failed.

The Clavicar drove them past Pillar Media where his dad worked. It was one of the tallest buildings in town, yet was dwarfed by the COO, a high-rise that dominated almost all of Central Square. The final portion of his training would be there, the main hub of Pillar's success – a prime example to the rest of the few cities left on earth.

His mom glanced at him over her shoulder. The look on her face was…unusual. "I know the work of an Elite Reformer is respectable but…"

Of course it was respectable and she should know because *she* was an Elite Reformer. She'd sent more people to Enab than anyone in Pillar's history. "But what?" Nash asked, brushing his finger along his NewsScreen. The front page of the WorldView Today, of which his dad was editor-in-chief, flashed onto the screen.

"Something has changed," she said.

"I see that," he said. As stated on the front page, the leader of the Accordance - who had escaped Necropolis' apprehension three months ago - had been sighted. In the picture, the man had a beard and a bright green shirt, which added to his rebellious look. "I'm looking forward to busting this guy once and for all. He's caused the city a lot of problems." And sending the troublemaker to Enab was going to help Pillar find the perfection it was destined for. That, and finding the Enchiridion of Emmanuel.

"Capturing the Accordance leader is not what I'm talking about," his mom said.

"So what *are* you talking about?"

She reached for his father's hand. "You know how I go to Enab every week to observe and report?"

"I'm familiar with your routine," Nash said, frowning slightly at their entwined hands.

"Yes. I suppose you are." She took a deep breath. "Anyway, several months ago, I was bitten by a snake. I was brought to this woman, who extracted the poison and applied anti-venom."

"A prisoner saved your life? You got lucky."

"Actually, I had to make a deal - a deal I really want to follow through on, not just for her, but for us."

Clearly there was still poison in her system and it was affecting her brain. She certainly didn't owe an Enabian anything. "So what was the deal? Does she want a pass off the island?"

"She *did* want to get off the island, but I wouldn't agree to that."

At least she was thinking halfway logically. "What did you agree to, then?"

"To find the Enchiridion of Emmanuel."

That was his goal as well, but he knew that his mom hadn't been chosen to help locate it – specifically because of her hesitation during the failed attempt to recover the 'Cord's leader and the girl. "So do you actually think a copy survived the worldwide effort to destroy all passion-inciting books?" Nash asked. He watched his mother's face closely.

"I do."

"How do you propose to find it?" Nash asked.

"Well, the woman gave me a key and claimed rather passionately," she smiled slightly, "that it's the key to life and death information - information the LAW doesn't want us to find out about."

Of course they didn't want anyone to read it. Just the rumor of its power and influence was enough to trigger a widespread rebellion. He also realized that what his mom was telling him could convict her of treason. "What do you mean exactly?"

She looked at him squarely through the rearview mirror. "What I mean is that I've never read the Enchiridion and that we've blindly accepted everything the LAW has told us about it. Maybe we shouldn't trust them." Pulling a piece of paper out of her pocket, she handed it back to him. "I found this when we raided Necropolis."

He scanned the journal entries. The last one, especially, piqued his attention. It said, "Peace? Destroying who we are isn't peace! Controlling us isn't peace! Peace comes from within our souls. But the LAW has hidden the truth…and they have found me. I pray someone finds these words, that they find the Enchiridion of Emmanuel. We are on the road to destruction, and there's only one way that we can be saved! "He sent out his word and healed them, snatching them from the door of death." A Psalm from the Enchiridion of Emmanuel."

The words promised things that would surely mislead the public and incite the passionate drive Pillar had worked so hard to avoid. He quickly shoved it into his pocket. "You should've given this to the authorities."

"But they are hiding something. I can feel it!" She pounded a fist against her heart.

Nash couldn't believe he was having this conversation. The LAW was the best policing group in history, an instrumental force in transforming Pillar from war-ridden and destitute to orderly. "So you think they're lying and you want to find the Enchiridion before they do. Is that what you're saying?"

She twisted in her seat, her eyes brighter than he'd ever seen. "Think about it Nash. What if the book really *is* the guide to a life that's more than…this? What if it holds the truth?" She splayed her left hand along the driver's side window, the motion highlighting a park where an empty swing twisted back and forth in the breeze. There was also a slide and a merry-go round, but not one child played there. But there weren't any gang members or drug dealers either, Nash thought. Why would she want to risk the security they'd all worked so hard to obtain?

"Maybe you should get your LifeChip checked out," Nash suggested.

"And maybe you should read the back page in the WorldView Today," his dad said. "We've done our research…used our reliable connections."

Nash shook his head at his dad's unusually harsh tone. What was this? A test of some kind that would round out his training? He forwarded through the pages. At the very bottom of the last page was a picture of a book with a pillar of fire on its cover. The bearded green-shirt guy, the leader of the 'Cords, was trying to rip it out of the hands of the Benefactor, Pillar's governor. The picture's caption said *Don't Let It Fall Into the Wrong Hands*.

It seemed that the search for the Enchiridion was being highlighted by someone other than the LAW - and after a glance at his father, the editor, Nash knew who was responsible. "This certainly changes things." He'd have to find his dad's sources in the WorldView's databank and do some digging.

"We were hoping you'd understand what's really at stake here," his mom said.

He *did* know what was at stake. "Pillar's future," he said with a nod. Only judging by what his parents had revealed, Nash's idea of assuring their future was different from theirs.

Yet his mom's smile was broader than he'd ever noticed as their Clavicar turned down J Street. The street was similar to most of the others in Pillar. It led to his neighborhood, one he'd vowed to protect. "What do you want from me?"

It was his dad's turn to twist around, his hand clutching the console between the two front seats. "We know that you're on the locator team and that you've done some undercover work already," his dad said. "And just last week, you had a LifeChip upgrade."

"And?"

"That, combined with the other information we've learned…" His mom looked at him again through the rearview mirror, the edges of her mouth lifted in a smile. "You'll really be able to save Pillar, son."

"What other information do you have?"

She looked over her shoulder at him, her stare unlike any he'd ever seen. It was strange, and concerning. "Before we tell you anything else," she said, "you'll have to promise to hand the book over to us when you find it."

He'd already made a promise to the LAW and to Pillar. "And if I don't agree?"

"It will be much more complicated. Our connections are…" Her voice softened, but there was still an edge of determination to it. "If you don't agree to our deal, your father and I will find it…or we'll die trying." Her chin tilted up even as tears swamped her eyes.

There was definitely a problem with their LifeChips, he thought, looking from one to the other. There was nothing wrong with his, however. And it was his duty as an Elite Reformer to do whatever it took to keep Pillar on the right track. He just hoped it didn't include turning his parents in to the authorities. "I'll find the Enchiridion," he said.

"And you'll turn it over to us?" his dad asked.

Nash wasn't about to make any promises he couldn't keep. He opened his mouth to tell them so, but all that came out was a gasp. Something…a car…was racing toward them at an outrageous speed.

"Key is under my desk chair…and find Miracle!" his mom yelled as she grabbed for the emergency shut off, which would switch the controls to manual. Only it was too late to make a difference. The sudden impact of the collision forced a cry from Nash's throat, catapulting him into the door on the opposite side. Their Clavicar flipped, his parents' screams and the crunching metal pierced his ears as everything went dark.

Chapter 16

After Mira and Vaughn had escaped the LAW at Necropolis, Vaughn had brought her to a place called The Compound where they had been greeted by two other rebels, Kya and Logan. Mira had grown quite fond of their little group over the past three months, but there were times she coveted her solitude...like today.

Mira watched the sun shift lower in the sky and beam through the windows of her studio. Before the war, this small room located above the Daly Theater had been a lookout area for the FBI. Now it was her artist's nook, a peaceful place to escape. Her visions had gotten increasingly un-peaceful, though, with Pillar inching ever closer to the gaping hole. Thankfully, last night a new image had woven its way into her mind, an image that was much more pleasant.

Mira turned her attention back to her latest project. "If only this guy will somehow lead me to the Enchiridion," she said, adding a much deeper brown to his hair. She stepped back to take a better look. Her subject looked to be around seventeen, or judging by his broad shoulders, maybe a bit older. His hair was close-cropped, but it looked like it could be curly if he grew it out. He wasn't smiling.

"Something's still not right." She picked up a fine-tipped brush and slowly lowered it to his left cheek. *Dot.* She managed a shaky smile. "I'm done with you mister whoever you are...for now anyway."

"Who are you done with?"

Mira whipped around, her paintbrush flipping out of her fingers. It tittered on the floor, leaving a smear of dark brown on the ceramic tile. "You scared me, Kya," Mira said, pressing a hand against her skittering heart.

"Sorry." Kya moved closer. "I take it you had another episode?"

Mira turned the painting so that she could see it. "Another Unknown." Unknown was a term their group had come up with for her people paintings.

"I'd say he's from Pillar with the hair and all, but," Kya frowned, "his eyes aren't really Pillar-esque. They don't have that…dead look."

Mira agreed. "Do you think he's one of the .1%?"

"He might be." Kya held out a pale grey square of material. "We'll search the databanks later. We have a little, ah, situation."

"Does this little situation have anything to do with Logan, by chance?" Logan did everything with gusto – whether it was showering her with attention, or obsessing with the databanks, or enlisting new 'Cords.

Kya sighed like an exasperated mother with a naughty child. "After he hit the alert button on his Notifier, we zoned in on his location and tapped into the feed from the Sweepers at the scene of the accident. An ambulance arrived for him a few minutes ago."

Mira took the grey square and turned it over in her hands. She hadn't left The Compound, the FBI mock town, since they'd moved in three months ago. She felt safe here, in the little chapel especially. And even though she'd started her training in the facility's combat gym, she didn't feel ready to go on any rescue mission, especially because it was in a city doomed to be sucked into an abyss at any moment. "I just don't know if I can."

Kya wrapped an arm around Mira's shoulders and tugged at the grey fabric. "Don't let your experience with Gabe stop you from doing what you need to do. Put the smock on and get back in the game."

Gabe…her last Unknown. Guilt crept up to choke her, but she swallowed it back. She couldn't let her true friends down again. "I'll do it."

"See you in a few, then." Kya shot her an encouraging smile then disappeared through the door.

The room suddenly felt different. It was quieter and lonelier, even though it was cluttered with paint paraphernalia and evidence of the busy training life of past FBI agents. As she stripped off her paint-splattered button-down shirt and put on the drab smock, she tried not to think about the risks of what they were about to do. But the danger was real, and she knew firsthand what awaited them all if they failed. Sucking back the terror, she slipped on the matching scrub trousers and refocused. She shouldn't have to be in hiding like a marked enemy just because she wanted the freedom to truly feel! She glanced back at the painting. Her Unknown's eyes…they almost seemed as if they were daring her. "I'll deal with you later," she promised, and hurried out the door.

Mira's shoes clunked as she made her way down the metal spiral staircase that ended in an area behind the Daly Theater's big screen. As she skirted around the white vinyl movie screen, she stopped. Kya sat in one of the red velvet seats, glancing at her watch. "You waited," Mira said.

Kya stood up. "I thought I'd have to come back for you."

They didn't trust her. Not that she blamed them, especially after what had happened with Gabe – but it still hurt. "You were wrong."

Kya studied her a moment. "I guess I was."

Mira didn't want to waste time worrying about it, so she shut it out of her head and followed Kya out the door and down the sidewalk. They passed the Suds 'n' Stuff and the post office, both fake businesses that created a front for their dorm of bedrooms. When they reached Dogwood Motors at the south end of the property, Mira stopped and rested her hand on one of the bogus, shell-only cars. "If something happens and we don't make it back, I just want you to know…"

But Kya didn't let her finish. "We *are* coming back. All of us. And we are going to end this all…soon." The determined look on Kya's face was reassuring.

"You're right." Mira hoped she was anyway - that the risks and the sacrifice would be worth it in the end.

"Ready then?" Kya asked, but she was already walking toward the dealership's showroom.

Mira followed her through the front doors of the fake business. Maneuvering around two halved cars with their intact sides facing the display window, they walked together into the supply closet located between the men's and women's bathrooms and continued to the shelves that stood against back wall. Mira stepped onto the bottom shelf, clutching the metal bar beside her. "I still hate this thing," she said, staring at the grimy grey wall.

Kya laughed as she scooted onto the shelf-step right beside her. "What? You don't like the secret shelf-a-vator? How else would we get to our getaway vehicles?"

"It would be a whole lot sneakier if it didn't squawk and groan all the way down," Mira grumbled.

Kya's grin was infectious as she pulled back the mop handle.

Mira smiled back, not even minding that the floor had opened with a loud screech. Even when the apparatus moaned its entire descent to the basement storage room, she felt okay…like she was really part of the team again.

"What do you know? We made it," Kya said, and jumped off the step before charging through the door.

Mira followed her, breathing through her mouth to avoid the overly strong smells of oil, rubber, automotive paint, and exhaust. She saw Vaughn sitting in one of the vehicles. It was parked by the exit, a garage door that opened into a tunnel. With the digital side panels and the Stint Transport logo, the van looked just like the real thing. She hesitated, a cold wisp of memory freezing her feet to the ground. She didn't want to go back to the Stint…not ever!

"*I'm so glad you're here,*" Vaughn sang from the driver's seat.

Vaughn's love of speaking in song always seemed to strike a chord in Mira – good or bad. This time, it prompted her to move. She climbed through the van's open back doors. As she closed them behind her, she noticed that the bench seats now lined the sidewalls, and fake monitors hung from the ceiling's corners. It was alike enough to the actual vehicle to make Mira feel like she was reliving her own trip.

"What song is that from?" she asked, trying to distract herself as she sat on the seat along the wall behind Kya.

"I made it up," he said, looking at her through the rearview mirror.

"Well, I *am* here, and I'm ready to move." She lifted her chin, and he nodded.

"It's good to have you on board," Vaughn said.

It was good to have him on board, too, Mira thought, her mind traveling back to that day in Necropolis when Gabe got into the line of the Reformer's fire so that Vaughn could escape. Vaughn had said he'd forgiven her, but it didn't change what had happened. Gabe was a traitor – and she had brought disaster to their door.

The passenger door of the van clicked shut and as Vaughn turned to glance at Kya, Mira caught sight of a little grooming detail he'd missed. She laughed out loud.

"What?" the pair said in unison, identical frowns on their faces.

"Vaughn, you've got a…" she grinned as she waved her hand beneath her chin, "a long piece of beard hanging."

Kya giggled. She reached into the glove compartment for a scissors. Snipping off Vaughn's errant strand, she said, "There. You're Pillar ready."

"Close-cropped, useless, heartless, and boring you mean?" Vaughn winked at Kya, but as always, sadness still lurked behind his playful expressions. Mira had asked him about it once, and he said he'd tell her someday…when he was ready.

"You'd never pass for boring, useless, or heartless," Kya said, although the last word was voiced in a whisper. She turned her gaze to the dash and cleared her throat. "More new inventions?"

Vaughn nodded once. "Just wait until you see them in action."

"I can't wait," Kya said with a smile.

Vaughn revved the engine and hit the remote to open the doors into the tunnel. "*We just keep movin' along,*" he sang as he drove the van up the incline that, after a quarter of a mile, leveled off into a tree-lined road.

Mira watched the closely spaced trunks as they passed. They reminded her of prison bars. "Your vehicles are definitely more useful than my paintings," Mira muttered. "They get us out of trouble, not into it."

Kya looked over her shoulder. "You didn't know that Gabe would turn us in to the LAW."

"But Vaughn had told me to stay put…and I didn't have to tell Gabe about my prophetic dreams…and I…" She snapped her mouth shut. Why did this dark feeling glom onto her every time she thought about what she'd done? Because she deserved it…that's why. Her paintings and her stupidity had gotten people killed. And some of the Accordance leaders had been sent to Enab because of her, too. It had set back their cause in a big way.

"I have good news for you." Vaughn glanced over his shoulder. "A new couple joined up with us and they have connections. They'll even be able to get us to the island to rescue our friends."

"It's sure to work out, then," Mira muttered, "because it has nothing to do with me."

"I thought that by coming with us, that meant you'd moved on." Vaughn's expression was stern as he looked at her again through the mirror.

"It's just…" Just what? That she couldn't forgive herself? That she was starting to think that the paintings she couldn't retrieve from her memory were the ones she needed? Or maybe the Enchiridion was only a fantasy and she was playing a game of fools?

Kya cleared her throat. "I think she's having trouble because she painted another Unknown. Male. About her age. Probably a citizen of Pillar."

Vaughn straightened, his right index finger tapping in a slow one-two-three-four pattern on the steering wheel. "I see."

What he thought about it, Mira couldn't even begin to guess. She looked out the window. They were already rolling into town. Her stomach cinched up, holding in place the crawly feeling that had settled there.

They turned onto Pillar's main drag, aptly and unoriginally named Main Street. Vaughn slowed the van to fifteen. He was a pro at blending in with the auto-piloted traffic, yet he must have been distracted because he wasn't slowing down enough.

"Red light!" Mira shouted.

"Shoot!" Vaughn slammed on the brakes. "Perfect timing, too," he said, grimacing. "We've got a Sweeper at eleven o'clock and it's heading our way."

"We can handle this," Kya said. "Blank faces for the camera everyone."

As the Sweeper inched closer, Mira noticed it was a new version. Instead of being a grey colored orb, it had chameleon-like skin stretched over its surface so it blended in with its environment. The once fat quills with eyes a half-inch in diameter were now thousands of clear quills tipped with high-tech lenses. The new and improved version was harder to spot and sent much clearer pictures to the Center Of Operations. And they were annoying.

The Sweeper veered to the right, caught a gust of wind, and as it twirled, slammed into Mira's window. The impact knocked something loose from the ceiling above her and it dropped onto her forehead, clinging there for a moment before scampering to her eyebrow then to her temple. Out of the corner of her eye, she could see an antenna twitching. Slowly, she reached for it, but with wispy fervor, it continued its scrabbling trek toward her ear. Memories of the Stint whooshed back. She squealed as she flung the critter to the floor and stomped, but missed it completely! It disappeared into the tiny space where the seat connected to the floor.

"It's not an Amender. Get control of yourself," Vaughn said, looking as calm as a sloth after a meal.

She'd done it again. She'd put them all in jeopardy over something she'd imagined to be true. When would she ever learn? Gabe hadn't been her soul-mate – or her key to the Enchiridion - and the brown-banded cockroach hadn't been an Amender, the device the Stint used to mess with a person's psyche all while working to erase their memories.

"I'm sorry," she said, rubbing her clammy hands on the seat. Even though her appearance had been altered after they'd escaped the Stint, she knew that if the Sweeper saw her freaking out, it would take several more pictures from various angles to compare her image to the watch list in the Sweeper's memory bank. The close look could easily turn up as a match.

"No worries," Vaughn whispered.

Mira met his gaze in the rearview mirror and was surprised to see the corner of his mouth curled up. He thought this was funny? "You're not the one who's under review," she growled.

"Neither are you," he said, circling his index finger over a switch in the dash. "The new Replicator I installed has you on a continuous loop," he muttered without moving his lips.

She looked out the window to where she'd last seen the Sweeper. It was still there. "Can it see me?"

"Yes and no. The window between you is actually a screen with your altered recorded image. So far, the Sweeper hasn't been able to pick up the low-frequency buzz, but the sooner we're out of here, the better."

"Amen to that," Kya said, "And hallelujah. We have a green light, ladies and gentlemen."

As if nothing was out of the ordinary, Vaughn inched through the intersection, using his knee to steer. Mira wanted to stick her tongue out at the Sweeper as they moved away, but it was a chance she couldn't bring herself to take right now.

"'Cords headed to the hospital to pull off a heist. Report to COO," Vaughn said in a robotic stutter.

"Totally not funny." Mira glared at him before glancing back at the Sweeper that hovered near the stoplight, its many eyes still watching them. Thankfully, the van was too far away now for it to pick up information.

Vaughn turned the corner and pulled the van behind a dented and rusted metal building. "Sometimes you come to a point where you have to choose which side you're going to focus on – the curses or the blessings." He shifted into park. "Our blessing in this is that we have a wonderful opportunity to swipe one of the LAW's biggest irritants – Logan - from right beneath their noses."

It was also an opportunity to show that the Accordance could trust her – that she *could* make good decisions. Mira smiled, refueled by the opportunity to prove herself. "I guess it's just one more day in the life of the Accordance, huh?"

Vaughn smiled back at her. "My sentiments exactly."

"Everyone remember the plan?" Kya studied the device on the dash that picked up the signal for the tracker Logan wore around his neck. "Because Logan's ambulance is close by."

They all knew this emergency plan by heart because they'd made it long ago and reviewed it often, just in case. "Ready," Mira said.

"Me too." Vaughn plopped a courier's cap on his head.

Chapter 17

Kya and Mira stepped out of the vehicle into the hot, humid air of summer. After checking for Sweepers and shoving aside her dark thoughts, Mira waved at Vaughn then started across the parking lot behind Kya. Their strides were unhurried, their faces masks of nonchalance, transforming them from family on a mission to employees returning from a late dinner break. They made it to the hospital entrance seconds before the ambulance did.

When the vehicle rolled to a stop, Kya opened its back doors like she knew exactly what she was doing. Inside, Logan's head popped up an inch. It was dimly lit, but Mira could see the puffiness around his eyes and the bloody gash on his cheek. He dropped his head back down and moaned softly.

The tightness in Mira's chest eased enough that her breathing was almost back to normal. Logan was safe. The LAW wasn't anywhere to be seen. And they *could* pull this off.

The driver, Chuck, his nametag said, got out of the ambulance and strolled to the back doors. He pulled out Logan's stretcher. "Accident happened near J Street, Patricia. One driver is stable. One person from the other car lived, too, but," he said, pointing over his shoulder at the remaining stretcher, "his parents didn't make it."

Mira turned her head so that her horror wouldn't show. Patricia, the admissions clerk who had come outside to jot down the information, said, "Got it," before clicking her pen against the clipboard and making a note of it. "We've had a few accidents this week," she said. "I wonder if there's some sort of glitch in the new Clavicar programming or maybe a malfunction in the LifeChips." She moved to sit on the bumper.

"Or maybe the 'Cords got a hold of a copy of that Enchiridion book," Chuck muttered. "Did you know they made a special locator team to find it?"

"Hadn't heard that," the woman said, glancing at the sheet-covered patients.

Mira reached into the ambulance for the remaining stretcher as she listened to the exchange, trying to keep her hand steady.

"It's true. Heard it from my neighbor who is one of the coaches at the Elite Reformer Training Center," Chuck said.

"Sounds important," Patricia said.

Understatement of the year, Mira thought, inching the stretcher to the edge.

"Nothing to worry about." Chuck ambled back to the driver's side door. "The search team is made up of some of the best Elites yet, so I'm sure Pillar will be back to normal in no time at all."

Even Pillar's citizens were talking about it! Panic swooped in like a fire in a forest of dead trees. Mira looked for Kya, who was already wheeling Logan through the hospital's patient entrance.

"I can take care of this patient if you want, Patricia," Mira said, nodding toward the Help desk where Vaughn stood in his courier garb. "I think you have a package to sign for."

Patricia only shrugged and wandered back inside to her desk.

Mira grabbed the bottom of the second patient's stretcher and yanked it out of the ambulance. The folded, wheeled legs dropped to the ground with a bang, snapping the guy's head over, giving her a clear view of his face.

She gasped. Heart hammering, Mira glanced at Chuck. She could see him in the driver's seat through the open back doors of the ambulance. He dug in his ear with his keys as he slowly gathered forms from a box sitting next to him. He hadn't heard her.

As he pulled up a page and scanned it with a hand-held device, Mira called out, "I'll take this one inside."

Her voice must have wobbled a bit because his head swung around and he dropped the scanner. She focused on tucking the blanket around the patient's feet.

After a moment, Chuck said, "Fine by me."

She pushed the stretcher ahead, surprised by how hard it was to move him. How big was this guy?

"Hey, wait," Chuck said from behind her.

Now what? Mira stopped, but kept her arms tucked in tightly so the approaching driver wouldn't notice her sweaty pits.

He scratched his head. "Sign these first, for both the patients, would ya?"

After a quick peek to make sure Vaughn was still keeping the attendant busy, Mira signed *Patricia* across the bottom. She glanced at the patients' names as she handed the release form back to Chuck. *Nash Montgomery* was written on the first line and Logan's was stamped *Unknown*. The irony was almost enough to make her smile…almost.

Chuck tucked the page beneath his arm and got back into the driver's seat, and after what seemed like forever, drove the ambulance across the parking lot toward the storage garage.

Feeling like she'd chugged five banned NRG drinks, Mira restricted her movements as she rolled Nash through the hospital doors and down the hallway. The Observation Room was the first room on her left, just like it was on their map of the facility. She paused. What was she doing? She should just stick to the plan. But as she looked at the realness of him - at the rise and fall of his chest - she couldn't do it. She took a deep breath and, after flipping the sheet over Nash's face, rolled him inside.

The smell hit her first – a sweet odor with a hint of electricity. She breathed through her mouth, but it still brought back the memories and made her gag. The Nervous System Examiner was in the far corner. Being in that chair was one thing she wished *had* been erased from her memories for good…the attachments, the storm of electric pulses that supposedly measured the limbic and the autonomic nervous systems. She could still hear the voices relaying her scores, scores that revealed her need for the Stint. Even though she'd met Vaughn there, she never wanted to end up in that place again.

Kya's hand covered her forearm. "Don't even look at that thing."

"I wish I could rip it apart, piece by piece."

"They'd only build a new one." Kya nodded toward the stretcher Mira was clutching. "You should've left him in the room across the hall."

"I know." She reached for the hem of her smock, fidgeting with the little double-folded edge.

"So why didn't you?"

Revealing him was harder than she thought. Mira's swallow seemed extra loud as she carefully peeled back the sheet.

Kya gasped when she saw Nash. "There's no way we can bring him to The Compound with us!"

"I think I've seen him somewhere before," Mira said, staring at the unconscious patient. Logan groaned as he stirred.

Frowning deeply, Kya went to check on Logan, her hands trembling as she reached out to adjust his sheet. "That's the guy you just painted, Mira! Of course he looks familiar!"

"I know. But that's not it. I'm quite sure..." her voice trailed as she ran her finger along the dull white fabric covering Nash's arm. Muscled. Warm. Real. "I think we should take him back with us."

A disbelieving gaze locked onto Mira. "You're kidding me, right?"

Logic rasped, "Leave him."

Something inside Mira, though, wouldn't let him go. "I'm serious," she said. Call it intuition. Call it insanity. Maybe it was both. "What if he can lead us to the Enchiridion?"

Kya moved to the far wall to peek through the slice of window that opened to the parking lot. "We need to be more careful, take our time, research him first."

"But we're running out of time," Mira said. "I need to do something!"

Closing her eyes, Kya was silent for several moments. Then she leaned back against the wall, arms crossed. "How about we start with what we know about him. Do we know *anything*?"

Mira's heart slowed down a little. "I know his name is Nash Montgomery."

"Hey. His parents just joined our team a little bit ago," Logan said from the shadowy tent of sheet he'd used to cover his head.

"But it doesn't mean their son did." Kya pulled away from the wall. "Maybe we can talk to them before we go any further."

Mira touched Nash's cheek with her palm. "We can't ask them," she said softly, unable to stop the tears.

"Why not?" Kya asked, frowning.

"Because they're dead."

"What?!" Logan groaned as he whipped the sheet off and turned his head to the side. His eyes were pinched with pain as he looked at them. "That can't be!"

"That's what the ambulance driver said."

"Hey – it's not *my* fault!! Someone hit me from behind and shoved me into this guy's car." Logan paused to catch his breath, then added, "I remember looking in my rearview mirror right as the car hit me. The guy driving it looked determined...like he knew exactly what he was doing."

"It wasn't an accident, then. The LAW *has* to be responsible." And it was another reason Mira couldn't let Nash go. There was no way she'd allow another one of their own to get into the hands of the LAW.

"Well I know it wasn't MY fault!" Logan wailed, and then whispered, "Not my fault. Not my fault," as he flipped the sheet over his face again.

"We'll talk to Vaughn," Kya said, moving again to peer out the window.

Mira knew it was a huge risk, that bringing Nash with them could eventually lead the LAW right to their hideout. Her decisions with Gabe had cost everyone, but her decision right now didn't have to. "I'll take him somewhere – so you and the hideout aren't compromised."

"Don't be dumb," Logan said.

"I'm not dumb."

"Just not thinking," Logan barked. "Where would you even take him?"

"To Freetown. I've been there before," she confessed. She only remembered little things about the place, and they were hazy at best, but it was a good alternative.

Both Kya and Logan were quiet – quiet enough to hear the rumble of the van's engine. "We'll talk to Vaughn," Kya repeated and hurried over to the wide docking style door. She pulled up on the handle. The cool air mixed with a hint of exhaust filtered inside as the door lifted.

As planned, Vaughn was there, the van perfectly parked. It stood, its open back doors flush against the building so they could step right inside it. Just like the LAW's transport van would do before taking the new patients to the Stint.

Kya helped Logan from his stretcher to a spot behind Vaughn. He sat heavily and leaned his head back against the window. His eyes closed, his breathing was shallow. He looked like crap, Mira thought. They'd have to x-ray him when they got back to The Compound.

Kya whispered something to Vaughn after she slipped into the front passenger seat.

Vaughn looked at Kya first, then his watch. He hurried through the back of the van and jumped into the Observation Room. He didn't look around, only at the patient. "Nash Montgomery, huh?" Vaughn studied Mira a moment. "I won't have you traipsing off by yourself, you know." He nodded to Kya. "Toss me the Detector."

Kya grabbed the watch-like device from the side pocket of the captain's chair and threw it to him. He caught it, and quickly scanned both of Nash's hands. The light flashed green over Nash's right hand. From the Detector's side panel, Vaughn flipped out a miniature scalpel and removed it from its disinfectant soaked cuff. "One LifeChip coming right up," he said as he made a tiny slit in Nash's skin. "Or out, rather." He pressed the device over the cut to seal the skin together. "And one sleeping pill to give us a little extra time to make our guest comfortable," he added, popping a tiny white pill into Nash's mouth.

"Let's get him into the van." Vaughn grabbed him beneath the arms and Mira grabbed his feet. Lugging Nash into the van, they maneuvered him into the seat.

Mira knelt to tie him in, and paused, the metal seat belt tongue resting against the buckle's opening. Even though she knew that the Detector would mark his location as being at the hospital, it was entirely possible that he would reveal his *own* location when he woke up. She couldn't live through another raid – or another attack on her hope of finding the Enchiridion. She really needed Nash to be the answer. With one more glance at her sleeping Unknown, she sealed her fate. *Click.*

Chapter 18

Nash's head throbbed and his mouth tasted like he'd eaten napkins for dinner, but the air that crossed his lips was refreshingly cool. And the blanket covering him softened the pain encasing his body. He struggled to open his eyes. Tiny slits were all he could manage. The room was unfamiliar…two closed doors right next to each other, a window on one wall with a desk beneath it. It was dark outside, so the only light in the room was from a floor lamp. The room suddenly began to spin. He squeezed his eyes shut and sucked in a deep breath. The nausea faded somewhat, but the breathing…he clutched his hand against his chest and bit the back of his lips to help keep the pain inside.

Delicate fingers caressed his cheek. "You're awake," said a soothing voice.

Nash opened his eyes again and tried to focus on the female standing next to him. The vertigo slowly diminished and finally faded away, but he was careful to keep his head still. He sipped in tiny bits of air, cognizant of his aching ribs as he studied her. Pretty, with golden skin and ocean blue eyes, bangs cut at a jagged angle, tipped with purple…and she had perfectly shaped red-tinted lips. He must be dreaming. He didn't recognize her at all. And she certainly didn't belong in his world.

She pushed a button to incline his bed. It hummed and squeaked as it lifted him up into a sitting position. Man, every inch of him hurt!

"How are you feeling?" she asked

What a strange question. "It's a toss-up between confused and like crap, I guess."

Her tiny smile was not expected, nor was his reaction. He instantly flung the blankets off, clenching his teeth against the pain. "This," he pointed to his bruised, now exposed chest, "is not something to smile about."

"You're right." The corners of her lips drooped as she laid a book entitled *An Artist's Love* on the nightstand next to him.

Nash frowned. With his high IQ, his Elite Reformer training, and his enhanced LifeChip, he should easily be able to make sense of this. But it didn't make any sense at all. His gaze traveled down her body to the frayed edges of her jeans.

"Where am I?"

"Safe." The girl bent over him to adjust his pillow. Her scent followed. His head suddenly seemed a bit better and…different. Like he was in a fog, yet…aware. As she stood back up, her hand bumped against his chest. A shiver spiraled out from the point of contact, leaving a web of heat trailing behind. He reached up so he could touch her, but she'd stepped back as she'd turned away. He dropped his arm and tucked his hands beneath his thighs.

"Do I know you?" he asked.

"Not yet." She twisted back toward him and lightly squeezed his forearm. His gaze shifted from her hair to her nails, which were overly short, like something had nibbled on them. They had patches of color here and there. Her fingers did too. "My name is Mira."

"Why am I here…in this *safe* place?"

Mira's lips parted slightly. "You don't remember?"

He fought for recall. He'd been riding with his parents after Elite training, talking to them about something – a book maybe? That's all he could come up with.

Nash squinted as he looked at her more closely. "Where are my parents?"

She looked down and away, but not before he saw her eyes turn glassy. He frowned. He'd seen tears before…in the videos they'd watched in school and in training maybe?

"They, um," she bit her lip, "they died in the car accident."

The news hit him like a slap in the face, only his entire body stung in reaction. Mira tucked her hand into his and squeezed. While he wanted to clasp it against him, he also wanted to fling it away. He did both and then pinched his eyes shut as details suddenly snapped back into focus. They'd been driving toward his family home on J Street when another car had skidded into the intersection, t-boning them. The screeching, the crunch of metal, the shattering glass, and the screams of his parents echoed in his ears. He could taste bitterness in the back of his throat and tried to swallow, but couldn't. "Did the other driver's Clavicar malfunction?" The words sounded raspy, but it was all he could manage.

"I'm not sure what happened, but..." she took a deep, shaky breath, "I'm so sorry."

Nash glanced up at Mira, whose cheeks displayed tear lines, and felt a ribbon of warmth slide down his own. He swiped at it with the back of his hand and glared, trembling chin and all, at the offensive wetness. "What the heck?"

She leaned down and kissed his forehead, skimmed his bare shoulder with her soft hand. "It'll be okay."

He shuddered. "No, it won't. My parents are dead." The tears were coming faster and his nose was starting to run.

Mira handed him a tissue, and used another one to dab at her own eyes. "Your feelings will lessen. Just give it a little time," she said.

Feelings? They weren't something he'd had to deal with...not intense ones like this anyway. No citizen of Pillar did. The LifeChips saw to that. "How would you know about my *feelings*?" Fire flamed up in his belly, an entirely different kind of heat than before.

Mira stood there looking at him, crying. She grabbed another tissue.

"Well. Answer me!"

She crumpled the tissue and threw it next to the others on the nightstand. "Okay. I'll answer you." Her eyes, though still damp, had transformed from smooth pebbles to cold sapphires. "I know exactly what it's like to be alone," she said, then turned to look out the window – like she was looking at something far away. "And I'm chipless. Like you."

"What are you talking about?" Nash scowled, and it hurt.

She glanced back at him with an unreadable expression that seemed much safer to him. More normal...like what he was used to.

"We removed your LifeChip so they couldn't track you here," she said.

He glanced at the precise slit amidst the scrapes covering his hand. It explained his behavior, but he didn't want to believe it. He wasn't prepared...he glanced down at his bruised skin, hands that trembled, and the tissues that had wiped his tears. How could he, top Elite Reformer trainee, not be prepared for this? He shook his head, ignoring the pain that sliced through it. "You're lying."

Her dark brow lifted. "Think about it. You hardly act like you have a LifeChip."

His brows pinched in reaction, which made his face hurt as much as his head and body. "No." This couldn't be happening! Something seemed to burn a hole inside his stomach and it was working its heat all the way into his throat.

"You're chip free, Nash Montgomery. Enjoy the freedom."

How did she know his name? He snagged the edge of his bed to keep from being sucked into the abyss of useless emotions he'd supposedly been taught about. The realness and intensity of them wasn't anything like he'd expected.

Through gritted teeth, he said, "Why would I want to be *free* from the most amazing, life-preserving invention since the war?" With a sweep of his arm, he shoved the pile of crumpled tissues from the end table onto the floor. "How long until I can get a replacement?"

"A while."

Nash's hysterical laugh turned to a growl. He twisted so that his feet hung from the side of the bed. Catching sight of those stupid tissues, he kicked at them with his feet. When they disappeared beneath the nightstand, he still didn't feel any better. He wanted something...no, needed something to relieve this torment. He latched onto Mira's book and with coiled energy, flung it at the desk. The resulting clunk preceding its fluttering drop to the floor only made him want to throw something else. But there wasn't anything. "I don't *want* this!"

A glance at the window had him considering a jump, but Mira stepped in front of him. She said quietly, "I know you don't want this. And I'll help you get your LifeChip back…if you still want it after you adjust."

He latched on to the calmness in her voice and the reassurance in her words. Suddenly more tired than he could ever remember, he plopped back onto the bed. Breathing heavily, he pressed his palms against his eyes to cover up the light that seemed to be getting brighter. He tensed when he heard the door open, but he didn't look at who'd come in. He'd never felt so out of control and he didn't like it one bit!

"Nothing negative popped up in the databank search. He's clean," came a low, hoarse voice.

"That's great news," Mira said softly.

"I have his meds," the guy said. "And Vaughn and Kya will stop by in a few minutes."

Nash put the names into memory, but they meant nothing to him. Then he felt something smooth run along the crease of his lips. "Swallow these. One is for the pain. The other is an Evener drug. It will take the edge off."

"I don't want to take the edge off." He did, but he didn't. "Don't you get it?" What he really wanted was to destroy this nightmare and return his life to normal, to his routine, to his family. And he wanted it now!

"I get it. That's why I want you to take these," she said firmly.

Who were these people? Why was he here? He should be at a hospital…or maybe at training. It dawned on him then. He moved his hands off his eyes and looked at Mira. "You're 'Cords," he spat out.

Her eyes widened slightly, but she still didn't lower the glass or the pills. "It will take a while to explain, but in the meantime…" She looked pointedly at the glass and pills.

Would the medications destroy him? Get information from him?

"We want to help you, not kill you," she said. "Think about it – we didn't even tie you down." Her tone lowered to a ragged whisper. "You can trust me, Nash."

Could he believe her? A sharp pain suddenly spiked into his skull, and he found he didn't care about anything but making it go away. He grabbed the glass and then the pills, tossed them down his throat. The accompanying swig of water tasted flat and dirty, like motes had bathed for weeks in the long-forgotten glass, but it got the job done. And it was better than the taste of napkins. He handed the glass back to her. When she moved to put it on the desk, the young man who'd brought the meds came into view. Dark hair, a gash across his cheek…

It was him. It had to be. He knew it in his bones, in his gut, and in his heart. "YOU." The sound hissed, unrecognizable, from Nash's own lips. "Murderer!"

The young man hobbled back toward the door, his eyes wide. "I'm sorry. It was an accident. I swear," the guy said, now trying to open the door with his shaky hands. "I was hit from behind…knocked into your car. We were hoping you could tell us why."

Something in Nash's head erupted, overriding every ache and every confusing emotion but one. Face flushed, a roar ripped from his throat and he catapulted from the bed. His fingers curled as he stormed across the room, the book he'd tossed tripping him up. He tumbled toward his prey, swinging awkwardly. Instead of smashing into the face of his enemy as he longed to do, his knuckles grazed the edge of the closing door…then landed squarely against Mira's shoulder.

Her squeal of pain did something to his insides that he wasn't prepared for. Nash staggered sideways and grabbed the desk to steady himself, his mess of emotions like a puzzle that had no fitting pieces. His heart swelled painfully, feeling like it was four sizes too big for his chest. He couldn't seem to bring himself to turn around. "Why did you get in my way?" he barked at the wall.

"I'd do it again," she said from behind him.

She wasn't cowering, if the strength of her voice was any indication. When he finally did turn around, he saw why. Mira had a knife, and it was pointed at him. Still his hands curled and uncurled, and his heart beat hard at the base of his constricted throat.

"We're not the enemies, you jerk," she said.

The words splashed him like cold water to the face. For some reason, he believed her. Maybe it was just because he wanted to. He didn't understand any of this. He didn't understand himself. He ran a hand over his face and cringed. All the energy, that had filled him to bursting just moments before, evaporated. He slid to the floor. Something was wedged under his butt, but he didn't have the energy to move it. Not quite knowing what to do, he cleared his throat. "Um, are you okay?"

"Better than you." She was staring at him, which made him fidget. "You feel like swinging still?" she asked.

His nervous laugh was followed with a frown. Finally he shook his head. "Not at you."

The knife clicked and slurped back into its housing. She shoved the compact weapon into her back pocket before lowering to the floor beside him. They both leaned back against the desk drawers. "I don't know exactly what happened with the accident yesterday but…" she began.

"Don't," he said between clenched teeth. He didn't want to go there, to become that monster again.

"We *will* talk about it, but later…when you're feeling better," she said.

Cool, tender fingers reached up to press against his cheek. Ah yes. He was feeling better already.

After several quiet moments, she whispered, "You know…you're even more beautiful than I imagined."

Beautiful? He'd never been called *that* before. And how had she imagined him? He had so many questions, and yet he couldn't seem to get them to come out of his mouth. All he could think about was her soft touch, the heat emanating from her leg which was flush against his, her pretty face, and blue eyes that changed their deepness of color and looked at him in a way he'd never been looked at before. Then she smiled. A shockwave zipped through him.

She must not have noticed because she stood up and reached into the desk's top drawer. Taking out a book, she held it out to him. "This will help you recognize your feelings and will give you tips on how to deal with them," she said.

He stared at the book for a moment, a symbol of a change he didn't want. He shoved it away with a grunt.

She shook her head as she put it back into the drawer. "It'll be here when you want it," she said. She sat on the edge of the desk, staring down at him, and again, he was swamped by a feeling that begged him to do something…only what?

"You're going to be okay, Nash," she said, holding her hand out to him.

He hoped so. Taking her hand, he stood up slowly. His heart had begun to pump faster than he ever remembered. When he raised his eyes from their linked hands to her face, it was all he could do to control the animal inside of him that was trying really hard to come out. Not monster. Just animal. And then she licked her bottom lip. His body felt it…like *he* was being caressed. All his pain seemed to drift away. He just *had* to kiss her.

Chapter 19

The awkward collapse of his lips against hers made her jerk back, only the desk behind her kept her from escaping. Before she could shove him away, though, his sloppy baby kiss matured to one of sensual exploration. She should end it now but…maybe she could use this to her advantage. Her eyes drifted shut.

Nash deepened the kiss, and made a little sound in the back of his throat that was half sigh, half growl. She peeked up and couldn't help but smile against his lips as his shifting expressions captured the wild spectrum of newly dawning emotions. He drew back to take a breath and to trail his fingers across her cheek. "So soft," he said. "So…" he didn't finish, but sank back into the kiss.

She was playing with fire, she knew, but with his eyes focused on her, alive and the exact color she'd painted, she couldn't help the hope that sprang to life. What would it be like to look into these eyes every day – to have him look at her like nothing mattered but loving her as they lived out their dreams together? She pulled back, yet for a moment she let herself believe that dream was possible. With an unsteady hand, she carefully covered his heart. Skin to skin, she felt its accelerated beat. It matched her own.

"I need to get closer," he said. He wrapped his arms around her and hugged her close. "What is this, Mira?" he whispered. "What am I feeling right now?"

Something dangerous. "It's nothing," she snapped. "Let me go." She tried to wiggle out of his grasp, but still he held on.

"It can't be nothing," he said. "And I don't want to let you go…ever."

"You have to."

He looked out the window and frowned. "I don't understand."

"You don't need to," she said. "Now let me go." Her heart squeezed at the pained look on his face. She shouldn't have let it get this far. Her purpose was to help him assimilate, and, through the process, discover how he fit into her goals. She didn't want to hurt him – nor to get hurt herself.

He took a small step back. "Letting you go seems really hard for me to do right now," he said, his frown even deeper than before. While one hand remained splayed across her back, the other he used to clutch his own chest. "And it hurts in here. Am I having a heart attack?"

She couldn't help but smile. "No. It's just the extreme emotions you feel when coming off of the LifeChip. They aren't real." She wiggled off the desk, putting some space between them. "All you need is a little time to figure them out."

"I don't believe you," he said, latching onto the back of the desk chair, his fingertips like grappling hooks over the edge of the checkered fabric. "What do I do now? My arms feel empty and useless," he said, eyes wide as he looked down at his hands and then to her.

She wanted to tell him she felt empty and useless more often than not – only it was deeper than just the physical. But it was dumb – to think, or to admit, so she tucked her hands into her pockets. "Give it a few days, Nash. Get to know our group. Read the book I showed you. Let your body and mind adjust to being chipless."

His grip on the chair grew tighter. "I doubt I could read when I'm like this. And I don't know if I can even stand this nonsense for another minute. How do I get out of here?"

She knew she couldn't let him leave. "Let the Evener medication work completely into your system before you decide."

"And how long will *that* take?"

She glanced at her watch. *It should be working by now!* "Another five minutes or so," she said, hoping she had given him a big enough dose. She went to the closet. "Until then, I have something that might keep your mind, um…distracted." Shoving the clothes aside, she saw what she wanted in the back corner. She grabbed it by the neck and swung around. "This will give you a taste of what it's like to have your creative nature free from that passion stifling LifeChip."

He ignored the acoustic guitar, his eyes never leaving her face. "Is that what you want from me? Just to give me a taste of what it's like in your world?" he asked.

"That's one thing."

"What else?"

"I'm not sure yet." That much was true. Before he could ask any more, she tilted the guitar closer to him. "The name inscribed on the pickguard is *Rave*. Want to try it out?"

After a moment's hesitation, he took the guitar, his gaze skimming along the neck and then the body. He traced the cross and the lettering etched across the guitar's copper pickguard. "I wonder why it's called Rave? And why the cross?" he whispered.

"I don't have an answer to that, but it's fun to think about, isn't it?"

"Yeah." He smiled slightly. "Yeah. I guess it is." His eyes remained locked on the guitar as his long fingers ran along the strings. He had strong, sure hands. She'd noticed before when holding his hand that he had calluses, but hadn't seen his nails. They were nicer than hers, which wasn't saying much. She wondered what his life was like before the accident.

He asked, "How does this thing work?"

"The guitar actually plays," she said with a grin, the pressure in her chest easing a little.

"Plays?"

Still smiling, she hurried back to the closet and snagged the other, smaller guitar. With it now tucked under her arm, she sat on the bed and propped her foot on the metal bed frame beneath it. "Watch." She pressed her fingertips on various points on the frets, clueless as to whether or not it would be an actual chord. At least it would make a noise, so she strummed. The dissonant sound bounced around the small room. "Well, what do you think?"

He chuckled. "That sounded awful."

A laugh burst from somewhere deep inside. It felt good. "It did, didn't it?"

"Can I try mine?"

"Sure."

He sat down beside her. Mimicking her earlier pose, he carefully pressed his fingers against the frets.

"Go ahead. Strum it," she said.

He did, and looked surprised. "That sounded so…" He cleared his throat. "It felt so…" He just shook his head.

"You're a natural." She smiled, absorbing the beauty of something as simple as discovering an internal music that has been locked away. "And this is just the beginning."

He continued to strum for a while, but then it transformed into a gentle plucking of the individual strings to create a solemn and questioning melody. Looking down at his fingers as they moved deftly over the strings, he asked, "So what brought you here in the first place?"

Mira didn't know if it was the song or what, but for some reason, she wanted to tell him everything – the whole naked truth about herself. Only, she reminded herself, along with revelations came vulnerability – a place she didn't want to be ever again. So she said simply, "I like to paint." She jumped off the bed and hurried to the closet. After returning the smaller guitar to its place, she grabbed the first shirt she touched.

Nash plucked one final note, then reached back to run his hand down the wall's bright teal colored stripe. His skin was flawless, she noticed, his muscles like chiseled perfection. He *was* more beautiful than in her painting! "So you risked your safe life in Pillar to come here and paint?" he asked, glancing up at her.

She leaned against the closet's doorframe, the t-shirt she'd picked now crumpled in a ball over her stomach. She could only nod. His face was a study of art, a million pictures in one - hungry, confused, and curious at the same time. Then with a shake of his head, he laid the guitar on the pillow and stood.

"Where'd you get this?" He slowly bent to pick up the book that he'd hurled at Logan.

"It was a gift from Vaughn."

"Who's he?"

"A friend."

With a short grunt, he tossed the paperback on his nightstand. "Maybe you joined the 'Cords," he said, his sharp tone at odds with his longing look as he traced the outline of the embracing couple on the cover of her book, "so you could read passion-inciting books, too."

Her objective was connected to both painting and books, but she was supposed to be the one figuring out *his* purpose, not the other way around. "Being free to feel and think has a lot of benefits," she said with a shrug, hoping the standard response would appease him. "You can wear this for now." She tossed him the shirt she'd been squeezing the life out of. "We had to cut yours off."

He snagged the shirt, but only held onto it as he approached her. Tilting her chin up, their eyes met. "Why me, Mira?" he whispered.

She smiled. "Because you were at the right place at the right time."

"That answer isn't good enough for me."

For someone who'd been emotionally dead for his entire life, he sure knew how to ask questions that got right to the heart. She'd have to tell him a little of the truth at least. "You're here because I painted you." She scooted around him and quickly hit the talk button on the intercom stationed beside the door. "Vaughn. I'm taking Nash on a tour of the grounds."

"He's evened out?" Vaughn's voice crackled through the intercom.

She glanced at Nash. "Yeah. His pain seems somewhat under control, too."

There was a pause on the other end.

"Vaughn? You still there?"

"Yeah." She could hear him take a deep breath. "Are you sure about this, Miracle?"

What did Vaughn think would happen? That Nash would hurt her? That he would run? She glanced at Nash, who wore a confused frown - not a threatening one. Besides, his background had been thoroughly checked out by Logan, who wouldn't have left her alone with Nash if he'd truly thought she couldn't handle him. "I'm sure." She released the button. "Put that on," she said, nodding at the shirt Nash still held.

"Can't we just stay here?" Nash asked.

She shook her head. "The main street through our town butts up to a river. It's the perfect place to explain about my painting." And it would give her a little breathing room. Mira reached for the doorknob, but Nash grabbed her hand and swung her around and gathered her into his arms. "And I'd really like to know more about this, too." He lowered his lips and captured her mouth in a kiss.

Chapter 20

He'd always thought kissing was a formality. Of course, he'd never tried it. Who'd have guessed it could be so amazing? Her lips were so soft and fit perfectly with his. And she tasted like nothing he could've ever dreamed. He could do this forever...or not.

Mira shoved him backwards. Off balance, he smacked into the intercom. "Ouch! Why'd you do that?" He rubbed his shoulder, waiting for an answer as he watched the lips he'd just kissed.

She bent to pick up the black t-shirt he'd dropped. Shoving it into his hands, she said, "We're wasting time."

While he was kissing her, he didn't think it was a waste of time, but maybe she was right. The t-shirt smelled different than the lye soap they used in Pillar, but he slipped it on anyway...slowly. His body cringed in protest – and the more he thought about it, the more he hurt. He'd ask for another pain pill, but he wanted to be alert...to be able to make better sense of all this. Maybe this trek would help.

He followed Mira...aka Miracle...into the hallway, but she'd trotted halfway down it by the time he'd shut the door to his room. It was almost like she was making a break for it – which he didn't get. Why bring him here and then try to get away from him? Nash's teeth clenched so hard, his jaw ached. "Could you slow down?"

Mira stopped and waited for him to catch up. "Sorry," she said, holding out her hand to him. "I keep forgetting that you're still recovering from your accident."

He focused on her hand as he trudged down the hallway, feeling strange about it – and about the name of the person it belonged to. When he caught up to her and took her hand, he figured out why. His parents had held hands in the Clavicar before the accident, which shouldn't have been normal for them. It *was* normal for the 'Cords. Had they been traitors, then? Did they want him to find this Miracle to become one himself? He wished he could remember their conversation more clearly – and yet, he didn't like to think about it at all, didn't like the intense pain that punched at his stomach when he did.

"Something wrong?" Mira asked.

"Just trying to piece everything together," he said, rubbing his free hand across his abdomen.

"It'll come." She pulled him along. "This is where people can stay when they visit," she said, fanning her arm out toward the many doors that lined the hallway. "We have twenty-four rooms in all, twelve on each side."

"You have a lot of visitors, then? People like me?"

She slowed. "Not yet. It's a new place for us."

He felt like a low dose of tranquilizer had just absorbed into his system as he looked down at their entwined hands. His skin was a lot darker than hers, but that wasn't the only difference. Hers was also scarred and blotched with various colors. She was definitely a 'Cord, his enemy, and yet when he looked at her, held her, kissed her, he felt like it just made sense that they were together. "Do you ever think that maybe you're on the wrong side?" he asked, wanting it to be so.

She squinted up at him. "I wouldn't be here if that was the case," she said and let go of his hand to slip through a door.

Note to self: she's here voluntarily. He followed her, stepping into a small room packed with two washers and two dryers, a square sink, and one metal basket on wheels. "A laundromat?" he asked, thinking it actually looked more like half a laundromat.

"We *do* wash our clothes – even though we don't have groom-bots to do it for us," she said before breezing out the front door like a gust of wind.

He rubbed his chin, feeling the prickliness as he watched her pass by the large front window. She was beautiful, her walk calling his attention, something that wouldn't have happened if he still had his LifeChip. He should go and get the thing replaced immediately before he made a mistake, but for some reason, he wasn't ready to yet. There was so much more he wanted to know.

Nash hurried outside. Pain shot up through his body with each press of foot to pavement, but he ignored it. He wasn't a stranger to pain, but he was a stranger to being chipless and these emotions affected him a lot differently than he'd imagined. When he caught up to her, they had just passed a structure called the Daly Theater.

"What is this place?" he asked, glancing back over his shoulder at what looked to be a town's main street, only without any people or Renovatrons.

"It's home. Only better," she said as they went by the last building on that block. "We have a chapel, a theater, a laundromat." She pointed at the structure covered with half chipped off purple stucco. Displayed on the front of it was a billboard picturing a couple in camouflage tank tops, their muscles pumped and smeared with paints, their sweaty grips locked onto guns. "And a combat gym…complete with weight machines, an obstacle course, and a rock climbing wall."

"Sounds…interesting," he said, unable to take his eyes off the picture that reminded him of the war he didn't want to repeat. What was he doing here? His stomach knotted.

Mira looped her arm through his, her touch breaking the spell he'd been under. All thoughts of war drifted away on the wind when he glanced down at her. Again, her appearance, her mannerisms affected him strangely. It pleased him with an intensity he couldn't explain…and redirected his thoughts to illogical things, like how her arms and legs would look without the cover of her clothing.

She led him across the street to where a river flowed powerfully over sporadic piles of rock – not unlike the gush of emotions crashing over every piece of his body. They stopped on the bank about a hundred yards from a wood-planked bridge.

"You're doing great, by the way," she said, giving his arm a short, gentle squeeze.

He tried to ignore the warmth that spread out from every spot she touched because it made him want to do crazy things. Before the wild images could take over, his gaze darted around looking for a way to escape this unknown force reaching for control over him. Dense trees were to the north. To the east was a rundown chapel that stood on the other side of the river. The ocean waved twenty yards behind it, but its beach was blocked off by the fence that surrounded the entire property. The way the river tapered and then twisted in the direction of the ocean, he determined he was somewhere north of the docks the Elites used. If he could climb the fence and follow the beach line to Pillar, he could be back home in a short amount of time. Only he didn't feel like doing that. He *liked* the warmth of the girl beside him. And he *liked* that something sparked inside him every time she spoke. And when he looked at her? All those escape plans were overridden with a need so strong that he'd risk everything just to have her fill it.

"I know the drug helps," he rasped, "but...how did you figure out what to do with all these..." He circled his hand in the air, trying to say the word he'd never thought to connect to himself. "All these feelings that don't even out?"

The corner of her mouth lifted. "The book...and trial and error." She looked as if she would say more, but instead plopped down onto the grass. She tugged on his hand.

He didn't know if he wanted to sit, but when she said, "Sit, and I'll answer your question about my painting," he sat. At least he'd get one of his questions answered.

"Now lay back." She let go of his hand to lie back on the grass and tucked her hands behind her head. "Like this."

He did as she said.

"Close your eyes, Nash."

He closed his eyes for a second and opened them again. Being outdoors was so different than being inside the small room. "I don't like it."

"If you want to understand, you have to close your eyes." She inched closer to him so that they were touching, side to side. "Try again."

His lids fluttered closed, but the darkness there made him feel like the world was too big and he was too small. His eyes popped open again. "Not working."

She shook her head and rose up onto her elbow, facing him. "I promise I won't let anything happen to you." She was so close, his heart instantly started to pound. Was that normal for the chipless? He tried to sit up like her, only to have her shove him back down again.

"Do you want to know about my paintings or not?" she asked.

"I do, but I also want..."

"One thing at a time," she interrupted. Reaching over, she pressed his eyelids shut. "Now take a deep breath and don't say anything for a sec. Just listen to the sounds. Inhale the smells."

It seemed ridiculous and lonely somehow, but he'd play her game for as long as he could. Her hand once again found his, and surprisingly, the tightness in his chest eased – a little. "Now what?"

She chuckled, and he had to smile, intrigued by the lightness it had left behind inside him. But when the sound of her laughter faded, a cacophony of sounds invaded his senses. It was almost unbearable at first, but just when he thought he couldn't stand it anymore, the sounds transformed into individual notes that he could pick out. It was...nice.

"What do you hear?" she whispered.

"A bird chirping. Loud gushing water nearby and crashing waves further away. The flutter of leaves. You rubbing your hand along your jeans."

The jean rubbing stopped, but the thumb of the hand that held his began running along his forefinger. "What do you smell?"

"The water. Grass, I guess. Salty air and...sweetness."

"Flowers?"

"No, you."

In the silence, he heard her breathing change…just slightly, but he'd heard it.

"Can you picture what everything looks like?"

He tried hard to imagine it. "Sort of, I guess. But what does any of this have to do with your painting?"

"I saw you…with my eyes closed." She cleared her throat. "I have these episodes that shut out the world and show me a new one. I feel the colors, the shadows, the contours. I hear things too. It's almost like the scene is in my heart – and I have to paint it. The image that came to me a few nights ago was you."

Did that mean they were somehow destined to be together? Maybe he was meant to be here – to bring her back over to the right side of things, to save Pillar for once and for all. "Am I the only one?"

She hesitated, then answered. "No."

The squeeze of his heart was almost unbearable. He opened his eyes to stare at the clouds. He couldn't bring himself to look at her. "How many others?"

She cleared her throat. "A memory extraction erased a portion of my memories, so I can't be sure."

Did he want to ask more? He had to know, to understand. "Do you paint only people?"

"I've painted scenes, too, many of which have become part of my past. Some are yet to be a part of my future."

He felt her shudder and wondered at what she'd all seen. Could her visions really tell the future? He may have heard of something about that before his accident, but he wasn't positive. "What other people have you painted?"

Mira rubbed her hand up and down her jeans again and added softly, "It doesn't matter."

"It does to me." He looked at her then, but her gaze was on the sky. "Was your last one male or female?"

Her ruby red lips pursed.

"Tell me."

"It was a guy named Gabe," she said. She peeked over at him, but then couldn't hold his gaze.

For a moment, he lay perfectly still, thinking he'd heard the name before. He stared at the curl of her lashes, the contours of her face, the curve of her neck. His heart started beating hard. Had she and Gabe lain here like this? Had they kissed? His gut twisted tighter and tighter as he clutched at the grass with his free hand and tore at it, blade by blade. "So where is he now?" *Please don't say he lives here.*

She remained silent.

"Answer my question!" His tone was dark and sharp like his insides. "Tell me!"

Her hand reached up to rest on the base of her throat. After a moment, she whispered, "He's dead."

Nash sat up so quickly, everything around him spun and sparked his vision with pinhead flickers of light. He paid no attention to Mira's hand on his arm and staggered to his feet. He swayed slightly, and then on impulse, started to run. The bridge was opposite of the direction he wanted to go and the river was too turbulent to cross, so he dashed toward the wooded area. Although he hurt so much he felt like puking, he kept pushing himself faster. Not even when Mira called out that he was different did he slow up. His lungs burned as did his throat. He had to escape these emotion-driven monsters!

He dipped into the cover of trees and headed in the direction of the ocean. Ignoring the pain stabbing every inch of his body, he latched onto the feeling that his freedom was right around the corner. But it lasted only a moment, only until his foot snagged on a stick and launched him headlong into a thick tree trunk.

Groaning, he scowled back at what had tripped him up. *What? No way!* The leg bone of a human stuck up at an angle. And beside it was a rectangular hole big enough to fit him. *Had* the grave been dug for him? A sudden intense fear seized him, strangling a cry from the depths of his soul. He had to get away from this place! As Nash scrambled to his feet, he heard a noise above him. He looked up in time to see Logan crouched on a tree limb…right before he pounced.

Chapter 21

She needed a do-over, Mira thought, sprinting after Nash who was already a hundred yards ahead of her. He'd disappeared into the wooded area they called the Bone Graveyard. *Way to go, Mira*, she thought. *Scare him off before you've even gotten any information from him.*

The only hope she had was to somehow reassure him that he was different from Gabe, but first she had to catch up to him. When she finally made it to the edge of the trees, she paused to catch her breath. Palm to trunk, she glanced right and left, seeing nothing. But then she heard…grunting? She took off toward the sound. When she dodged the big orange tree near the dig site, she saw him – and Logan.

"Stop!" she screamed. But they just kept thrashing around.

Logan suddenly roared and knocked Nash into the grave the FBI had used for forensic practice. Before he could jump in after him, Mira dove. Her chin whacked Logan's bony shoulder as they toppled to the ground next to the deep hole Nash was crawling out of.

"Darn it, Mira!" Logan pushed her away, but didn't go after the escaping Nash. "This is just great!" He glared at her. "I try to help you and you turn on me."

Inside she was torn. "Beating the crap out of him wasn't going to help anything." She stood up, keeping Nash in her peripheral as he inched deeper into the woods.

Logan got to his feet. "What was I supposed to do? Let him go?" He spit off to the side. She noticed the blood dripping from his nose and felt a twinge of regret.

"Yes," she said.

"Seriously?"

Logan's question had her second-guessing the strategy that had just popped into her head.

Nash, who was watching the exchange from behind a tree asked, "So you don't care if I leave right now?"

She did care, but if she was in his shoes, a choice would make her more willing to stay and cooperate. Prison would prompt her to focus on escape. "Stay. Leave. It's up to you, Nash," she said, going with her gut.

Logan threw up his hands, his face a mottled red. "Unbelievable! Let's just let him go back and report us all."

"I thought you said he was clear," Mira said, her confidence faltering as she frowned at Logan.

His voice dropped to a near whisper. "He checked out okay, but who knows…maybe it's a cover."

She rolled her eyes. "You and your overactive imagination. Save it for the theater."

"Whatever." Logan sighed and slipped his arm across her shoulders. "I don't really want him here anyway."

"But I do," she said, watching Nash out of the corner of her eye. *Please choose to stay.*

Logan's smile was now a pout. "Seriously?" He pulled away from her and crossed his arms over his chest. "You're choosing him over me?"

With a wet leaf stuck to his cheek, he looked more like a little boy who was refusing to come inside and wash up than a scorned friend. "I can have more than one friend, can't I?" She gently peeled off the leaf. "Besides, I'm just doing what I think is right." And hoping that it *was* right and conducive to finding the Enchiridion of Emmanuel.

Sniffing, Logan ran a hand under his bloodied nose. "Don't you think I was doing the same thing?"

"I guess."

Logan took a deep breath and then shrugged. "You're not mad at me now, are you?"

She smiled. "No. I'm not mad at you." Mira noticed that Nash was edging closer as she brushed the debris off Logan's green and yellow checked button down shirt.

"Good." Logan grinned. "How about dinner with me tonight, Mira?" He watched her carefully. "I'll plan a picnic by the chapel. I know how much…" His gaze snapped up to a spot over her head. Both his eyes and mouth opened wide.

"Stay away from her," Nash said from behind her. The menace in his voice was unmistakable.

She twisted around. Nash's chest heaved and his eyes zeroed in on Logan. She knew the look even if Nash didn't. While his jealousy was kind of endearing, it could definitely get way out of hand. Mira reached for him, but her touch went unnoticed.

"I don't answer to you, newbie," Logan said through his teeth.

"Shut up, Logan," she said over her shoulder. She turned back to Nash whose eyes, if they had been lasers, would have left Logan with two holes burned through his head. In as soothing a voice as she could muster, she said, "It's okay." She glared back at Logan. "Logan and I are only friends."

Nash's shoulders relaxed a little, but not much. The sooner she got him and Logan separated the better.

"So are you staying?" she asked, crossing her fingers.

Nash shoved his hands into his front pockets. "I don't know why, but I want to." Then he laughed, albeit humorlessly. "Inside, I feel like I don't have any other choice."

"Whatever the reason," she said with a smile, "I'm glad you are." She tucked her arm through his and led him back toward The Compound, leaving a scowling Logan behind.

Chapter 22

Nash chased the last spaghetti noodle around his plate with his fork before shoving it over the edge and onto the spoon he'd propped beneath it. He was really enjoying his meal in the place they called The Deli, especially because that idiot Logan wasn't there to interfere. "This is delicious," he said, sucking the noodle into his mouth, relishing the weird sensation on his tongue.

"Glad you like it," Kya said, wiping her mouth with a napkin.

"So where do you get your food?" Nash asked. Everyone knew that rations in Pillar could only be picked up if a person had a LifeChip. He looked at each one of the strangers sitting around the table. They'd nursed him, fed him, housed him. Risky – just like the 'Cords. He was very eager to find out how they worked and what they wanted from him.

Finally, Vaughn said, "We have MRE's leftover from the military. They last forever."

Picking up a strawberry, Nash popped it into his mouth. "And the fresh food?"

This time, it was Kya who answered. "We have a community greenhouse…do some trading…that sort of thing."

Nash chomped down on his last bite of corn on the cob. As the kernels exploded in his mouth, he couldn't help but grin. "Is this greenhouse close by? I'd like to see what other fruit and vegetables you have."

"We'll show it to you sometime," Kya stood up and carried her plate to the sink located behind the counter. She turned on the water and squirted in some bright blue soap.

"That would be…nice," Nash said. If he could find out the main source of their food supply, he could bring the Accordance down for good. Yet when he glanced at Mira, who was picking up the rest of the empty plates, he felt an ache in his chest at the thought.

Vaughn took the stack of dishes from her and brought them to the sink. He plunged them into the water now piled up with bubbles.

Nash started to get up, wanting to touch the white fluffy mess, but sat back down when Kya suggested dessert – something that was against the rules of Pillar.

Nash watched Mira walk to the refrigerator. At the moment, he didn't really care if she brought him dessert or not. He just liked to take in all her nuances, all her expressions. And there was just something about her that she could make him feel so weak, yet so driven at the same time. He wanted to figure it out – figure *them* out. The rest could wait, and he could easily justify it as an investigative situation when he later filled out his report.

"Do you want ice cream with your apple pie?" Mira asked him, slipping the triangular piece onto a small plate.

"I'm not familiar with it, but sure. Why not?" He rubbed his stomach, glad he wouldn't have to log this meal onto the Regimen Monitor.

She brought it back to the table and laid the dessert in front of him. "The trick is to scoop a little pie and a little ice cream in each bite."

He picked up his fork. "Aren't you having any?"

She smiled and his heart flipped. "You have the last piece."

For a moment, he paused and stared at it, a niggling feeling tickling the base of his throat.

"If you don't want it, I'd be happy to take it off your hands," she said, reaching for it.

But he snatched it away from her and dug in. The moment the flaky sweetness and the cold creaminess hit his taste buds, he couldn't help but close his eyes. He tried to remind himself that food was only to sustain them and give them energy. Food for pleasure was where problems started – like gluttony, greed, poor health. Pillar's system was better, but man, this was an experience he'd never forget!

Vaughn, who was washing the dishes with Kya, said, "I hear Mira told you how you ended up with us. You okay with that?"

His chewing slowed, his eyes opened. "For now." Nash pointed his fork at Vaughn, who'd turned around. "And it also depends on what you all want from me," he dared to say.

For a second, the air sizzled with silence, then Mira blurted, "What *I* want from you is the last bite of your apple pie." She swiped it off his plate and grinned at him as she popped it into her mouth. His insides surged with a flood of emotion, though now familiar, he still couldn't name. The feeling overpowered his unease at the situation *and* his irritation at being cheated out of his last piece of dessert. He couldn't tear his eyes off her mouth and the sweetness it could promise.

While the dishwater burbled down the drain, Vaughn said, "Actually, what we want from you right now is all the information we can get."

Information about what? Nash tried to get his mind back in the game, but it was really hard with Mira looking at him like that.

"Do you remember much from before the accident, Nash?"

Ah. The accident. Nash had recovered quite a bit of his memory, but he wasn't ready to tell them that. "Not really."

The clunk of dishes being placed in the drying rack did nothing to drown out Kya's next words. "Did you know that your parents had been working for us?"

How much should he tell these people? "I'd suspected, but wasn't sure until our...last car trip."

Mira scooted her chair up next to him. "Did your parents mention anything about the Enchiridion of Emmanuel?" she asked, blinking up at him.

Again, he was drawn in by her, like he couldn't help but say what she would want to hear. "They mentioned that the Benefactor was forming a locator crew to find it, possibly because of some picture my dad posted in the WorldView." That much information they probably already knew. "The Enchiridion was in the picture." He tore his gaze from Mira and looked at Vaughn. "And so were you."

Vaughn sighed, even as Kya and Mira gasped.

"You know we all do things in the name of revival," Vaughn muttered.

"Even things like putting yourself in the WorldView for everyone to see?" Kya railed.

He shrugged. "People need to be aware."

Kya slapped her dishtowel onto the counter. "Of all the dumb..." she began, but Vaughn sliced his hand through the air, effectively stopping whatever she was going to say.

"We weigh out the risks," he continued, his blue eyes piercing as they focused on Nash. "One of which is you, Nash. We're hoping you'll help us. Will you?"

Nash stood up, the motion knocking his chair over. "I can't make any promises right now." He rubbed his temples with his fingertips, trying to ward off the headache he felt coming on. Mira stood, too, and reached for his hand. After bringing it down to rest between them, she tugged him toward the door. Strangely, he felt better – and he wanted to leave...with her.

Vaughn approached the table, which was now several feet behind them. "We were hoping that by coming here, you'd realize what you're missing, that you'd see what your parents had seen in our cause." He picked up the chair and set it back up. "But you'll probably need a little more time to decide."

Nash looked at all their faces. If he could decipher them, he'd have an advantage. Yet he was so out of his element, he couldn't understand them. He couldn't even seem to think past the hand that was holding his. "What if I decide I want to go back to my old life and my LifeChip?"

"It'll be done," Vaughn said.

"And if I decide to stay, to help you find the Enchiridion?"

Vaughn sat down and folded his hands on top of the table. "*We find family*," he sang, "*in the most unusual places.*" He leaned back in his chair and smiled.

Nash had already had a family. "I'm tired. I'll need to sleep on it." He escaped out the door, but Mira followed right behind him. He wanted to be alone…and yet he didn't. And he found no energy to object when she took his hand again, but he was grateful she remained silent. He needed time to think.

As they went inside the Suds 'n' Stuff laundromat, something struck Nash as odd. He said, "You have your freedom here." He spread his hands out wide and shook his head. "I don't get why you want to find the Enchiridion so badly. What's in it for you?"

She looked into his eyes as if searching for something. He didn't know what, but he knew that when she looked at him like that, he felt a burst of power – one driven to help her find what she was looking for.

"I hope by finding it that I'll be free of my…episodes, for one," she said.

He noticed the shading beneath her eyes had grown darker throughout the day. "They're that bad?"

"Yes and no." She nibbled on her bottom lip as she headed into the dormitory. "I could do without the one where Pillar slides into this deep pit, like it's swallowed by the earth."

As they continued to his room, he thought about that. "Do you think that's possible?"

She shrugged. "It seems very, very real…to me, at least." Taking a deep breath, she blew it out in one big huff. "And then there's the other image." She stopped, leaning back against the wall near his door. "It makes me want something," she explained, pressing her hand gently on his chest, which immediately started to pound a quicker beat. "It's a place, a feeling that is opposite of the other, and it's like there's a war going on between them. I feel…I hope…that if I *do* find the Enchiridion, the good will win out."

He stared at her hand, her touch that connected them, and found it difficult to keep his thoughts straight. "You think those two scenarios hinge on the Enchiridion of Emmanuel?"

"That, or the man in my vision who had told me to find it," she said, looking up at him with bright eyes. "But I'm not entirely sure."

"I want good to win out, too." Which was exactly what he planned to make happen, whatever it took. Pressing his hand over hers, he let it rest there because it felt nice. It felt right.

"There's another reason I need to find the Enchiridion," she said.

"What's that?" he said softly.

"I have a memory of my mom where I see her pleading with me to promise to find it."

"And you made that promise."

She nodded.

Nash had made a promise too - to protect Pillar. Releasing her hand, he opened the door to his room. He stepped inside, hoping she'd follow. He had so many questions – yet even without answers to those, he wanted her to stay. "Do you know where your mom is now?"

Mira stopped in his doorway to lean against the jamb. "No," she said, her entire body seeming to droop.

He watched her carefully. "When did you see her last?"

"My last vivid memory is of her fiddling with a key on her neck chain as she watched me paint. I don't remember anything else about it, but I know that it happened more than three months ago." She looked down at her feet. Her face had paled, and her eyes looked full of an emotion he couldn't name.

Nash felt a pang travel from his heart to his throat. "So the feelings will get worse then?"

She looked up at him again, her brows knitted. "What feelings would those be?"

"Sadness…over losing my parents."

She shook her head. "With time, it gets easier, actually."

"It's not…" he paused, rubbing his hand down his face as he tried to form his words right, "it's not that hard for me right now, Mira. Their deaths are like a fact, a change in routine." He slumped down onto his bed. "For some reason, that seems wrong - like there's something wrong with *me*!"

She moved into the room, each of her approaching steps making his heart thrum faster. He swallowed hard as she sat on the bed, wanting her closer but afraid of what that meant.

"I don't think there's anything wrong with you," she said, folding her feet beneath her. "The way I see it is this; the LifeChip prevents a person from feeling anything deeply – including love. Relationships, families, friends -they all become more like business arrangements."

"So what do *we* have, then?" He stared at her mouth, which at that moment, curled up just enough to make his heart sing.

She ran her hand over the multi-colored quilt. "We're building a deeper relationship, I suppose."

He wanted to ask what kind of relationship, but the words wouldn't come out.

Mira cleared her throat then patted the mattress twice before standing up.

She was leaving? Suddenly he couldn't catch his breath. "Don't go," he said, reaching for her.

"You need to get some sleep."

"I don't want to sleep. I want to figure things out."

Her answering smile felt like fresh air that had swept through his room, reviving every one of his senses – including unease at the thought of her leaving. "Don't worry," she said. "I won't leave you all alone to face this world you don't know anything about."

But she was leaving now!

She walked to the door. "Besides, time will help you figure things out too. So will sleep. And of course the book about feelings." She stepped through the doorway and his stomach dropped and twisted.

"Wait." He didn't want her to leave! "I just remembered something my mom told me."

She turned around, her perfectly shaped brow lifted high over her right eye. "What do you remember?"

He wished he still had the journal entries with the excerpts from the Enchiridion that his mom had given him, but it was probably at the salvage yard along with their crashed Clavicar. What else could he tell Mira that would keep her with him? "It was about a woman on Enab who convinced her that the Enchiridion still exists. And she gave her a key."

She took a step closer to him. He felt better when she did, but the tension in his body strangely increased. "Do you know what the key was for?" she asked softly, her eyes wide.

"No." Even though he didn't know *exactly* what it opened, his answer hadn't been entirely true. And for some reason, when he'd told her no, something blipped in his chest and squeezed really hard, making him regret his mistruth.

"Do you happen to have the key? Do you know where it is?" she asked.

She'd come near enough for him to touch her, so he reached out his hand to grasp hers. She didn't pull away. "Sorry. No," he said, answering the first of her questions.

She stepped closer. He could smell apple pie.

"Do you think the key could be back at your house?" she asked.

It probably would be, and if he could get Mira away from this place and the rest of the group, maybe he could convince her to find the Enchiridion with him and turn it over to the LAW. "I would assume so, and my mom also kept notes about her trips to Enab." He searched her eyes. It felt like he was floating, weightless in a turquoise sea of warmth. And it felt really, really good.

"Tell me. Do you remember anything else? Anything at all?" she whispered.

He took a moment to gather his thoughts. "Right as the car crashed into us," he said, "she shouted the word Miracle."

A tiny gasp escaped Mira's lips and brushed over his, making him shiver – and react. He swept in for a kiss, wanting to change the world for her...wanting her to change his. He pulled her tightly against him, but couldn't seem to get close enough. He squeezed her harder. She squeaked.

He loosened his hold. "Sorry," he said.

She extracted herself from his embrace, which he didn't like much at all. "We need to take this slowly, Nash," she said and started backing toward the door.

She couldn't leave. Not now. "Slow is for LifeChippers."

She shook her head. "Slow is good...and acting on emotion alone is stupid."

His hands curled as he fought to understand. "Aren't freely expressed emotions the main goal of being chipless?"

"Not exactly." She swept through the doorway. "Get some sleep, Nash. I'll see you in the morning." She swung the door shut. A faint *click* followed her escape.

"No way!" He raced to the door. Sure enough, it was locked. "Mira! Open this door!" Nash tried punching a few number patterns into the code pad, but he knew that finding the correct sequence would be impossible. He slammed his fist against the door's raised panel.

"Mira...you said it was my choice to stay or leave. I want out!" Silence was his only answer. His heart hammered inside his chest, the rhythm of it shaking him to the core. As he stalked around the room, he found he couldn't get Mira – or his predicament – out of his head. He pulled at the ribbing around the neck of his sweat-dampened shirt and marched to the window. He jerked up the sash. When it didn't budge, he roared, trying to release some of the intensity of what he was feeling.

A loud knock grabbed his attention. He strode back across the room, but instead of the door flinging open, a one-inch square packet, red in color, shot out beneath it. On this packet was written, *take this and you'll feel better.*

He flung the packet across the room and tried the knob again, shaking it as he yelled, "Mira. Come back!" When nothing happened, he charged against the solid door, shoulder first. The result was nothing more than a painful vibration, which rebounded back into his already sore body. His hands clenched, his eyes darted around the room, looking for a way to find relief. The packet…it was lying on the floor beside his nightstand.

He stalked over to it and snatched it up. Desperate, he ripped it open and poured it into his mouth. When immediate comfort didn't come, he dropped to the floor, falling back on the routine he'd had since he was fourteen. Palms flat against the tile, feet propped shoulder width apart, he formed a plank then lowered himself until his nose touched the floor. Intense pain eclipsed his body, but he couldn't tell where the physical aches ended and the mental torment began. His arms shook as he pushed himself up.

"One," he said, "I'm locked in this stupid room." Sweat dripped from his nose as he dropped back down to the floor. Hovering an inch from the tile, he fought the nausea that was creeping up his throat. "Two," he growled, pushing up as hard as he could. "I'm locked in these stupid emotions!" He lowered himself again. "Three…I need to power through it. I've done it before in training." Only it had been nothing like this. He continued his pushups until he'd done more than ever before. Fatigue finally hit, and hit him hard.

He twisted into a sitting position and leaned back against the footboard of his bed. His heart rate and breath rate were elevated, his body felt bruised but calm. He felt better now…more in control. And yet that inner want to be with Mira didn't leave him. Slowly, he stood up and went to the desk. He grabbed the book about feelings out of the drawer and began flipping through its pages. Wandering to his bed, he plopped down onto the quilted fabric. He'd study all their feeling definitions and beat them at their own game!

"Fear...an unpleasant emotion caused by the belief that someone or something is dangerous, likely to cause pain," he read then glanced at the expression of the woman in the book then turned the page. He did the same thing for each emotion, from simple to complex, until he got to the last page. "Love," he read, "is an intense feeling of deep affection." There were several expressions that went along with this emotion, which confused him. He stood up and raked his hands through his hair, feeling each and every one of those emotions - yet one in particular loomed inside him, more powerful than the others. That's when he noticed the book on his nightstand. The embracing couple on the cover of *An Artist's Love* connected with him somehow. He snatched it up and plopped onto the bed, adjusting the pillow behind him.

He read the first sentence and was hooked. "Now, we're getting somewhere," he said with a smile.

Chapter 23

Mira escaped into the cool night, thankful for the breeze. Her mom could actually be alive! Who else could've been on Enab with the key? And that the woman had also said the word miracle...it was just too big to be a coincidence.

She skipped past the theater and down the riverbank to the bridge, wondering how Nash fit into all this. Maybe she'd painted him just for this information, but she had to admit, she wanted it to be more than that. She *was* attracted to him - no chipless woman wouldn't be. And he could still be very useful...*if* his emotions were under control and *if* she was careful not to totally fall for him.

"I hope the evener powder works for him." She glanced at the dorm area and then to chapel in the distance. "And that he forgives me." Using the coded lock to keep him in his room *had* gone against her own rules, but he'd been overly emotional, and she didn't want him making a mistake he'd regret, right? As she moved onto the bridge, though, she had to admit her excuse was a weak one. The truth was she couldn't think clearly with him around – and she needed to come up with a plan!

With cautious steps and a firm grip on the rope sides of the shifting bridge, she inched along the rotting wooden planks. *There has to be a way onto the island to find out if the woman was my mom*, she thought. Unfortunately, all boats were property of the LAW, and even if she could manage to steal one to get onto Enab, the guards stationed there would surely stop her before she could start looking.

Mira ignored the inky blackness of the rushing water beneath the swaying planks as she navigated to the opposite bank. Once she was on firmer ground, she ran the rest of the way to the chapel. She was the only one in their group who seemed to like the small stone church, which was fine by her. It gave her a place where she could think and not be interrupted. She stood, silent and still, in front of the chapel's tall wooden doors. How could a place make her feel like she belonged there, yet so filled with emotions she didn't understand? She knew it would be like that the moment she opened the doors, and that the quietness would eventually help her figure things out. She couldn't explain this anomaly and had given up trying to. She just accepted it.

Opening the door on the right, she took a second to absorb the welcome. Inhaling deeply, she smelled cedar and dust, so familiar to her. Everything was going her way now. She grinned, twirling down the aisle, humming an odd tune as she envisioned the reunion with her mom. Would she be the same as she remembered her? The tune suddenly caught in her throat, her dance wilting to a shuffle as reality weaved its way into her utopian imaginings. She could barely remember her mom at all! And instead of jubilation, all Mira could picture was disappointment in her mom's eyes over not finding the Enchiridion. Mira skirted around the pews to the only clear window in the chapel. Pressing her forehead against the glass, she gazed across the fence to where the moon cast a sliver of light across the dark waves of the ocean.

"Maybe before I try to find her, I should find the Enchiridion, like I promised." Her mind shifted to the key Nash had told her about. Hope blossomed once again, but she needed to make a plan. Finding the key was imperative, so she'd have to go to Nash's house...tonight. She'd read through his mom's notes and it would lead her right to the Enchiridion.

"The glitch is that I don't have a clue where he lives, or where his mom would've kept her things." Her mouth twisted. "Bringing Nash along would definitely help make my search easier." She turned to sit on the windowsill. "So I guess my safest bet is for us to go together." She wasn't really too upset about spending more time with him but wondered how to best present the idea – especially after locking him in his room. She stared at the pulpit standing only ten feet from her as she contemplated how to proceed. Was it worth the risk?

Being out in the open could spark Nash's conscience and she could find herself back at the Stint in no time at all.

Pushing herself away from the window, she said, "I'll just have to make him trust me implicitly...and then make him forget everything he's learned." She grinned, the percolating ideas bubbling into a robust and doable plan. Thirty minutes later, Mira left the chapel, ecstatic that, again, the quiet place had given her the answers she'd needed. Once she was back in the dorm hallway, she bypassed her room and continued to Vaughn's suite to give him an update.

She knocked, silently counting to twenty. She knocked again, hoping he hadn't been sleeping already. This time, though, she heard his hurried footsteps as he approached.

The door opened. Vaughn wore a t-shirt with a smiling mouse on the front that didn't match up with the glare on his face. "I looked for you earlier and all I found was your room empty and a new code on Nash's locked dorm room with no one answering. What were you thinking?"

"Do you think that..." She couldn't finish the thought when the look on Vaughn's face told her exactly what he'd thought she'd been doing. "Not that it's any of your business," she said, crossing her arms over her chest, "but I locked Nash in his room and went to the chapel." She swung around, only to be snagged by Vaughn mid-turn.

"We're not done talking, young lady."

She stared at his hand on her arm then looked up into his eyes. "I'll talk, alright." Sharp anger sliced through her. "You aren't responsible for any of us, even though you lead the Accordance team and supply us with your fancy scientific gadgets." Her eyes narrowed. "Don't pretend that we're your family. We don't need your parenting," she snarled. He opened his mouth to speak, but she wasn't done. "In fact, I don't even have to talk to you if I don't want to, and I'm free to leave at any time." Heat infused her face as rage smothered all the excitement she'd been feeling. "Or are we prisoners like the citizens of Pillar are?"

The red tightness of his face suddenly melted into one that looked haggard and old. He let go of her arm. "I care about you – all of you! I was worried, okay?" He rubbed a hand across his forehead. "And we all know Nash is emotionally unstable right now. Anything could've happened. Admit it."

She wasn't about to admit it, even if after Gabe her judgment couldn't be trusted. Sighing, she said, "I don't need this." Once again, she turned to walk away, half wondering if it wouldn't be better for her to go out on her own so her every move wouldn't be second-guessed.

"Wait."

Mira paused, the ache inside her stomach almost unbearable.

"I'm really sorry, Mira. Let's start over again. Will you tell me what it was you came to talk to me about?"

A glance told her he was sincere. And going solo was much more daunting than she cared to admit. She took a deep breath, feeling a little calmer. "I've got news and a plan."

He managed a smile. *"Keepin' hope alive, hope alive,"* he sang and then nodded toward his kitchen. "Will you please come back and tell me about it?"

With a trip to Nash's house on her agenda, she could really use the backup, so she said, "I guess." Marching past him, she went down the short hallway then turned left into the kitchen. She sat down on the middle bar stool tucked beneath the eat-in bar.

Vaughn went into the kitchen, the orange flecked bar countertop between them. "So tell me what's going on."

"Well." Because of his high-handedness, she decided to tell him only what would benefit her situation. She crossed her right leg over her left. "Nash told me his mom had a key, and the key has something to do with unlocking the Enchiridion." Her leg bobbed up and down, one pant leg swishing against the other. "Did his parents mention anything about it to you?"

He frowned, but it was a much more composed reaction than she'd expected. "I've heard about the key, only not from them," he said. "And unfortunately it doesn't do us any good until we know where the Enchiridion is hidden." He pointed to the teapot on the stove behind him. "Want some tea?"

"No, thanks," she said, propping her elbow on the citrus colored Formica and resting her chin on her hand, her dangling foot now jiggling left to right beneath the bar.

Vaughn turned to open the refrigerator. "How about some really sour lemonade?"

"Is Kya rationing your sugar again?" Mira said with half a smile.

"That she is." He grinned as he took out a smiley-faced jug and carefully poured lemonade into the glass sitting on the counter between them. "So did Nash say anything else?"

"Only that his mom kept a record of her trips…and that she'd obtained the key from a woman on Enab." Mira lowered her hands, clasping them together. "It could've been my mom, Vaughn. She could be alive!" When he didn't respond, she said, "Did you hear me?"

He leaned forward onto his elbows. "Don't get your hopes up," he said.

Unbelievable! It was the best news they'd had in forever. "Well my hopes are up already," she said, smacking her hand on the counter. "I don't know why yours aren't," she said, glaring at him, "but I'm going to find her – and the Enchiridion…using this very *unhopeful* information."

Vaughn pursed his lips as he reached into the drawer beside him. Grabbing out a packet of Pro-ten, he said, "A few notes won't get you a boat to Enab and it certainly won't get you past the guards on the docks." Vaughn stared at her as he slowly ripped open the packet.

She tried to calm down. Taking a deep breath, she said, "I think you underestimate my abilities." As she stood, she tucked her hands into her pockets. The smooth feel of her knife handle fitting perfectly in her palm emboldened her. "I have my ways of making things happen."

"Don't do anything stupid."

She snorted, even though the jab – and the reminder - stung. "You mean like put my picture in the WorldView?" She clenched her teeth. "We all do things in the name of revival," she said, repeating the excuse he'd given them for his own risky decision.

His jaw was tight as he spoke. "Listen to me, young lady. You will not risk your life to find this woman." He shook the powder over his drink. Half of it landed on the counter.

His double standard infuriated her. "I'm going to find her," she said, regretting that she'd mentioned anything to him. She started for the door, but he grabbed her before she turned the corner.

"I don't know how to tell you this, so I'll just come right out and say it." He cleared his throat and looked over his shoulder into the living room. "Your mom is dead."

Mira's heart dropped to her shoes. "You can't know that."

He let go of her and tucked his hands into the pockets of his sweats. "After you joined the 'Cords, I did some investigating," he said softly. "That's how I ended up with that book I gave you. *An Artist's Love* was your mom's book, Mira, not one I just happened to find at the trade market."

"What does that have to do with anything?" she asked, not really wanting the answer, but needing to hear it.

He looked her directly in the eyes then. "I know about your trip with your mom to Freetown. I also discovered you were with her at Pillar Media, a place I assume you did some painting because the curtain was splotched with paint." He frowned, his voice trembling as he spoke. "And I know two bodies were found, burned, just outside of Pillar shortly after. Word in Freetown was that it was your mom and a guy named Nick."

Hands folded like in prayer, Mira pressed them against her lips until her teeth gouged her tender skin. The taste of blood…the spill of hot tears…they all enhanced her pain rather than diffused it. "Why didn't you tell me any of this before?"

"Because I couldn't stand to hurt you anymore than you already had been."

She looked at him through her tears, anger winding its way into her heart. "Or maybe you thought I'd give up if I knew." She sniffed and ran her sleeve beneath her nose. "Is that it? Is that the real truth?"

Vaughn's eyes glistened. "I know you won't give up. That's what scares me." He blew out a long breath and looked away. "I'm not sure how someone on Enab ended up with the fabled key, but I can guarantee it wasn't your mom."

She was sick inside. Half of her wanted to curl up in a ball and weep like a baby. The other half wanted to kick out every window at the COO. "I need to go to my room," she said, careful to keep any emotion from her tone.

He frowned down at her. "I'm sorry, Mira."

"Yeah. Me too."

As she walked toward the door, he asked, "You going to be okay?"

"I'll live," she said, and slipped out the door, letting it close behind her with a soft click. Dazed, she wandered back to her room. Once inside, she leaned back against the cold metal door. The hope and energy she'd felt when she'd thought her mom was alive had been smothered in an instant. It almost felt like she was buried beneath the dirt, and it was so heavy that she was suffocating.

Just breathe in and breathe out, she told herself. After a few minutes it became a little easier. She'd get through this like she had everything else. As she went to the dresser for her pajamas, she paused. Had her mom been killed because of her? Did it have something to do with the key and the Enchiridion of Emmanuel? Perhaps all of the above.

Mira went to the closet and dragged her bug-out bag off the top shelf. Vaughn always made her keep it packed and ready, just in case they needed to leave in a hurry. She needed it now.

"I won't let your death be for nothing, mom," she vowed. She'd find the Enchiridion and make whoever was responsible pay dearly.

After changing into black jeans and sweatshirt, she flung the backpack over her shoulders and snuck into the hallway. When she stood in front of Nash's room, she listened. The crumple of turning pages was all she heard. The powder must have worked. She smiled with relief as she knocked.

"Yeah?" came Nash's abrupt answer.

"It's me. Can I come in?"

"I guess. Not like I have a choice."

She cringed as she let herself inside. "Sorry...I just thought it was important that you stay put until you got your emotions under control. It was only temporary."

He stared at her for a moment, the intensity of it making her fidget. Then he said, "Understood."

He didn't look angry. Her shoulders relaxed, a little of their emotional load lifted. "Thanks," she said with a hint of a smile.

He didn't smile back, but lifted up the book he was reading. "I have a couple of questions about this."

At the sight of her mom's book, Mira was overwhelmed by a deep pang of hurt in her heart once again. Chest heavy and throat thick, she said, "I'll answer your questions as soon as we're on our way."

"On our way where?" Nash asked.

She straightened her shoulders, the items in the backpack clinking. "To your house to find the key and your mom's records." And whatever other clues she could find. The way she figured it, her mom wouldn't be dead if she hadn't been on to something big – and the same went for Nash's parents. And Mira was going to get to the bottom of it and hopefully find the Enchiridion in the process.

Chapter 24

Nash followed her without saying a word, which she appreciated. When they got to Dogwood Motors at the edge of the property, though, he asked, "Are we coming back?"

That question could never be answered with a definite yes, but she didn't want to scare him. Fear might freeze him up, despite the evener drugs in his system. "We'll be back."

He nodded at her bug-out bag as they wove through the cars in the lot. "What's the backpack for, then?"

"It has stuff for emergencies…first aid kit, a tarp, a flashlight, dine-a-cubes…that kind of thing." They went inside the showroom.

"Dine-a-cubes?"

She reached into the side pocket and pulled out a foil and cellophane wrapped cube and handed it to him. "It's a meal in a cube, calorie load and all," she said with a smile. "We have a lot of intelligent, creative people working for us."

He twisted the tiny cube around and around between his fingers. "Am I supposed to eat this thing?"

"Yep. It's a Thanksgiving meal, I think," she said, leading him to the supply closet where the hidden elevator would take them to their escape vehicle. Had it only been a few days since she and Kya had used it on their mission to rescue Logan? So much had happened since then, it was hard to believe.

Mira gave Nash a quick rundown of how the elevator worked. It was risky showing him all this stuff, but with the Alpha-Kinase packed in her bag, she wouldn't have to worry. Whatever she showed him, whatever she said, all of it would be erased by the anti-mem drug after their adventure was over. Well, at least six hours of it would be, which should give her plenty of time. She checked her watch. Nine o'clock – Pillar's citywide curfew was ten. They would make it work. There was no way she was waiting until tomorrow.

"This way," she said, directing him onto the shelves of their disguised elevator. As they rode down on them and into the garage, she noticed he was still toying around with the dine-a-cube. "Aren't you going to eat it?" she asked, grabbing the keys for the car that looked almost identical to a Clavicar.

"You first." He held it out to her.

"Just because I'm stealing you away doesn't mean you can't trust me," she said with a chuckle. She bit off the end of the cube and handed the rest back to him. "It's safe, really."

As they both got into the car, he said, "I know that, I guess. For a second there," he shrugged, "I thought you might be like the woman in this book."

She raised a brow at that. "It's just a book – not real life," she said. The heroine in the story had given her lover a sleeping pill so she didn't have to say good-bye to him – only she'd left him with a broken heart because he'd thought she'd chosen her art over him. "Besides, they end up together anyway."

"They do?" Nash glanced down at the novel clutched in his left hand.

She nodded. "Now eat. You won't regret it."

He slipped the dine-a-cube into his mouth and slowly started to chew. His eyes widened, and then he grinned. "Wow. This is amazing!"

"I hope I didn't eat all the turkey." She laughed when his eyes closed and the corners of his mouth curled up. "Did you get to the pumpkin pie yet?"

"No. Cranberries. Didn't know cranberries could taste this good."

"There's a whole world of things to discover when you're chipless." She started the engine, wondering what he'd be like when his true nature came out entirely. Would she even be around to see it?

As she drove through the doors and up the incline, Nash's eyes opened and looked all around. "How long has this been here?"

She reminded herself that her secrets were safe with him because this part of his memory would be gone soon anyway. "It's been around a long time. It worked pretty well for the FBI, I imagine."

"FBI?"

"You know - Federal Bureau of Investigations - a government intelligence and security service." They rolled onto the level road, and she punched on the gas. The curtain of trees flew by as they sped toward Pillar. "Our hideout used to be their academy."

He rubbed his hands up and down his jeaned thighs, the book sitting forgotten on the seat between his legs. When they came out of the trees to open road, he said, "All this time, so much going on right around me, and I hadn't even noticed."

"With the LifeChip, people miss out on the details because they haven't lived them – and they can't think like someone chipless." She turned onto Highway Number One. "What street is your house on?"

"B Street." He stared out the window. "Having the LifeChip was easier, I think."

"But was it better?"

His dark brows furrowed for a moment, but then he reached over to rest his fingers lightly on her neck. "I'm not sure," he said, his fingertips grazing the sensitive skin from her ear to her collarbone.

Instantly, she got goosebumps, yet inside her confidence had taken a nosedive. "Will you want your LifeChip back, then?" If he said yes, she had some work to do.

"Not yet." His hungry eyes traced her profile, yet after a few sizzling seconds, he tore his gaze away and dropped his hands back into his lap. "But maybe it's my selfish nature coming out. And maybe repressing our emotions is just the sacrifice we have to make for a better world."

He sounded like a Reformer, but at least he was being honest. "Well, the LifeChip quit working on me when I was thirteen," she admitted, the turkey flavor in her mouth turning sour. "And the Amender Bug – the memory cell extractor - only worked a little."

Wide eyes locked onto her face.

"Yeah, I'm supposed to be on Enab," she said, thankful for the Alpha-Kinase in her bag.

Nash frowned. "But you're...not like them. Not at all."

"And you know them personally?" She shook her head. "I think there are a lot of things we don't know the truth about."

He stared down at his now clasped hands. "Mira?"

"Hmm?"

"What if you find the Enchiridion and it causes another war?"

"At least people will have a choice."

"But think about the pain it could cause...worse than for the guy in this book."

He was second-guessing himself, something she'd done several times herself. She had to convince him somehow...or she'd have to make sure he didn't stand in her way. "It was worth it in the book. Read it to the end and you'll see." She turned the corner into Pillar. "Want to know a secret I've never told anyone?"

"Yes."

She clutched the steering wheel down low and took a deep breath. "Remember that guy I'd mentioned? The other Unknown?"

"Yes," he said in a tone so low she barely heard him.

Even though she told herself that the confession would be to gain his trust, it was more than that. She wanted to unload the full truth to someone...someone who would forget it and not judge her for it later. So she told him about being with Gabe on the rooftop - every last detail, including the journal page, how it had given her hope...a hope that included a future with Gabe. How she'd felt about Gabe before and after his betrayal was harder to admit than she'd thought, even knowing Nash wouldn't remember it after the Alpha-kinase.

"So you loved him then?" Nash asked.

She cringed. "I guess I thought I did."

He stared out the window, wearing a deep frown, his right hand now clutched onto his door handle. "It sounds like another reason LifeChips are the way to go," he finally said. When she started to make excuses, he slammed his right hand against the dash and turned his blazing eyes in her direction. "He hurt you, Mira, and just thinking about you and him together drives me insane."

She covered his left hand with her own and squeezed. He relaxed a little. "Can I tell you another secret?"

"If it's not about another guy," he muttered.

She had to smile at that. "It's not."

He flipped his hand so that they were palm to palm, their fingers entwined. She could see the tightness of his mouth, but he didn't shut her down. "I'm listening," he said.

His bold stare made her nervous so she focused on the empty streets in front of her as she shared what Vaughn had told her about Freetown and about how her mom had disappeared from Pillar Media. She didn't mention the burned bodies that had turned up because she didn't want to believe it herself. But she did tell him about her tattoo. "I know that the fiery pillar is on the front of the Enchiridion," she said, "but why tattoo it onto me? There had to be *some* reason for it."

He looked at her thoughtfully. "Maybe your mother put it there, maybe as a permanent clue that couldn't be erased, even if your memories were."

She hadn't thought of that. "You might be right."

"Well we need to figure it out. We *will* figure it out."

"Yes. We will," she said, feeling a layer of anxiety drop away with his confidence. She just hoped they'd get it figured out within the next six hours! She glanced over at him. The moment their gazes locked, the haze shadowing his green eyes shifted, leaving behind a vibrant force that nearly melted her into her seat.

"Do you feel that?" he asked.

"What?"

"That we're connected somehow – or are supposed to be," he said, frowning down at their entwined hands.

"I don't know, but what I do know is that I like who you are," she said, meaning it. "And I'm glad you're on my team tonight."

"I like who you are, too." His tender smile flashed in her direction. "And I hope we're on the same team for much longer than just tonight."

She didn't really know what to say. Her heart said *yes please* and her head said *don't be stupid*. "All I can promise is to take it one day at a time."

"That's enough for now." His smile broadened and he looked like a guy that knew things were going to go his way.

His confidence was enticing and frightening at the same time. As she turned the car onto B Street, Nash's jaw dropped. "My house…" Haunted eyes almost instantly transformed to fire.

Mira followed his gaze to the city lot where his house should've been. All that was left of the structure was burned rubble. "I'm so sorry," she said. "We should go back." She slowed the car to a crawl and looked for a place to turn around. If they headed back right now, they could be back at The Compound before curfew with no one the wiser.

But Nash said, "No." He pointed to a garage across the street. "Park over there."

"But…"

"Just do it." His nostrils flared as he stared out the window, but she could see a sheen of moisture in his eyes too.

Suddenly his pain felt like it was hers. "Okay." She pulled the car behind the garage and shoved the car into park. After stuffing her knife and the Alpha-Kinase into her front pockets, she said, "Now what?"

"We find what we came for."

She nodded and opened her door. He did the same and bolted before she even closed hers. She chased after him, following him across the street to a row of trees that edged the lot of smoldering ashes. They weaved between two trees with identical trunks and stopped just short of where his house had been. Nash knelt beside a half-burned desk chair, but he didn't look at it, or at anything on the ground. He was too busy checking out the perimeter.

But Mira had noticed something on the ground right beside him. She picked it up. "It's a Compatimate identifier card," she whispered just loud enough for him to hear her. Nash turned, and after a quick look at it, he stood back up. Taking the plastic identification card from her, he shoved it into his pocket.

It had to be *his* Compatimate, she thought, surprised by how much it hurt to imagine Nash married to the girl. She'd looked so pretty…and so normal and safe. And she must mean something to him because why else would he keep the identifier card? Her body flooded with pain and confusion as she tried to grasp onto a thread of hope. She looked at him for a sign.

But he was looking everywhere but at her. "Something's not right," Nash said, frowning. "I just can't…" He slammed Mira to the ground as tree bark exploded above their heads.

Chapter 25

She was so small beneath him, he was afraid he was crushing her, but it was better that than dead. Heck, the shot had barely missed them. "Let's get out of here," he whispered, rolling off her. The key his mom had kept hidden beneath her desk chair was now safely tucked into his pocket, so he had what he'd come for.

Rising into a crouch, he scrambled into the dense treed area that lined the property. He glanced back. A shadowy figure stood amidst the rubble, aiming a light toward the trees. Could he see them? Heart pounding, Nash suddenly felt unsure. He looked to Mira, who was right behind him. "Hurry," he said.

The wide open space between them and their car wouldn't give them enough cover. The only other place his frantic brain could think to hide was the culvert that sat between his parents' lot and his neighbors'. Nash headed that direction. As they wove through the treed area, though, he spotted a broad crescent swath of light swinging a wide arc just north of where they were. He picked up the pace. Nash knew exactly what the methodical pattern meant – that an Elite Reformer was on the other end of the spotlight. He knew their tactics, and he knew what consequences he and Mira would face if they were caught. But his training *hadn't* prepared him for what he felt right now. He slowed then stopped. What was he doing here with this Accordance woman, running from a man who was doing the job Nash himself had been trained to do?

He felt a touch against his arm. Glancing down at Mira, Nash's doubts began to fade. It was insane, yet the will to keep her safe had pushed its way to front and center in his mind. Only could he trust himself in this emotional state? He didn't know. *I'll think it all through later*, he told himself as he drove ahead at a full run, *when our lives aren't at risk.*

Thankfully, it wasn't much further to the culvert. Their labored breaths mingled with the breeze as they knelt in front of their only hope of escape. Nash slipped into the black space headfirst. Crawling on his belly, inchworm style, he didn't stop until there was enough room behind him to fit Mira. When she was tucked safely inside, a little of the pressure in his chest eased. The cylinder seemed too narrow, though, and it stunk like dead leaves, which he decided he hated a lot at the moment. Grabbing two fistfuls, he tossed the leaf mush to the side, hitting the meat of his hand hard against the metal rung. "Blast it!"

"Shhh!"

At Mira's reprimand, he realized his outburst might have given them away. Insides jumping like hail onto concrete, he scrambled deeper into the cylinder. When he thought he'd gone far enough, he looked back. Mira hadn't moved, and her palms were pressed against the metal sidewall as if it was about to fall in on her.

"What's going on?" He'd tried to whisper, but it had come out more like a squeak.

"Nothing. Shut up," came her hushed, but harsh reply.

Shut up? He frowned. Before he could even begin to make sense of it, Mira had moved up alongside him. She didn't say anything, only nudged at the sludgy debris to make a pile at their feet. Even if their pursuers looked inside, they wouldn't be able to see them.

He had to admit it was a good idea, and tried to help with the little room he had. When the barricade was high enough to hide them from view, they stopped to listen. To Nash, the silence was unnerving, and the metal ridges began to irritate, digging into his side while the stagnant water seeped into his clothes. A spot on his back started to itch. He tried to ignore it. It didn't work. He tried to scratch it, but couldn't reach. Suddenly, he wanted air…he wanted out!

Mira reached over him and scraped her nails along the center of his back and within moments, found the itchy spot. He sighed. She smiled…and just like that, the uncomfortable world around him melted away. Nash couldn't understand what he was feeling. Was this what it was like to totally be his true self — a knot of numerous emotions, strands of which flipped out of him at random times? Nash vowed to figure it all out before getting his new LifeChip.

With her gaze aimed toward the culvert's opening, which was barely visible over the debris pile, Mira said in a tone no louder than a breath, "I should've worn a Notifier. We could use a well-timed distraction about now."

He frowned. "What's a Notifier?"

"It's something we can wear that tracks our location and allows us to call for help if we need it."

It sounded like a useful device. "And we don't have one because…?"

She pursed her lips. "Because I was torked at Vaughn and wanted to prove I could do this on my own."

Another surge of protectiveness toward her spiked his confidence. "We *can* do this," he said. After all, he had an advantage. He knew exactly how the Elite Reformers worked. His lips a breath away from her ear he said, "But I think it's best to make sure they're gone before we risk heading back to the car." Another swath of light scraped across the culvert's opening, then disappeared.

Mira clutched the front of his shirt with her free hand. This time, it was her lips by his ear. "They're getting closer, aren't they? The light seemed brighter."

He wasn't used to seeing her afraid, and his own fear wiggled to the forefront. What if they were caught? Would he ever see her again? Would he remember any of this if he was sent to the Stint? Would they even live? The bright beam of light, that was at the moment shining directly into the culvert, prompted him to carefully cinch Mira in close. He held her like a swaddled blanket around a baby, feeling the knock of her heart. Or was it his?

The light hovered at the opening. Nash's urge to storm their enemy grew stronger. He fought to control the illogical thought. Elites had weapons. He did not. Staying hidden was their best bet. And he couldn't fathom allowing anyone to get to Mira…even though he was promised to another…even though a part of him felt it was his duty to go back to being an Elite Reformer – and his old life.

The light suddenly disappeared and she relaxed a little in his arms, but tensed again when footsteps sounded on the metal above them. They waited, motionless, until everything became eerily quiet.

Mira shifted. "I think now would be a good time to get out," she said.

He didn't let her go. "Not yet." Would their barely audible whispers carry out into the night and alert their pursuer? He didn't think so, especially with the gusty wind to help mask the sounds.

"Oh no," she whispered, tugging at her neckline. "Not now." Her breathing speed almost doubled.

"What?" He nudged her. "What's going on?"

She didn't answer, only started to shake and whimper. And then her eyes rolled back into her head.

Chapter 26

Someone was shaking her, but she didn't want to give up the vision just yet. The ramifications were huge. This was the connection she'd been waiting for. Although she wanted to revisit the sweet details over and over again, the shaking continued to interrupt.

"Stop," she groaned, peeking through the slits of her eyes at a very worried Nash.

"Mira." Her name was spoken in a whisper as he gathered her close. "I'm so glad you're okay."

"It was just one of my episodes." Her cheeks flushed, imagining a state of convulsing and drooling. Not the best look to impress someone she thought could actually be her soulmate. "Bet I looked pretty stupid, huh?"

Nash shook his head. "I thought I was losing you." She could see dampness on his cheeks. "And I hated feeling it."

"I'm sorry I worried you," she said, speaking past the lump in her throat. Then she remembered where they were. "Are they gone?" She pointed upward.

"Haven't heard anything for quite a while and haven't seen the beam of light either," he whispered. He leaned back to look at her face. "So what did you see in your vision?"

Them together…that's what she'd seen. Her heart and her head were finally united. Nash and she belonged together. She was sure of it. Otherwise he wouldn't keep popping up in her visions. "You and I…we were in my childhood room – I know because I saw the purple stuffed elephant trunk poking out of the stacks of folded tan shirts. We were looking up at the ceiling panel. It had a pillar of fire painted on it."

"A purple stuffed elephant?"

She actually smiled. "I found it in an abandoned house in Rag Town."

"That's outside the city. No one is supposed to go there."

"Well...that's a story for another time. We need to worry about what I saw in my vision."

"Do you think the Enchiridion is hidden behind the panel?"

"Maybe...or at least clues to find it." She smiled. "Any which way, we were meant to find it together." And she was thrilled at how much more confident she felt just knowing she had a true partner who would help her through the ups and downs of her search.

For several moments, Nash was quiet, making circles on her back with his palm. Part of her was anxious to go. Another part of her was fully enjoying just being with him and basking in the hope that her vision had rejuvenated.

Then Nash interrupted the silence. "I think I know where the key to unlocking the Enchiridion is."

"Are you serious?" she asked, almost too afraid to hope.

"Yes." He smiled softly at her.

Her answering grin trembled as a sudden jolt of energy intoxicated her body. The pieces were all coming together and she felt like she was ready to take on the world if she needed to. But first she had to take care of the irritating creepy crawly thing tickling her ankle. She swung her hand down to swat it, only the frayed seam of her black jeans was bugless...and entirely soaked. "What the heck?" Mira looked past the pile of debris toward the opening of the culvert just as a deluge of water burst through the hole.

Chapter 27

Nash grabbed her waist and shoved her up ahead of him. "Move Mira," he ordered, his training kicking in.

She scrambled forward, but then stopped.

"What are you doing?" His heart sounded tremendously loud in his ears, louder than the gushing water. "Don't stop!"

Looking over her shoulder at him, she shouted, "The other side is blocked!"

The freezing water continued to gush into the culvert and his limbs had started to tingle.

"Come out and I'll let you live," boomed a voice from the culvert's entrance.

Nash looked at Mira who had continued to the end and was frantically clawing at the packed dirt. His heart grew heavier with each gouge. He didn't want them to die. He didn't want them to go to the Stint. Not now. Not after all that had happened. But the reality of the situation was that their chances of escape were about nil. The only spark of hope he had was that maybe he could help Mira get away. "Good-bye…my love," he called out, only the words sounded like they'd been forced through vocal chords scraped raw. She hadn't heard him. He tried to say it again, but his throat was squeezed too tightly to get the words out.

He hoped she knew, that what he was about to do would prove how he felt about her. With limbs that felt as heavy as his heart, he crawled backward against the rushing water. When his feet neared the opening, he yelled out, "I'm coming out and I'm unarmed."

The gushing water lessened then dwindled to a trickle, so he shimmied the rest of the way out of the culvert and slowly got to his feet. Raising his hands, he turned around. He frowned at the moonlit scene. Where was the Elite Reformer?

The mud-encrusted nozzle of the discharge hose had been shoved aside. Nash followed its length to the edge of the tree line. He could see it continue across the neighbor's yard and driveway. The end of it was attached to a Renovatruck, but he saw no one. It didn't make sense.

Taking cautious steps, he moved through the trees, hoping to find a sign. The Reformers were a forceful group, yet predictable and straightforward when it came to capture. They should be easy to spot! Finding nothing, Nash frowned, and turned to retrace his steps. As he neared his starting point, he looked up. He gasped. Standing with his foot propped on top of the culvert was a masked man, his gun aimed into the opening. Nash had been so sure their pursuer was a Reformer…but this guy wasn't acting like one! Now what?

Nash took a quiet step toward the man, then another, and another. One more step and he'd be close enough to pounce. He pressed his foot down again, carefully. *Snap!*

At the tree branch's alert, the man swung around, his gun now aimed at Nash. For a moment, the masked man stood there, staring. Then he said in a low, hoarse voice, "Call the girl out."

Nash swallowed hard. "She's…she's gone."

"No. She's not." The man waved the gun across the culvert's opening. "Call her out here, or I'll shoot."

"I wouldn't if I were you," Nash growled. His insides felt coiled, painful almost. He didn't doubt that he could kill the man if it meant keeping Mira safe.

The gun swung back toward Nash. "I can make this very unpleasant," the man said, "for both of you."

The surge of fear and desperation cut the last thread of control he had. Nash sprang toward the gunman, his powerful leap interrupted by the gun's loud *crack*. As their bodies collided, searing pain ripped through Nash's side, yet it was nothing compared to what he felt *in*side. His hate and terror exploded as he smashed the thug to the ground. His hands snapped around the man's neck like shackles, his fingertips gouging into the thick flesh as he pressed his weight downward on his windpipe. The man thrashed, clawing at Nash's hands, but his grip was solid and relentless.

"You don't deserve to live," Nash sneered.

The guy reached up, and struggling, wrenched his mask off his face. Nash froze.

"Uncle Rand? Professor?" Nash loosened his grip and released his uncle's neck, but didn't get up.

"Get off of me." Rand's demand was weak and gravelly.

Nash's head spun with questions as rage continued to pulse from his fingertips. "Explain first. And it had better be a good one."

"Definitely no LifeChip." Rand spat off to the side. "We thought you'd been murdered, like your parents. And since your house burned, I've been keeping watch…in case the 'Cords returned to the scene of the crime. Passionate but illogical. Or have you forgotten?"

Nash held perfectly still. "Keep talking."

"Your parents were spying for us. The Accordance found out and killed them." He shook his head. "I warned your folks, said it was too dangerous to deal with the 'Cords, but they insisted they had connections and that their plan would work."

Was it true? Was the Accordance responsible? Nash slowly slid off his uncle. Kneeling now, he clutched his side, which felt like it was on fire. A warm, stickiness oozed between his fingers. He swallowed back his sudden nausea. "Even if what you're telling me is true…" he paused, remembering his last conversation with his parents, "there are secrets I need to uncover – without your interference."

Rand looked into the distance as he got to his feet. "Unbelievable," he muttered. After brushing at the mud on his shirt, he kicked the cylinder's metal edge. "Come on out, Miss Miracle. Your game is over."

Nash frowned. "You know her?" he asked, grabbing his throbbing side as he used the culvert to get to his feet.

Rand, an arm's length away with the culvert between them, nodded once. "Gabe led us to Necropolis, but she escaped, and then kidnapped you from the hospital. Now she's using her visions to get what she wants."

That was all true. Mira had admitted as much to him. And what about his parents? Could've they actually been spies? He had to admit, it was all possible. Filled with all sorts of conflicting emotions, Nash stared at the culvert opening, hoping that somehow the answers would come. But all it brought was the darkness of uncertainty. "Maybe you're right," he said finally, doubt seeping into every recess of his mind.

"Don't listen to him!" Mira popped out of the far end of the culvert, her face and clothes smeared with mud. "He's lying." Her left pant leg brushed rhythmically against the metal rungs as she inched toward Nash.

His uncle waved the gun in her direction. "Don't let her fool you when you're not in your right mind," he said. "All she wants is to use you and your overactive emotions to get the power she's been denied."

"They're the ones who want the power," she growled out through clenched teeth.

That's when Nash spotted the flash of the blade in Mira's hand. He shook as he staggered to the side, away from her. As he took another shaky step, his foot caught on the hose. Arms flailing, he stumbled sideways. He tried to regain his balance, but over-corrected, pitching forward. "Ahhhhh!" Just before his face planted into the leaf-strewn ground, sure hands grabbed him. "Easy there," Mira whispered, maneuvering him to an upright kneel. She put a hand on his shoulder to steady him.

"Ah. Isn't that touching," his uncle said. "But it's not real, Nash. She's playing with your emotions, trying to make you feel like she cares about you." He moved in close to them and raised his gun. Pointing it an inch from Nash's temple, he said, "Let's see just how much she really cares about you, shall we?"

Nash knew his uncle was counting on the chipless Mira being impulsive and emotion-driven, but when Rand's dare was met with silence, Nash doubts about her surged. He began to sweat, and the ache in his side reached all the way into his heart. From the corner of his eye, he could see his uncle apply more pressure to the trigger and he knew that he wouldn't hesitate to pull it if he truly believed it was for the greater good of their city. Nash couldn't watch, couldn't deal with the reality he faced. He squeezed his eyes shut only to feel Mira's hand leave his shoulder. The jolt of her choice made him scream the only words he thought would save him, "It's in the ceiling of her childhood room."

"Nash...no!" Mira cried out.

He opened his eyes at the sound of her voice. She had his uncle face down beneath her, her knife pressed against his throat, his arms trapped by her knees.

"How...how?" Nash didn't know what to do – or even what to think. And she stared at him like he'd done something horrible to hurt her. His stomach curled.

Mira pursed her lips and, after muttering something under her breath, flipped her knife back into her pocket and pulled out a cylindrical tube.

"What are you doing? Stop her, Nash!" his uncle ordered, squirming beneath her.

She ground her knees into his arms as his flailing body jerked her back and forth. But she was determined, and quick. She slapped a hand over his mouth and held the tube beneath his nose. "Time to go to sleep now," she said.

Nash couldn't believe this was happening. "Was that poison? Did you kill him?" He tried to get to his feet, but failed.

"Three, two, one," she said, shoving at Rand's shoulders as she stood up. "The only thing I killed was his memory of the past six hours with something called Alpha-Kinase." After scanning the area, she approached Nash. "I know you thought I was going to let him shoot you." She inhaled, then exhaled loudly through her nose. "If you'd have kept your eyes open, you'd have seen that wasn't the case. *He's* the one playing with your mind."

She held a hand out to him. He didn't take it. "I can't think straight right now," Nash said, his mouth tightening as his stomach threatened to release his turkey dinner. "I'm not feeling so well."

She let her hand drop. "I need to check out your injury before we head out. Can I?"

He didn't answer, yet she bent to peel his shirt from his side anyway. She was being so careful, but he couldn't help but flinch as the cool air jagged across his wound. "Looks like it's only a flesh wound." She looked at him. "Do you know if your uncle would use bullets or NBD darts?"

The neuromuscular-blocking drug tipped darts were the weapon of choice for most Elites, his uncle included...especially when dealing with high-risk 'Cords. "Darts, mostly. Probably the new X4 model," he answered with a grimace.

"Then we need to get you out of here before the drug sets in. Even a small graze can paralyze you for a long while." Again, she held her hand out to him. "And there's no way I'll be able to carry you."

He was already feeling woozy. His side was getting worse, the intense pain matching the one in his stomach...and his heart. "I told him your secret." He crawled to a nearby tree and used it to get to his feet. "Maybe you should leave me here."

"Well he doesn't know it anymore, and I'm not leaving you." She grabbed his arm, the one not holding onto the tree, and wrapped it over her shoulders. "Move it, soldier."

He dug in his feet. At least he thought he did. "Maybe I don't *want* to go back with you."

She paused to stare up at him. He couldn't look her in the eye.

"You don't trust me," she said.

It was a statement, not a question. "I just don't know what to believe," he said.

Her nostrils flared as she looked out across the road toward the garage that hid their car. "I told you things I've never told anyone else. I only want to help you *and* Pillar. And to do that, we need to disappear before you pass out or your uncle wakes up. We'll figure out the rest later."

Nash wanted to believe her, but after another glance at Rand's lifeless form, he said, "How do I know what you told me is true? Or even if I'm the only one you told? You could be lying about the whole thing."

She sighed heavily and her arm dropped from around his waist. The moonlight poking through the trees gave him a good view as she lifted the edge of her shirt an inch to expose a tattoo right above her jeans' waistline. "Proof enough?"

The pillar of fire was there, so at least a portion of what she'd said was true. When he reached for it – to feel the realness of it beneath his own fingertips - she tucked her shirt back into her jeans and stepped away from him.

Nash swayed, barely managing to stay upright.

With an arm now crossed over her stomach, she said, "I don't want to leave you here, but I will. Decide."

When it came right down to it, she was still his best bet to find the Enchiridion and his answers – even if she wasn't being totally truthful. "I'm with you," he said and held out his arms.

She immediately stepped into them and wrapped her arms around his waist. He couldn't help but sigh…and cringe because of the pain slashing through his side.

"Promise you won't pass out until we're in the car," she said against his chest.

"I won't."

"You won't promise, or you won't pass out?"

She smiled up at him. He managed to work up a wobbly grin.

"It's going to be okay, Nash," she said softly. Moving beside him, Mira propped his arm over her shoulders again. As they stepped forward, a hiss escaped his lips. Heck, his side hurt. And walking like this, with her being a too short crutch, wasn't helping anything. He let go of her and clutched his side.

She didn't say a word, only hovered close, watching his every step.

He was drenched from the culvert's water and the only warmth he felt was coming from the wound's blood. He tried not to think about how miserable he was and concentrated on putting one foot in front of the other.

"We're almost there," she said.

Almost wasn't close enough. As they approached the garage, the edge of it seemed to wobble. He reached out, finding it steady enough to lean against. So he did. He sucked in several gulps of air before rolling around the corner to where he knew their getaway car waited. But when he looked…

"It's gone?" he whispered, then slid to the ground. The shadows he'd been holding off suddenly eclipsed his vision, so he just gave in to them and closed his eyes. He heard Mira yelp, but an invisible force dragged him the rest of the way under before he could do anything about it.

Chapter 28

"Well, well, well. Looks like I found the owners of the dandy vehicle you left for me," breathed a voice into Mira's ear.

She hadn't heard him come up behind them, but she was very aware of the cold blade now pressed beneath her jaw line. She moved only her eyes to see if she'd get any help from Nash. He was out cold at her feet. "And you need to give the dandy vehicle back so we can go home," she said, covering up her fear with a cavalier parroting of his drawl.

"Sassy, are we?"

She immediately realized her mistake. Her one reckless remark had given away her chiplessness. "Sassy? No. Just tired. We're on the cleanup crew for that burned down house. It's too dark to work, so we're headed home," she said in an attempt to cover up her goof.

"What's with yer partner?" The guy's sock-covered toe nudged Nash's prone form.

"He's really tired too, I guess."

The man's quiet laughter surprised her as did the shifting knife. She squeaked. She couldn't help it. Before she could try to explain that one, her captor released her. She whipped around only to find the man tucking his knife into his belt. "You're letting us go?"

"Ya won't get far with that one." He nodded toward Nash.

"You aren't kidding," she muttered.

He chuckled. "Vaughn sent out an alert. He thought ya might be comin' my way. Just didn't know it was gonna be such an interestin' way of meetin' up."

She glanced back at where she'd left Rand. The area was dark and quiet. "Vaughn told you I was going to be here?" She shifted to her other foot.

"We have a secure line set up. He only suspected you'd come, but I promised to take care of ya if ya did – and yer friend there, too."

She didn't have much choice but to trust what he was saying and admittedly, she was so tired - emotionally and otherwise - his help was more than welcome. "I'd appreciate it. Who are you?"

He reached his hand out to her. "Hayes. Vaughn is my brother."

"What?! I didn't know he had a brother."

He grinned, which made him look a lot more like Vaughn. "Because of our positions in the Accordance," he said, "it's best that we keep our close friends and families secret. Never know when they can be used against us."

It made sense. She glanced back toward the culvert, hoping she wouldn't have to worry about Nash's family anytime soon. "You got a place for us to hide?"

Hayes nodded and put his hands beneath Nash's arms. "I've got a place to stitch him up, too." Lifting him up, he said, "Ya shoulda picked someone smaller. Grab his feet, would ya?"

Mira did as he asked, and together, they lugged Nash across the small backyard. They stopped several meters from a house that looked just the same as all the others in the neighborhood. Split foyers. Permanent siding. Only Hayes stopped ten feet from the house's back door, reached down into the grass and opened a sod-covered trap door. In the dim light, she could see cement stairs leading down into the darkness.

"Clever," she said, liking him already.

"Ya ain't seen nothin' yet, darlin'."

They struggled down the narrow stairwell with Nash's dead weight bumping down the steps between them. With his shoulder, Hayes nudged open the door at the bottom. They stepped inside and lowered Nash to the floor. Mira kicked the door shut behind her.

"We could use some help here," Hayes yelled toward the stairs, which were to the right of the fireplace on the wall opposite of where they stood.

Mira removed her wet shoes as she absorbed the warmth of the crackly fire with its wildly waving flames. She checked out the place, curious. In the far right corner was a fireplace, with a small couch angled to face it. The door for the steps, located to the left of the stone structure, was open, blocking her view of the hallway next to it. On the wall to Mira's left was a closet door and a huge picture of the Benefactor. She quickly looked away from the hideous thing. The wall on her right housed two tall cabinets. And directly behind her, next to the door they'd come through, stood a small desk.

"Let's put 'im over here." Hayes had pulled a sheet-covered table out of a closet and had positioned in front of the cabinets.

Mira took a deep breath and lifted with every ounce of energy she owned to help Hayes get Nash over to and up onto the table.

When they finally got it done, Hayes cut Nash's shirt right down the middle. "Mel, Mira and Nash are here. Where are ya?" He glanced at Mira. "Mel's my wife, by the way."

A roundish smiling woman bustled down the steps and into the room, closing the door behind her. Her hair was a deep red but cut in the typical Pillar fashion, her hands were propped on her hips. When she caught sight of Nash, she hurried over to the cabinets and opened them. "What happened to you poor dears?" she asked, turning to Nash and placing her hand an inch over his mouth and nose.

Mira wasn't about to blurt out the entire story, but she felt she owed them an explanation. "We went to search Nash's house. His uncle Rand, an Elite I guess, was watching the place. He shot at him," she said. "Then we managed to escape and make our way here."

"Good thing you did. We've heard some bad things about Rand Montgomery," Hayes said.

Mel flashed a pen light across Nash's eyes as she pulled back his lids. "His breathing is normal." Mel paused to glance at Mira. "I've heard this Rand fellow is an Elite Reformer trainer, bent on obtaining the Enchiridion of Emmanuel at any cost."

Could Rand have influenced Nash? Mira's gut twisted as she realized she knew very little about Nash's past. And now he knew several of her secrets...ones that could cost her the Enchiridion, her friends, and maybe even her life. Her eyes shifted to her partner-could-be-enemy as Mel peeled away his blood-soaked shirt. Tears forced their way out and clouded Mira's vision. She wanted him to be the good guy, her guy, she realized. But was she just in love with the idea...with who she wanted him to be?

"Looks like a surface wound from a bullet, not a dart," Mel said. She picked up his limp arm and let it drop. "But appears that whatever it was, it was tipped in NBD."

Mira brushed the wetness from the corners of her eyes. "What will happen to him?" she sniffed.

Mel quickly put an arm around her. "Don't worry, dear." The woman's eyes crinkled in the corners and just like that, she'd transformed from ordinary to beautiful. "He'll be fine in no time."

"That drug will keep him sedated while we stitch him up," Hayes added. "Then we can hook him up to a nerve stimulator to help the NBD wear off faster." Hayes lifted his thick brow. "Or not. Up to you."

Even though they didn't seem at all worried, the faster Nash woke up, the better she'd feel...at least once she gave him a piece of her mind. Unless... "You wouldn't happen to have any Alpha-Kinase around, would you?"

"No, we don't," Hayes said. "And it'd be risky givin' it to him in this condition."

She wasn't about to take a risk like that. "Use the nerve stimulator then...after the stitching."

"Sounds like we have a plan." Mel ushered her over to the paisley couch and covered a section of it with an oversized towel. "You just sit here and rest and I'll find you a nice warm wash cloth." She paused. "unless you want a shower."

"I'm too tired," Mira said. She sat down on the couch and leaned back, relieved that the portrait was behind her and that Nash was only a couple of feet in front of her. The fire's warmth started to wick away the moisture in her clothes and it lulled her with its mesmerizing flames.

Hayes grabbed a plastic wrapped towel from one of the shelves. He sliced open the package. "We have something called the Stitcher that works like a charm for stuff like this. Did ya know we patched up Vaughn a time or two?"

She shook her head.

"We sew disguises for the Accordance and patch up clothes, too," Mel added.

Hayes chuckled. "Your group goes through clothes like a baby through diapers," he said.

Mira smiled. "I'm sure we do."

Mel smiled back in a motherly way that made Mira think of her own mom – and her promises.

"I'll go get the Stitcher and the washcloth now." Mel hurried into the hallway, her fading whistled tune familiar. Vaughn had whistled it many times. It made Mira immediately feel at home yet lonely and regretful at the same time.

Hayes dabbed at Nash's wound with a square of gauze saturated with something orange. "So did ya find anything interesting out there? Or did the Enchiridion Locator Search Crew get to it first?"

She looked at him questioningly.

"They've already been through half the houses in Pillar looking for the Enchiridion."

She tensed, hoping that her vision hadn't come too late. "Nash's house is pretty much all burned up. Nothing really left to find."

"Hmm." Hayes resumed his application of the orange goop on Nash's skin, but said nothing else.

His continued silence was killing her. "So was Vaughn mad when he called you?"

He glanced at her. "A bit. Mostly just agitated 'cause he doesn't want to lose anyone else close ta him."

She sat up and leaned forward, her elbows on her knees. "He worries too much," she said, but inside it made her feel good - and guilty.

"He's lost a lot, darlin'," Hayes said, balling up the now red-soaked gauze.

"Like what?"

He studied her a moment. "I'll tell ya some of it if you promise not to tell him that I did."

Mel hurried back into the room and after handing Mira the warm square cloth, plopped what looked like an over-sized button into Hayes' hand. "Why does stitching people up make you want to blab a bunch of secrets?"

He only laughed.

"I won't say a word to Vaughn about it. I promise," Mira said, slowly wiping the steamy cloth across her face. It felt awesome!

Mel shook her head, but went to the desk to type on a laptop computer sitting on top of it.

"A few years back, well quite a few," Hayes said, grabbing a bottle from the shelf next to the gauze and spraying the underside of the Stitcher. The needle that poked out was curved. He laid it onto Nash's stomach. "Our family owned a little place on an island close to here." He flipped a switch on top of the contraption, staring at it as it started to move. "It was taken over by the LAW. Fer strategic purposes, they said." The button inched along Nash's torn flesh in time to the clicking of Mel's computer keys. "Turns out the LAW needed a place for the folks who couldn't be controlled by the LifeChip."

Mira jerked her head back in surprise. "Your island is Enab?"

The Stitcher continued to inch across the gash. "Yup." Hayes wiped his hand on a clean towel he grabbed from the shelf. "Anyways, they dragged our parents away that day. I was sixteen, Vaughn was eighteen."

Vaughn had been her age. Maybe that's why he was being so protective of her. "What happened then?" she asked, taking one final swipe across her face, neck, and arms with the now cool washcloth. She felt much better.

"We hid out in the woods 'til it was dark, then we took a rowboat 'cross to the mainland." Hayes removed the Stitcher, wiped it off, sprayed it and wiped it with a new square of material. "Kinda rough waters, but we made it. Then we hiked ta this abandoned cabin we'd found when we were out exploring one time."

Mel snapped the laptop shut, put it into a black bag and wandered over to Hayes' side. "But the cabin wasn't exactly empty," she said.

Hayes' eyes softened when he looked at his wife. "A girl was inside, cryin', so we knew she was chipless." He kissed Mel's palm before putting the Stitcher into it. "It was love at first sight for Vaughn."

Mira actually smiled at that. He probably wanted to fix everything for her, like he had when he'd first met Mira. "So did you all live together in the cabin, then?"

"No. She just came around every day with somethin' for us." Hayes carefully put a bandage over Nash's wound then stuck two electrodes to the skin on either side of it. Slim wires extended from the square patches. He connected them into the nerve stimulator lying on the table beside Nash. "Blankets, food, books - those sorts of things."

Mel returned to Hayes' side after putting the items away. When she rested a hand on his shoulder, he continued. "She and Vaughn'd go off together and work on their plans to shake up the LAW's system. I didn't know how serious he was about her, though, 'til he told me he was gonna marry her."

Mira frowned. Vaughn had told her that he'd never been married and would never marry. "What happened to her?"

He glanced at Mel, who nodded. "A month before the wedding, she came by ta tell him she couldn't marry him."

In her heart, Mira could almost feel Vaughn's world crumbling. Carefully, she laid the cloth on the coffee table in front of her. "Why couldn't she?"

After punching a couple of buttons on the nerve stimulator, Hayes pulled a folded sheet from the cabinet shelves. "Vaughn was gone when she stopped by and all I got outa her was that she was going to marry her Compatimate."

It was dumb to think a computer could pick a perfect match, but looking at the choices she'd made so far… She glanced at Nash, wondering. When this was over, would he go back to his old life? Would he choose *his* Compatimate – logic and LifeChip over love and passion? "Why the change of heart, do you think?" she asked, her tone choked with emotion.

"Doubt we'll ever know. The lass wanted to meet up with him one last time so she could explain." Hayes sighed as he laid the blanket over Nash. "But Vaughn said whatever her reasons, they weren't good enough. And seeing her one more time – knowing she'd never be his – it would kill him, so he didn't go to the meetin' spot she'd set up."

He prevented a last good-bye, like the main character in the paperback Vaughn had given her. "Then how did he end up being the leader of the Accordance?"

"Vaughn didn't really care about anything anymore, so he picked the most risky thing he could think of – leading a group of rebels to terrorize the system that, in his mind, caused him to lose the woman he loved," Mel said, reaching for Hayes' hand.

"And then several years later, someone in Freetown told him his love was still alive on Enab."

Then it dawned on her. "That's why he got caught? So he'd be sent to where his true love was?" Mira asked.

Hayes nodded.

"But why did Vaughn change his mind, then? Why did he rescue me?"

Hayes looked at Mel who shook her head. "That's somethin' he needs to tell ya himself." He tossed the bloodied towels onto the floor beneath the table. It opened like a mouth. The towels disappeared with a quiet hiss, which was interrupted by a hard knock.

Mira looked around for the source and noticed the couple's focus was on a small monitor on the wall near the fireplace. It had lit up.

The knock came again, more insistent this time.

"Looks like we got company," Hayes said, moving toward the steps. As he opened the door in front of them, he peeked over his shoulder at Mira. "Mel will show ya to the safe room. Normally, I wouldn't worry, but it looks as if Rand has a partner – and it's someone we've had some trouble with before."

"This way," Mel said with a wave of her arm.

Mira wound around the couch toward her, but kept glancing toward the monitor screen that showed two men standing at the front door. The one was definitely Rand. The other she only got a glimpse of, but there was something about him that seemed eerily familiar - his creepy eyes perhaps? No two people would have those, would they? She wished she could remember where she'd seen him before.

"This is the entrance to our safe room," Mel said, drawing her attention to the life-sized portrait of the LAW's Benefactor. She flicked his nose. The image slid to the side, like a pocket door.

Despite the seriousness of the situation, Mira giggled.

"There's nothing better than a secret hideout right beneath our governor's nose, right?" Mel said with a grin.

"What about Nash?" He was still out cold.

"The opening's big enough to wheel him through."

Mira nodded. After hurrying to put on her shoes, she grabbed Nash's shirt. "Anything else I should know?" she asked, taking one last look to make sure no sign of their visit remained.

"There's a switch to your right that turns on the lights. It'll shut the portrait door behind you too," she explained. "And then there's Deidre." Mel let out a long, drawn-out sigh.

Mira went to Nash, laid the shirt on his legs then grabbed the end of the rolling table. "Who's Deidre?"

"Well, she came to us a few weeks ago. She's a…unique girl." Mel glanced down the hallway as she headed toward the stairs. "I don't know if she'll join you or not, but I just didn't want you to be scared silly if she happens to pop in."

Mira wheeled Nash close to the opening. "Got it."

"We'll join you when the coast is clear," Mel said, edging toward the stairs.

"And if you don't come back?" Mira asked.

"That's doubtful." Mel paused to look over her shoulder. "But just in case, there's a tunnel behind the tapestry that will lead you to the Unified Church. Pastor Ettreim will take care of you."

Mira had met Pastor Ettreim before. She really liked him. "Thanks," she said.

Mel nodded and went to the first door in the hall. She knocked softly, a rhythmic pattern – probably a code. Then she hurried to the stairs and closed the heavily padded door behind her.

Mira turned back to her task and gave Nash's bed a hard shove, but it stalled in the doorway. Her eyes darted from one side of the wheeled table to the next. "It should fit!" It had to fit! Positioning herself at the head of the narrow table, she propped her foot on its edge to try again. "One, two, three," she said, giving it a good solid kick. But all it did was twist a little to the side. "Stupid piece of crap," she growled. *Why can't anything be easy?* she thought.

She glanced at the monitor. The Elite Reformers were still outside, and it appeared as though they were deep in conversation with Hayes and Mel. Hands on hips, lips pursed, Mira stared at Nash's inert form. Maybe she could drag him. No. He'd been way too heavy for her when she'd carried just his feet. Maybe if she propped him up and rolled him, somersault style into the hideout. It was worth a shot. She grabbed his shoulders and tried to sit him up.

"Stop!" Nash blurted, startling her.

Even though his eyes were still closed, she noticed his brows were knitted tightly and his mouth was set into a firm line. And he looked a little green.

"We have to hide, Nash." She carefully laid him back down. "Help me get you into our safe room, okay?" His hands moved, and she looked for a thumbs up. Nope. He had a death grip on the edges of the doorway.

When she realized that *he* was the source of her trouble, she muttered, "You cause me so much grief," and with shaky hands began to pry his fingers off the metal jamb. They finally loosened and dropped to his sides. She skirted back around him so she could push again. "Hold on," she said. But right as she gave it a shove, he rolled off it. The bed whizzed, unencumbered, into the safe room.

A short bark of laughter burst from somewhere deep inside her. Maybe it was her nerves, maybe exasperation. But it quickly died when she looked up into his face.

Chapter 29

The only thing keeping Nash from falling was the wall his shoulder was propped against. Eyes half closed, he looked around, clutching his side as he tried to get his bearings. A bandage wasn't the only thing beneath his fingers. He glanced down. Grabbing the two wires that hung from the square things stuck onto his skin, he yanked, ripping them off. The sharp pain forced his eyes to close and his jaw to clench. The contraption clunked onto the floor.

"That was the nerve stimulator." A hand touched his bare shoulder. "You okay?"

It was Mira's voice, but when he looked at her, he couldn't seem to get his eyes to focus. Images floated like confetti in his mind. He tried to force the shredded pieces back together, but it wasn't working. "Define okay," he said.

"Do you think you can make it into the safe room?" She nodded her head toward the dark space she'd been trying to shove him into. "You can lie down again in there."

It didn't look safe to him. He pressed a hand against his queasy stomach. "You go first."

Rolling her eyes, she said, "Whatever." She snatched something off the floor and then disappeared into the dark room. After a few seconds, she called out, "You coming?" She popped back into the doorway and held out her hand.

Hesitantly, he took it, and let her guide his stumbling feet inside. Man, his body felt like stomped garbage and his head felt like mush.

Mira reached past him to flip on a switch. A dim light buzzed to life and then something whirred behind him. He tripped a little as he turned around. A mirror had slid across the opening they'd just come through. He cringed when he saw his reflection.

"A nice shower and a hot meal and you'll be feeling back to normal," she said from behind him.

He tried to swallow, but his mouth was desert dry. "A drink right now would be good," he said. Carefully, he traced the edges of the gauze bandage that covered a good portion of his side. Memories poked at the fringes of his fuzzy brain. "What happened to me?"

"You don't remember?" She came up next to him and handed him a bottle of water.

"It's coming back but…" He took the water, glancing over his shoulder to see where she might have gotten it. The back wall was covered with shelves stocked with supplies. "Want to fill me in?"

He opened the bottle and as he brought it to his lips, Mira blurted, "Rand Montgomery shot you. You told him my secret. I erased the last six hours from his memory." She shrugged. "That about sums it up."

Her words hammered into his sensitive skull. He tilted his head back, letting the cool liquid rush down his parched throat. After he drank it all, he ran a hand down his clammy face. His memory was becoming clearer and he didn't like what it was telling him. Not at all. "You were going to let him shoot me in the head," he croaked, the pain of that worse than anything he ever remembered feeling.

"Look at me, Nash."

Slowly, he did as she said. Her fists were propped on her hips and she'd come so close to him that her stagnant leaf smell overrode his antiseptic. "I had two choices. One," she held up a finger, "I could jump in front of you and take the bullet. Or two," she said, jutting her chin upwards, "I could use the swing kick Vaughn taught me a couple of months ago to knock the *gun* out of your uncle's hand and knock *him* down." Her eyes glittered as they stared up at him. "I chose the second." She took a deep breath. "And you need to remember…he was the one with the weapon. He's the one that did the threatening."

Nash didn't know what to think - only knew he needed to sit down. Spotting a chair to his left, he took two clumsy steps and plopped into it. After a moment, he said softly, "I don't know who to trust anymore."

"I know the feeling," she muttered. She drifted over to him and, resting her hands on his knees, leaned in so they were eye to eye. The silver in her blue-eyed gaze sparked and branched out from her pupils like lightning barbs. "And *I* don't know if I can trust *you*." She gave the ribbed neckline of her shirt a gentle tug. "Every day, I wonder if you'll turn me in. I question if you'll destroy the Enchiridion if we find it. And I worry you'll go back to your old life and your LifeChip." The heat in her tone was unmistakable. She meant what she said. He reached up to rub his temples, trying to think past the ache.

"And do you know what else I can't help but think about?" The sharp barbs in her eyes transformed into soft feathers layered with dew. "If you'll marry your Compatimate and break my heart."

Something inside him twisted, making him feel like he couldn't get quite a deep enough breath. "I don't want to break your heart."

"What *do* you want, Nash?"

"I don't know. I mean..." He frowned, trying to find a way to put his thoughts into words. "I guess what I really want is to find the truth. For myself, for you." His eyes grazed along her face then rested on her slightly parted lips. He swallowed, frozen in place except for the wild beat of a heart that wanted more of something he didn't understand. "And I want to do the right thing."

Slowly, she stood up. Tucking her hands into her pockets, she backed toward the leftmost shelf crowded with jars and baskets housed at her chest level. As she turned around to face it, she skimmed her hand across the fronts of the jars. "And what if that causes you to lose everything...your whole way of thinking...your occupation...your old life?"

He sat forward in the chair. The lines that had been very clear to him no longer were. Clasping his hands together between his knees, he said, "I don't really know what my whole way of thinking is anymore and I can't make any promises. What I *do* know is that I feel like I care about you."

"Well..." After clearing her throat, she said, "I care about you, too, Nash." She turned to lean back against the shelves and offered him a crooked smile that went straight to his heart. "And I *did* see you and me together in my vision."

He squeezed his hands together more tightly. "Have your visions ever been wrong?"

"Not so far." Her eyes took on a sober, but determined gleam.

"So," he said shakily, "are you going to tell me why we're here? Or is that a secret I can't be trusted with?"

She crossed her feet in front of her. "You did blab to your uncle, you know."

He cringed, a powerful ache digging its tentacles into his heart. "I know. I'm sorry. I thought..."

She held up her hand. "I don't like it but I get it." She wandered over to a ten-foot rack filled with hanging clothes. "We are currently in the house we parked behind. It's owned by Hayes, who happens to be Vaughn's brother. He stitched you up." Hangers screeched along the metal rod as she shoved them over. "Then when Rand and his partner came looking for us, Mel, Hayes' wife, told us to hide in here."

He recognized their names and realized he was surrounded by some big players in the Accordance group. The truth...he needed it more than ever now. "Rand had a partner?" He didn't remember seeing anyone else in the area, not by the Renovatruck either.

"I saw him on a surveillance screen when they came to look for us." She fiddled with a shirt's sleeve. "And I just remembered who he is," she whispered, dropping the sleeve to clutch the bar. "His name is Burt Guyver."

The name sounded familiar. "What does he look like?"

She turned, holding her curved hand about a half foot above her head. "He's about this tall." Her arm dropped to her side. "His hair is a buzzed gray with the hairline of a monkey. He's got these spooky eyes that are like an almost transparent blue but with fire-like orange encircling his pupil. He gives me the creeps."

Nash knew him – and didn't like him. The further away from him they could get, the better. He scanned the walls…shelves, a tapestry, the racks of clothes. "Is there a way out of here?"

"Yeah. There's a tunnel leading to the Unified Church but…" she frowned. "I think we should wait a little bit, make sure that Hayes and Mel are okay."

They *had* stitched him up. Nash leaned back again, but couldn't lose the uneasy feeling. "You want to throw me one of those shirts. It's kind of cold in here."

She pulled out a black pinstriped suit coat and hung it sideways on the tops of the other hangers. After brushing the collar, she threw it to him.

Nash didn't hesitate to put it on.

"Warmed up and cozy?"

"Not warm enough," he said, opening his arms, hoping she would come to him. He needed her right now.

She smiled as she walked toward him, but stopped when the mirrored door whooshed open behind them. Nash turned. They had company – and she was stunningly beautiful…and familiar.

Chapter 30

The girl swished her long blonde hair to the side as she stepped into the room. Hayes and Mel came in behind her. "Sweet. I love visitors," the tall thin girl said, the feather hanging from her hair fluttering as she checked out both Mira and Nash.

She was gorgeous, Mira thought. Obviously Nash thought so too because he couldn't take his eyes off her.

"I see our patient is up and at 'em," Hayes said with a smile. Hand on Mel's lower back, he ushered her over to a food basket. She dug in with a smile of her own. Hayes nodded toward miss perfect. "This here is Deidre."

Deidre sauntered over to a box of hats. After pulling out a floppy one, she sashayed over to the blue overstuffed chair sitting next to a tapestry - one that covered half of the north wall. "Haven't been here long, but Hayes and Mel have made me feel right at home." She plopped the turquoise hat on her head, slouched into the chair and hooked her leg over the arm.

"Pastor Ettreim sent her through the tunnel," Mel said, peeling the plastic off a cookie she'd taken from one of the food baskets. "She was quite the...surprise."

Deidre chuckled. "I didn't realize being chipless could be so much fun." After carefully arranging her long blonde hair over her shoulder and adjusting her low-cut shirt so that it exposed more skin, Deidre peeked over at Nash. "Why didn't anyone tell me he was so cute? I'd have been down here a lot sooner."

Hayes shook his head. Ignoring Deidre's question, he said, "The Reformers are outa the house, but they're still hanging around outside." He wrapped his arms around his wife's waist and tugged her close. "We let Vaughn know you were alright and to be ready for a call to come pick ya up at the church."

The room's air seemed to thicken with the cloying scent of the girl. And it was way too crowded to feel comfortable, Mira thought. "Maybe we should get going then," she said, taking Nash's hand. "We can wait it out in the church."

"Or maybe we should stay a while," he said.

What? Mira glanced at Nash and then followed his gaze to where Deidre was busy preening. For the first time in her life, Mira was jealous…intensely, insanely jealous. And she didn't like it at all. "I really want to go *now*. Nash…you can stay if you want," she said sharply, snagging her hand away from his.

The girl smoothed her hair again as she smiled. "Or I could join you two and help out. I've had some nurse training, you know."

No way *that* was going to happen! Mira marched toward the tapestry-covered tunnel, which happened to be right where Deidre was sitting. "That isn't necessary." Had she sounded sincere? It didn't matter. "Either he stays – and gets nursed here, or he comes with me, alone," Mira said.

Mel lifted the cookie to Hayes' smirking lips. He took a bite and chewed, not saying a word.

Wanting to escape, Mira hoisted the edge of the tapestry. When she bent to go inside, her butt bumped into someone behind her. She turned with a frown. Nash. "I thought you were staying," she said.

"Not without you."

Those three words soothed her like nothing else would. "Okay then."

Mel smiled and said, "I'll give Pastor Ettreim a heads up." She pulled the laptop out of the bag she'd taken along and started to type. "He's asleep, I'm sure, but the message will beep on his end and alert him."

As she waited for Mel to finish, Mira glanced down at her muddy clothes. She looked like a rag doll that had been dragged through the dirt. Until now, she hadn't really cared.

"There we go. Message was received," Mel said. "I'll send Vaughn a quick note, too."

While she typed, Hayes came over to them. Holding back the tapestry for them, he said, "Flashlights are hanging on the wall to the left."

"Perfect." Mira popped her head into a cement tunnel and grabbed the first one she saw. "Any more tips?"

Hayes nodded. "The ladder that leads up ta the church is the first one ya all will come to. About nine hundred steps down the way."

"Thanks." She turned to hug Hayes. "For everything," she whispered. When she pulled back, he was smiling fondly.

"Nice to meet ya, girlie," he said, ruffling her hair.

"You too," she said as she ducked inside the tunnel. Nash was right behind her, but Deidre grabbed his arm and pulled him back.

The tapestry flopped into place with Nash on the other side. "I'll see you later maybe?" Mira heard him say.

To which Deidre's answer was, "Absolutely. When?"

"I'm not listening to any more of this crap," Mira muttered to herself. Flipping on the flashlight, she stalked off into the dark tunnel. She was several yards in before she heard the whoosh of the tapestry as it flapped back into place. She picked up her pace.

"Hey. Wait up." Nash's voice floated to her ears.

She just kept walking.

"If you'll recall, I'm not really functioning at my best."

"You seemed to be functioning just perfectly with Deidre back there." Her voice was sharper than she'd intended, but whatever.

He grunted. "Slow down. Please." When she heard his labored breathing she felt a little guilty. Finally she stopped.

"I'm waiting," she said, tapping her foot.

"I know. I can see you – and the light you're holding."

She was tempted to turn off the flashlight, but she didn't. When he finally caught up, he reached out for her hand. She wanted his touch in the worst way, but she wanted the pain, too, so she'd remember to keep her heart out of her decisions. How stupid she'd been to believe he'd only be attracted to her! No matter what she'd seen of them together in her vision, she had to remember that she had been the only girl Nash's age that he'd seen since being chipless. Who knew how many other girls, like Deidre, there could be?

She turned around and started walking again. After hiking in silence for a while, she blurted, "I doubt Deidre would like it if we held hands."

They walked for a while longer before he responded. "I don't care about Deidre, but I *did* recognize her."

Mira stopped. Swinging around, she grabbed the lapels of his jacket. "What did you say?"

"I've seen her somewhere before," he said.

"Who is she?"

"I'm not really sure yet." Nash touched her cheek tenderly. "But I *am* sure that I think you're really cute when you're mad."

"I'm not mad."

"What do you call it then? My emotion vocabulary is rather…limited." She could see the glow of his perfect teeth in the dimness.

"I'm jealous, okay. She's beautiful – and what I thought we'd had between us disappeared as soon as she came along. This," she rolled her hand between them, "attraction is simply that, and it was dumb of me to make it out to be anything more. It's not real."

"I see it much differently, my little tiger." He dipped his head in close so that his lips were a breath away from hers. "I'm going to kiss you now," he said.

She knew she shouldn't let him, but she didn't stop him as his mouth molded to hers. They felt like velvet on bare skin - only better. Even though the tunnel was dark and cold, it was like she was being bathed in sunshine and hope. Her stomach fluttered and her arms came up to wind around his neck.

He groaned low in his throat before pulling back. "Deidre is nothing compared to you, sweetheart."

His whispered words sounded sincere and made her heart beat double time. But was she only making him out to be what she wanted him to be, like she'd done with Gabe? She put a little space between them. "What about your Compatimate? Why did you keep her picture?"

He inhaled deeply and blew out a long breath. "Look. It was part of my life, Mira, a life I hardly remember…a life I'm giving up in order to find the Enchiridion…with you. That has to count for something."

"We've all had to give up a lot," she said past the lump in her throat.

"Then why are you making this harder than it has to be?" He tucked her into his arms and rested his cheek on top of her head. "Do you know what I think?"

She shook her head. She didn't know what to think anymore.

"I think that you painted me right into your life, and I'm not going anywhere. And the sooner you get that into your beautiful head, the better." Nash tugged the flashlight from her hand and angled it at her face. It flickered and dimmed. "I don't understand what's going on between us, but I can't get enough of the feeling."

She smiled, the pressure in her chest easing. "We'd better get going. The pastor will start worrying if we don't show up shortly."

He kissed her cheek, then said, "Lead the way, oh flashlight bearer."

She started walking again, her legs wobbly, her heart light. Her hopes and dreams seemed almost reachable at the moment. The light flickered again.

"The flashlight's getting dimmer," she said. "How many more steps do we have?"

"I wasn't counting."

"Great. Me either." The flashlight chose that moment to go out completely. She stopped and hit it against her palm, but after one hopeful flicker of light, it died again.

"Should we go back and start over – and make sure we count this time?" he asked.

He sounded serious. "And double my chance of running into a hungry rat that's ready to gnaw on my leg? No way."

His laughter drifted past her ear like the pied piper's magic song. "I wouldn't blame them. You are very sweet," he said, and after a few silent moments, he found her hand. "I still have more questions about that book - *The Artist's Love* - you know."

The soft tenor of his voice hinted at his curiosity and something deeper. "I don't know if I'll be able to answer them," she said honestly.

"Maybe we can figure them out together, then." He pulled her ahead, taking the lead, which, judging by his uneven gait, was no easy task.

"Are you feeling okay?" she asked, worried that she'd pushed him too hard.

"I'll survive," he said, giving her hand a reassuring squeeze.

She was glad for his ability to see in the dark as she followed. Her night vision stunk, and she kept stepping on his heels. He didn't complain, but she felt bad. "How much longer do you think?" she asked after catching his heel for the tenth time.

He stopped, and she ran right into him. He turned, and putting his hands on her shoulders, shifted her sideways. "Reach out," he said, nudging her forward.

Her hands connected with a cold metal rung. "We're here?"

He laughed. "You want to go first? Or should I?"

"I'll go," she said. She climbed the rungs. When she reached the top, she crawled out onto the platform. Unfortunately, it was too dark for her to figure out where to go next. "I can't see anything up here, either."

"On my way," Nash said. She heard his stifled grunt and strained breathing as he climbed up to join her. He paused, the platform shifting beneath his weight as he pressed his hand against his bandaged side. At least that's what she thought she'd seen.

"Does it hurt a lot?" she asked.

"Yes," he said. "But it's nothing I can't manage." He took her hand once again. "Ready?"

"Yes," she whispered, anxious to be out of the dark and headed back to The Compound.

Nash reached out and opened a door. Ducking beneath the doorway, he led her into what she hoped was the church.

"I have some news to share with you kids. Hurry," came a deep voice from the shadowed office.

Chapter 31

An older man with prominent jowls and wearing a misbuttoned shirt grabbed a book off one of the chairs facing his desk. It was entitled *The Unified Church City Center Guests*. "Sit down," he said, pointing to the chairs as he shoved the book onto his desk.

Mira and Nash sat.

"There was a broadcast earlier tonight," the pastor said, shuffling over to a file cabinet. The book he'd just propped on the desk fell to the floor behind him.

Nash stood up to get it, but the man sighed and shook his head. "Leave it. It's not important right now."

Maybe the book wasn't, but the Unified Church was, Nash thought. Because religious passions had started the war, the government had required the churches to unify and to have a core curriculum. It was a great peacemaker, even if very few people made an effort to go to the local churches any more. Nash sat back down.

The man reached inside the cabinet drawer. "I'm Pastor Ettreim, by the way. Mel said you two would be stopping by. Couldn't be better timing." He pulled out a Newscreen tablet and turned it on.

"Why is that?" Nash asked.

"Because," the pastor said, attempting to finger comb his tuft of tangled hair as he watched the tablet blink to life. "The LAW's locator crew has searched over half of Pillar this past week already, so it's only a matter of time until..." He gave up on his hair, his jowls hanging low like a scalloped curtain. Then he shook his head. "But that doesn't matter because we have this young lady's gift to help us find it before they do."

Mira smiled slightly as he handed them the tablet. Sitting down on the edge of his desk, the pastor said, "Now watch. Then we'll see if we can come up with a plan of action."

On the monitor was the Benefactor. He stood behind a podium with a video billboard as his backdrop. Nash pushed play.

"This, citizens of Pillar," the Benefactor said into his mike, "is what Enab has come to." He pointed over his shoulder to the video that had begun to play behind him. It showed Enab and a group of the island's inhabitants. "These people are like animals – fighting, stealing, murdering. And disease is rampant," he said.

The pastor studied him and Mira as they watched. Nash shifted uncomfortably, even though he had no clue as to what the older man was looking for.

Mira brought the screen in closer, as if she was searching for something. Her mom perhaps?

"We're in the process of using more drastic measures to reform this group," the Benefactor said, "but in order to do it right, we have to locate the Enchiridion of Emmanuel, a passion-inciting book we think might have been preserved somehow despite our efforts to rid our society of them. If this book falls into the wrong hands, it could cause a whole lot of trouble for Pillar." He leaned forward to say in a hushed tone, "Just knowing about the Book has emboldened the Enabians and the Accordance. They want to convince you all that a passionate life without the LifeChip would be so much better." He stood up straight and pointed behind him. "But look at what it's actually done for them." In the first scene, a woman knelt as a cleaver slashed down on her neck, beheading her in one fell swoop. The second was of a man, his beard scalped from his face before a cloaked guard pushed him off a roof to his death.

Mira gasped, pressing a hand against her throat. Nash felt sick. "Is this really the life we're working to accomplish?" he asked softly.

"It's a lie," Mira growled. "He's a liar!"

Not sure what to believe, Nash felt for the key in the pocket of his jeans. It was still there, snuggly held where he'd tucked it into the loop on the back of his Compatimate identifier card. He looked back at the screen. The Benefactor ended his segment by offering free high-qual food for a year and a new house with the latest and best conveniences for anyone who found the Enchiridion and turned it in to him.

"That's dumb," Mira said, turning off the tablet. "People already use their LifeChip IDs to get their food rations. And even if the food and housing he's promising is better, because of the LifeChips' dulling properties, none of them have any motivation." Mira held the Newscreen out to the pastor.

He took it and laid it on the desk. "But seeing his warning on the screen is persuasive. And there's always the possibility that someone chipless will turn it in."

"I suppose that could happen," Mira said with a frown.

"Why would they do something like that?" Nash jumped up and started to pace. "I thought the 'Cords all believed passionately in finding the Enchiridion."

"Only some do," the pastor said, running a weathered hand across the wooden edge of the desk behind him. "Many don't even know what the Enchiridion is about, so they don't really care if it's found or not. They just want to be free to do what they want."

"And that's better than what we have in Pillar?" Nash asked.

After studying Nash for a long moment, the pastor walked to the room's only window. "Our selfish emotions show up when our subconscious prompts us to act out selfish patterns and ideas."

"What's that supposed to mean?" Nash frowned.

Glancing out at the moonlit street, the pastor sighed. "Without the example of love and direction from the Author of the Enchiridion of Emmanuel, our self-serving nature will win out time and again." He looked at Nash. "I only hope we find the book soon so that people can learn the truth about what is actually happening…what they are heading for if they don't change directions."

Nash wandered over to the window and stood beside the pastor. They peered out to the dimly lit empty street. The truth, to him, looked like the world was moving along with very little resistance with the exception of the 'Cords. "What do *you* see happening?" Nash asked, curious.

The pastor was quick to answer. "Evil working everywhere – even through Pillar's apathy." He pressed his hand against the glass. "When's the last time you heard a song playing on the subway, or children laughing in a park, or saw a painting? I tell you, we are *not* meant to live like this. Life has completely lost all its color and its true purpose – and the people don't even realize it! Do you hear what I'm saying?" His voice was intense, his fists clenched, his eyes hard and resolute.

"It's better than the *color* of robbing and murdering," Nash said, trying to make them see how it might not be for the best to allow passion back into their world, even if he ached inside at considering giving up his feelings for Mira.

"I disagree. Just yesterday, I saw a little boy fall as he crossed the street. A Clavicar ran him over." The man's troubled eyes turned fierce. "Not only did no one move to help, but his own mother didn't even react. Not one tear! Then the Keepers came to take care of the body, the Renovatrons took care of the mess, and life went on as if that little boy hadn't even been a part of it."

"That's horrible," Mira said.

The Keepers, a motorized remains-cleanup crew, had probably come for Nash's parents after their accident, too. If he had been conscious at that time, would he have reacted any differently than the woman losing her son? He'd like to think so, that life would be more precious to him than that, but deep down, he didn't know. Nash rubbed the ache in his chest, wishing he could somehow make the feeling go away. "So what happens if we don't find the Enchiridion?"

The pastor wiped a hand across his tired face. "We'll be left with no purpose, hardened hearts, and souls doomed for eternity."

"The pit in my vision…" Mira rasped. "Pillar was inching toward a dark pit that had only a torturous lonely road surrounded by sounds of people in agony."

Even though Mira had painted him before he came into her life, Nash was still having trouble believing that without the book, they would be doomed for destruction and despair. He looked at both of them skeptically. "And what do you think will happen if we *do* find the Enchiridion of Emmanuel?"

The tight lines of the pastor's face relaxed into a smile. "We'll find our connection to the only one who can give us true life - and we'll gain the wisdom and heart that will allow us to live passionately in the love-filled way we were made for."

Mira laughed, the sound musical to Nash's ears. She pressed a hand against his shoulder and looked at him with a bright gleam in her eyes. "That world is so amazing Nash – so full of beauty, and adventure. Love and laughter are everywhere!"

Nash frowned. He knew Pillar wasn't perfect, but could a world such as they described be possible? Could the Enchiridion of Emmanuel actually help them make it a reality?

The pastor wandered to his desk and sank into the chair behind it. Taking off his glasses, he rubbed his eyes. "Now I know you two are working together to find the Enchiridion," he said. He put the glasses back on, looking at them both. "Please tell me you're getting close to finding it. I need good news."

Nash was tempted to mention the key, but he didn't.

Mira slid to the edge of her chair. "We *are* getting close."

The pastor perked up. "You are?"

Mira stood and began to pace across the length of the small room. "I had an episode…and I think the answers are hidden in my childhood room."

"Tell me more," the pastor grinned.

Before she could explain further, the office's two doors opened in unison. Out of the door that led to the tunnel came Deidre. On the opposite side of the room, in the doorway that led outside, Logan loomed. A gush of cool air swirled through the room between them, and even though the draft had disappeared when both doors slammed shut, Nash still felt a residual coldness, one that he couldn't shake.

"Deidre…I'm glad you made it," Logan said, smiling across the room at her. Deidre smiled back and joined him at the door.

Mira gasped. "You know each other?"

"She's on our team – and I know everyone," Logan said. "Let's get out of here. It's been a long night with Vaughn-the-agitated." He shook his head. "Never seen him stew about anyone like he does Mira."

"She does have a remarkable gift," the pastor said.

Logan just smiled, his face softening when he looked at her. "That she does, pastor, that she does."

Nash scooted in between the pair, his fists automatically clenching. But the pastor put a hand on his arm before he could do, or say, anything else.

"Prayers for you all," he said, "and keep me posted, alright?"

"Thanks, pastor, and we will," Mira said, but instead of heading for the door, she frowned at Logan and Deidre, who were whispering between themselves.

Nash leaned in close to Mira and whispered, "It'll be okay. We'll be okay."

"You really think so?" Her direct stare made him fidget, the information tottering back and forth in his mind. Was he letting his feelings get in the way of doing what was right? Because at the moment, his feelings were shoving their way to the front of his mind, making him want nothing more than to protect her and to follow through on this quest just so he could be with her in the world she imagined. With either scenario, though, finding the Enchiridion was imperative. And maybe he didn't have to decide, yet, what he'd do with the book when they found it.

"I really *do* think it will be okay," he said.

The corner of her mouth curled, and his insides curled in reaction. "Let's get out of here," she said, and walked with him across the room. As they approached the door, Logan and Deidre stopped their hushed conversation. They didn't move out the door, nor did they stand aside.

"Mira, um…" Logan looked from Mira to Nash and back again.

"What?" she said, frowning at him. "Let's move out. We have some planning to do."

Logan rubbed his hand along his jaw, squinting his right eye, which was still marked with bruises. "Yeah. Alright. It's nothing that can't wait a bit longer." He headed outside, Deidre walking closely behind.

Mira scowled at the retreating pair. "I still don't like her," she said, tugging Nash out the door to follow.

Nash glanced at his fingers wound with Mira's. He hoped she'd never let go, but knew she probably would…because he just remembered where he'd seen Deidre.

Chapter 32

Vaughn rushed to hug Mira right as she walked through the Deli's glass front doors. She was glad to see him, but it wasn't just a quick, friendly hug. With her cheek crushed against his chest, she muttered, "You can let go now. I'm fine." He hesitated but then slowly let her go.

He went to the table and picked up a pencil. "Don't ever go out without our help and a plan again," he growled through clenched teeth, the pencil snapping in half in his hand. But then he sat down. The pencil pieces, he carefully positioned between the top two lines of the notebook paper lying on the table. Adjusting the mug that sat beside it, he said, "Now, Pastor Ettreim said you had a vision about the Enchiridion." Propping his elbows on the table, he steepled his fingers, the two index fingers resting against his chin. He caught her gaze. "Come and sit down."

His schizophrenic switches confused her. First elated to see her, then upset, now all business. What was with him? And he hadn't even said anything about Deidre. Mira looked at Nash, who seemed more worried than anything else. Logan and Deidre had already taken seats at the table as if they were sitting down to a nice family meal.

"Okay," Mira finally said, hoping she'd get some answers of her own. The soles of her shoes squeaked against the tile as she made her way to the table. She took the seat next to Vaughn. Nash sat on her left and immediately found her hand. She weaved her fingers through his, calmed by his warm, solid presence. Then she glanced up at Deidre sitting right across from her, and the warm feeling cooled considerably. No one else seemed to have a problem with her though, except maybe Nash, who kept glancing at the girl.

"My brother filled me in on your little escapade, so let's start with the vision," Vaughn said, picking up the sharpened half of the pencil. "What did you see, exactly?"

Mira frowned. "I'm not saying a word in front of Deidre."

"That's rich." Deidre laughed. "It isn't me you should be worrying about, Miss Perfect." She looked pointedly at Nash. "He's the Elite - one that worked undercover in Freetown."

Mira turned her head ever so slightly. Nash did the same until their eyes met. She saw...guilt. "It's true then?" she said as she yanked her hand from his grasp.

"It's not what you think!" he shouted.

"Easy now." Vaughn stood up, bobbing both hands downward like he was dribbling invisible basketballs. "First tell us what you know, Deidre."

Deidre's gaze drifted to the coffee mug in front of her. "Oh, it's probably worse than you think."

Nash's chair scraped back as if it was a growl of warning, but Deidre kept talking. "He was in Freetown when you and your mom were there, Mira. I was there, too and I saw you make the trade with Millie." She pointed at Nash. "He was there to follow you and figure out a way to use you to find the Enchiridion."

"No!" Nash lurched to his feet. His chair crashed to the floor.

"Stay where you are, Nash, and let her talk." Logan glared at him as he leaned back in his chair, arms crossed. "We want the truth, don't we?"

Mira was too stunned to say anything.

"It's true. I swear." Deidre glanced at Mira, her expression one of pity.

"Don't listen to her." Nash's nostrils flared, and when he spoke, his voice was hushed and quivering. "You know me, Mira...in your heart. I know you do."

"But you recognized her," Mira said, barely able to get the words out. Her mind was racing with the possibilities. Nash's car accident could've been a setup...he could've alerted his uncle about the house search....and he could've even been responsible for her mom's and Nick's deaths! "I really *don't* know you."

Nash latched onto her arm, his sweaty palms giving away his nervousness. "I *was* there," he said, "but I need to explain…in private."

If only she could remember more about that time in Freetown, she could better figure out what kind of man she was dealing with. But she didn't remember it. One thing she did know, however, was that she couldn't take a chance when it came to securing the Enchiridion. Tears filled her eyes. "I think you need to leave now."

After several tense moments, Nash got to his feet. "So you're going to believe some stranger without hearing my side?"

She wanted to hear his side, but she was afraid she wouldn't be able to discern the truth from him, or from Deidre for that matter. "I'll listen, only not now. I have much more important things to do here," she sniffed.

She glanced at the empty notebook page and then chanced a look at Nash, who stood unmoving, his eyes closed, his Adam's apple working in his throat. "What about the vision in the culvert? The one about us finding the Enchiridion together," he said.

She didn't know how to answer. Her visions had never been wrong – and yet how could she let him come with her? If only she had more time to decide if she could really trust him. But she didn't trust him and the locator search crew was closing in. Pillar was nearing the edge of the crater and their ultimate destruction. "I lied," she said, "You weren't really there."

Nash stared at her for a long moment then walked to the door. As he reached for the handle, he looked back. His eyes were clouded with grief and begging her to change her mind. She tore her gaze away before she did.

"For what it's worth," he said, "I don't believe you." The door swung open, the gust of air dousing her with the cold reality of dreams lost for good. She felt like she was dying inside and she wanted to run away. But she had to finish this.

"Logan, follow him back and lock him in his room," Vaughn said. "Mira…give him the new code." He handed her a piece of paper and a pencil.

She picked up the pencil. Did she really want to do this? Her feelings…her gut instinct…her logic – all were at war. Gabe's betrayal hovered in her thoughts and pushed her over the edge. With shaking hands, she wrote down the number, folded it and handed it to Logan.

"You're making the right decision, Mira." Logan stood up and after a glance at the code, shoved it into his pocket.

Kya came around the table and placed a comforting hand on Mira's back. "Logan, you can show Deidre to her room, too," she said.

"No way!" Deidre spat.

Logan only chuckled and grabbed her by the arm. She squawked and argued, but he dragged her to the door anyway. "Just shut up," he said, and ushered her out the door.

Chapter 33

After three hours of discussion with Kya and Vaughn in the Deli, Mira escaped outside for some fresh air. Tucking her hands into her pockets, she strolled along the sidewalk flanking the shops. She counted the steps between cracks. Five…five of her steps between each - just like there were five steps to their plan, one that had already been set into motion. Her legs suddenly shaky, Mira stopped to lean back against the brick on the dorm's edge. Thoughts of Nash pervaded her mind. If he was looking out his window in the fading light, he wouldn't be able to see her…but was he thinking about her? Had she frustrated his plans – or ruined her own?

Closing her eyes, she rested her head back against the rough rectangular block. It gouged into her head, but the sun's stored heat emanating from it felt nice. "I am so tired of thinking," she muttered under her breath. She'd replayed so many of her chats with Nash that she felt like she was going insane. And thinking about confronting him only ended up being a revolving door of faux conversations that didn't resolve anything - they only spiked her aggravation.

She pushed herself away from the wall. She wanted to quit thinking about Nash for a while and she needed to concentrate on their new plan. Who would believe that it would come to this - that at midnight, she'd be facing her father at the band shell, and that the entire future of Pillar was dependent on the outcome of that exchange? There were so, so many ways it could go wrong.

Wanting to find peace with her decision, Mira wandered across the road to the bridge. The river was as turbulent as she was feeling, its white-tipped frothy fingers clamoring over each other like clusters of snakes doing the rumba. "Must have rained a ton up north," she said, trying to distract her brain as she crossed the planks. When she stepped onto solid ground, she glanced at the chapel, hoping it was just what she needed. In fact, she was counting on it.

Jogging the rest of the way, she hurried inside its doors, only she didn't feel quite the same as she'd anticipated. It seemed almost as if she was out of place. As she made her way to the front bench, cool drafts of air seemed to cover her, making her shiver. Sitting down, she tried to reassure herself that the chill was a coincidence, but as she stared at the pulpit, she couldn't help but think that they'd made the wrong decision – that *she* had. It was too late to do anything about it, though. At this very minute, Vaughn and Kya were rounding up a watch-crew for her midnight venture – and she'd already sent the letter by messenger to her childhood home…and her father had signed for it.

"Ahhh," she growled, bouncing her head back against the hard wooden lip of oak as she tried to shut out the words she'd written – and sent. But they were still there, emblazoned in her memory. Her idea, her words, her responsibility.

Father – I can't take living like this anymore. If you can arrange a house for me on Enab, I will exchange it for the Enchiridion of Emmanuel. Meet me under the band shell at midnight if you agree to my terms. Come alone or the deal is off. – Mira

Mira groaned and bent forward, pressing the heels of her hands against her eyes. What if her father didn't show up? What if the Enchiridion wasn't really hidden in her room? What if they didn't get enough recorded evidence from her father to convince Pillar to change - to give the Enchiridion of Emmanuel a fair shot? What if she *did* need Nash with her?

The strain of the day…no, of the last three and a half months…poured over her. She needed courage…a big dose of it! Her mind reached for images from her childhood, trying to remember the worst times. It wasn't long until the misery and loneliness returned with abandon. She would not let her father win! Only was this the best way?

Panic wiggled its way inside until taking a breath felt like she was sucking air through a clogged hose. Maybe she *should* go with what her vision had prophesied. Perhaps talking to Nash before she met up with her father tonight was the right thing to do. No! She shook her head. Her visions had only managed to bring her heartache and she couldn't trust that Nash wouldn't betray her. She had to remember that! Conjuring up the feeling she'd had when she realized Gabe - who was not even a Reformer - had betrayed them, she latched onto it. Bitterness swept in to replace her fear and doubt. She straightened her shoulders, clutching the edge of the pew. Darkness overshadowed her thoughts and hate consumed her heart. She would exact retribution on her father for all he had done!

"I'll be in control this time," she growled. And she couldn't wait to see the look on her father's face when he realized it. She'd escaped the power of the LifeChip and she'd escaped from him and from the Stint. Their plan would work – and then she'd be free of this entire mess. She laughed in triumph, the vicious sound unpleasant to her own ears. Had that been her own voice?

Pain slashed across her forehead as if to answer. Her brain seemed to swell, her temples throbbed. Her wail filled the chapel as she curled up in a ball on the bench. Clutching her head, she pulled on the short strands as she tried to stop the torturous images from coming, yet they came anyway. The abyss in her mind's eye loomed deep and dark, the hints of fire and smoke inhibiting her view – except for the view of her father. She could see him clearly, standing on an outcropping about ten feet down the steeply sloping surface of the pit. Arms crossed over his chest, he stared at her as if daring her to come and get him. The will to do that was so strong, she couldn't keep from taking a step closer to the edge. Her hands clenched and unclenched as her desire to shove him into the void grew. Nash's voice rang out from somewhere, ordering her to stop, to think about what she was doing, but she was through taking orders from *any*one. Then a more confident voice begged her to turn back, that it wasn't too late, that he could save her. She paused, but only for a moment because the hate for her father was so powerful and demanded revenge. As she took another step toward the man she detested and longed to destroy, something, someone grabbed her arm, keeping her in place. "Let me go," she cried out, yanking free from the firm grasp. "I don't want these stupid visions! LEAVE ME ALONE," she screamed.

And just like a door slamming shut, the images disappeared, and so did her urge to paint what she'd seen. The sudden silence, the emptiness she felt, weighed in on her until tears filled her eyes. What had just happened? What had she done? After a few minutes, she willed herself to move. She wiped her eyes and sat back up. Running her sleeve under her nose, she pulled herself to her feet and staggered outside.

Chapter 34

"Resetting your route?"

Mira glanced over her shoulder at Logan as she slapped the tape on a small pink rock jutting from the far edge of the climbing wall. "Setting up challenging routes means limitless opportunities to overcome all my weaknesses." The truth was, that after her experience in the chapel, she'd needed something to help her refocus. A tough workout was the best she could come up with, so she'd changed into her black spandex shorts and her favorite climbing tank top that said *The Best View Comes After the Toughest Climb* and headed to the gym.

"I didn't know you were so serious about climbing," he said, sitting on one of the weight benches as he watched her. "Need some help?"

"No," she said, trying to rip off a piece of the marking tape but failing. She whipped the roll across the room. It smashed into the boxing bag and then dropped to the floor with a thud.

"Want to talk about it?"

She didn't want to talk about it…and yet she did. Rubbing her arms, she asked, "Is Nash still locked in his room?"

"Just checked on him," Logan said with a nod. "He's playing guitar again. You going to go talk to him?"

She grabbed the towel she'd brought, and dabbed her sweaty neck as she walked toward Logan. Sitting down beside him on the bench, she said, "Maybe later."

He cocked his head to the side and raised an eyebrow. "Why wait?"

She took a few moments to blot her face. Then she said, "Quite frankly, I don't know if I'll be able to tell if he's being truthful, so I want to go through with the plan first."

"Hmm." Logan crossed an ankle over his knee. "Are you sure you don't want me to help out tonight? I'd rather search your house for the Enchiridion than babysit Nash. You think the book is somewhere in the house you grew up in, right?"

She smiled, knowing Logan would love to be part of the action, but someone had to make sure Nash didn't interfere – and she certainly didn't trust Deidre to do it. "You know I want to be the one to confront my father – and if I don't uncover the Enchiridion after all this time?" She shook her head. "I just need to do it."

"I understand." He frowned at his jiggling foot. "I know tonight is risky for us all, and if I don't say this now, I might never get a chance."

She glanced at his stoic face. "What are you talking about?"

He reached into the inside pocket of the lime green velvet sport coat he was wearing and pulled out two little boxes, both wrapped in colorful paper. He cleared his throat. "I have a question to ask you. If you say yes, one box is yours. If you say no, then you get the other. Are you ready for the question?"

"I guess."

Running his fingers over the edge of one of the boxes, he said, "I didn't count on feeling this way, Mira. I really didn't. But because I do, this is the only way I can handle it." He looked over at her. "What I want is to be with you forever. Will you marry me?"

She pressed a hand against her lips.

"I know this seems like it's coming out of the blue, but I've been thinking about it for a long time." He shifted on the bench, the leather creaking. "And if I've learned one thing about being in the Accordance, it's that each day is a gift not to be wasted." He reached up to cup her cheek. "I don't want to waste another minute pretending I don't want to be with you."

"I...I don't know what to say."

"Say yes. We'll be good together." His eyes were alight with hope.

Mira knew that Logan would be there for her. He always had been. But there was something missing between them that she couldn't explain. "I'm sorry Logan. I can't."

His hand slid from her cheek, his mouth hardening as he looked back at the rock wall. Mira hadn't thought she could feel any worse today, but now she did.

"Don't worry about it," he said, tucking one of the boxes into his pocket. "It's not what I'd hoped, but I'd be lying if I said it wasn't what I'd expected." He took a deep breath as he rested the second box on her knee. "Open it and I'll explain."

"I don't deserve a present," she said, guilt gnawing a hole in her stomach.

"I'll consider it a present to me if you'll wear it." He nodded. "Open it."

With shaking fingers, she pried the little box open. Inside, resting on a square of cotton, was a double heart pendant on a sturdy silver chain.

"It's an unlocked heart necklace – so you know mine is always open for you," he said.

To Mira, the woven strands forming the outer heart looked like a web and reminded her of spiders. Yuck! She hated spiders, but she didn't want to hurt his feelings any more than she already had. "You are so sweet!" She tilted it to the side, trying to get a better look. It appeared as though the center heart was dotted with emeralds. "Where did you get this?"

"I had it specially made for you. Want me to help you put it on?"

She couldn't say no. So she nodded.

Logan draped it over her neck and hooked the clasp. "Can I see how it looks?"

She turned toward him, her heart was pounding and aching at the same time. His eyes drifted downward to rest on the pendant hanging over the shiny black tank top she wore.

"Thank you, Mira," he said softly and after shifting his gaze up to her eyes for a few moments, he stood up. "Back to guard duty," he said, and with a salute, he was gone.

Chapter 35

Nash paced around his bed…again. He didn't know if he could stand even another minute in the tiny room that had become his jail. The pads of his fingers were red and throbbing from playing the guitar for hours. His muscles ached from doing so many pushups. And his mind was delirious from rehashing, over and over again, what he'd tell Mira when she came to talk to him. He glanced at the clock. It was nearing midnight and she hadn't shown up yet. He had to face reality. She probably never would. Just the thought of never seeing her again - knowing that she thought he'd betrayed her - was driving him insane. He had to get out, find her, force her to listen.

Nash pounded on the locked door.

The muffled sound of crunching filtered through the door.

Nash pounded again, harder this time.

"You're interrupting my eating." Logan took an even louder bite. "Does my apple eating make you want some pie, traitor?"

He would not let Logan get to him, but the guy's attitude prodded at Nash – as did his mere presence. "Tell me where Mira is!"

Logan snickered. "She's out."

Nash fought to control the beast inside him that threatened to come out. He needed information. "But it's almost midnight."

The chewing ended with a loud swallow. "Glad you can tell time, Smudge. Now, enough questions." Logan started whistling, the unrecognizable tune growing softer as did his retreating footsteps.

Nash tried the door one more time. Of course it was still locked. He turned to lean against it, frowning down at the grout lines in the tile. The nickname Logan had used – Smudge - it tickled his memory. Nash straightened as his memories began to connect. Even though Logan's hair was now black, he remembered him. He was the guy in Freetown…the one that had tried to pursue Mira…the loser whose efforts Nash had thwarted. His fists clenched as he recalled it all in detail. He'd disliked Logan in Freetown. He hated him now.

"It doesn't matter," he told himself. But finding Mira did.

Nash hurried to the window and shoved hard against the frame. The stupid thing didn't budge. He spun around and with a growl, snatched up the desk chair. Lifting it high over his shoulder, he charged toward the window. "Ahhh!" he yelled, swinging the metal legs at the glass. But it bounced back, smacking him in the face. With a yelp, he let the chair drop from his grasp and clatter to the floor. Ignoring his swelling eye and the blood dripping down his cheek, Nash kicked the chair out of his way and stormed over to the closet.

"This isn't fair!" he yelled, snagging fistfuls of clothing. The hangers screeched across the closet rod as he wrested them from their home. A terrorizing agony egged him on. He flung the clothes onto the floor behind him then grabbed the smaller guitar resting in the corner of the closet. He was ready to tear the strings off, one by one, but the moment he touched the smooth finish on the neck, he paused. Sweet memories of Mira attempting to play it came rushing back and brought with them a poignant despair that made him tremble. He couldn't lose her. He just couldn't!

Nash slumped to the floor inside the closet and tried to compose himself enough to come up with a plan. He ran his blistered fingers across the rough grout, first one tile and then another. He cringed at the discomfort, but the even repetition settled him, so he continued. Up, over, down, back to the starting point. He moved to tile number three…up, over, down, back to the starting point. Scooting to the edge of the closet next to the Rave guitar, he sat back. As he contemplated his options, he started up his tile tracing again. Up, over, down…. He frowned and glanced down. The tile's grout was raised slightly higher than its neighboring lines and it was a shade darker than what was in the rest of the closet. His breathing quickened as he ran his fingers down the seam again. He stopped halfway.

Heart tripping, he pried at the tiny indentation. The tile shifted. He pulled harder, joggling it as he did. *Pop!* It jerked upwards, stagnant air wafting up through the two by two foot opening it had left behind. He shoved the four-squared covering off to the side, poked his head through the hole, and peeked into the crawlspace. The dirt-packed area wasn't deep, but it was big enough to fit him. "I really hope the former FBI used this for a way out rather than as a holding cell," he said. Though his first impulse was to take a chance and dive in, Nash shot over to his bed. He needed insurance for what he planned to do. Snagging the key and the Compatimate identifier card he shoved them into the pocket of his jeans. He grabbed a black hooded-sweatshirt from the heap of clothes on the floor. Shaking with emotion, he slipped it on, yet inside he was resolute.

Thirty seconds later, he was in the tunnel. After replacing the tiled lid, he took a few moments to allow his eyes to adjust to the darkness then scurried ahead – mostly by feel. The dirt sides scraped at his sleeves, bringing to life the dust motes that had long lay dormant. The pathway seemed to run straight, and if his guess was correct, it extended directly underneath the hallway between the dorms.

Adrenalin kept his pace swift as the underground passage took a sharp curve to the right and then stopped. Crouching at the dead end, the air seemed to grow dense. Nash pushed at the side walls and the wall in front of him. They seemed solid, so it was either move upward somehow or turn around and head back. He reached up, shoving hard against wood ceiling he hoped was underlayment – and a doorway to freedom. The overhead section squeaked, then jerked free. A slim ray of light shone through the crack.

He grinned, wanting to yell out, but he held back to listen. The quiet of the room above him was a welcome sound. With jittery hands, he shoved the overhead covering off to the side. *Crash!* Nash froze as he tried to hear over the sound of his wild heartbeat for anyone who might have heard. But no one came to investigate. He poked his head up through the opening that was located between the sink and counter. His gaze grazed across tile similar to the kind in his room and locked onto the cause of the clatter. He'd knocked over the garbage can!

Nash crawled out of the tunnel, staying hunched over as he peeked around the Deli's counter. Thankfully, he was alone. Wanting to leave no evidence of his escape, he first shoved the flooring back into place. Next, he righted the metal bin and began dumping the refuse back into it - wrappers, a couple of cans, a banana peel. The last item he picked up was a crumpled piece of notebook paper, the same type of paper that had been on the table before he'd been sent away. He quickly brought it close to the sink where a single light had been left on. He flattened the page out against the tile. Ignoring the crossed out words, his eyes shot right to the circled ones. Mira was going to make a deal with her father tonight at the band shell and then she was planning to retrieve the Enchiridion of Emmanuel from her childhood home. Nash didn't know the location of her childhood home, but he did know where the band shell was. And he was going to be there whether she wanted him to be or not.

Chapter 36

The slice of moon cast an eerie shadow across the band shell stage as Mira stood tucked behind a tree just steps north of the structure. Even though a group of ten people hid in strategic places all around the meeting site, something inside her sensed that the concert on this stage would end up being hers to perform alone. Her nerves were as taut as guitar strings, causing her hands to shake, so she shoved them into the pockets of her midnight blue cloak. Tonight would be the first time she'd seen her father in person since he'd taken her to the Stint. He was a powerful man, and there was so much riding on this moment. And there were so many ways this could go wrong, so many ways she could end up the loser. Curling her fingers around the handle of her knife, she was somewhat calmed by its presence, but not nearly enough.

Vaughn wasn't helping any either. He stood beside her, repeating his motions in a sequence, like he had some compulsive disorder. Tuck hands in pockets, pull them out and cross over chest, shift feet, clear throat, turn in a circle, repeat…again and again. It was driving her crazy. Finally, she couldn't stand it anymore. She bumped into him mid foot-shifting.

He scowled down at her, but as soon as their eyes met, his expression softened. "Kya said everyone is in place and the cameras are set to roll. Are you sure you want to do this?" he whispered.

She glanced at the empty band shell, feeling her own swell of emptiness, one she hoped would change after tonight. "I need to do this," she said.

"Somehow I knew you'd say that," he said with a sigh. His gaze combed the area, over and over before he looked back down at her. "There's something I need to tell you, Mira."

She frowned at his confessionary tone. "Can't it wait? I need to concentrate." And her plate of things to deal with was already full to brimming.

He said nothing further because Kya was running toward them. "He's coming," she said, her high-pitched timbre colored with breathiness.

Mira's own breath stalled, her hands fisted up then released as she stared out across the lawn. The man's unhurried gait as he approached the band shell was deliberate and confident. He was definitely her father. She pressed her hand against the tree, the rough bark gouging into her skin as she watched him get closer and closer to the stage. Each step plunged her deeper into her memories. She could feel once again the stark loneliness of being his child. She could smell the drug he'd forced into her lungs and taste the bitterness of being abandoned at the Stint. The paintings she'd done in the basement of Pillar Media were right on the edge of her thoughts, but fear kept them locked in place. Perhaps she didn't really want to see if he would win, this man she knew would stop at nothing for the sake of his cause.

Vaughn handed her a thick book – their fake Enchiridion. "Don't give this to him or let him see the title – just taunt him with it so he makes the deal, okay?" Vaughn said into her ear.

She took the leather bound dictionary and clutched it against her stomach, which felt like it had been wrung out then refilled with acidic balls of fire.

"Mira," Vaughn whispered, shaking her shoulder. "He's on the platform. Time to go."

She nodded. She couldn't let her father crush her, couldn't let him win. Taking one step, then two, then five more. Finally, she was out of the protective covering of the trees. Her legs felt numb as she continued toward the stairs, yet the weak limbs managed to somehow keep moving on their own. When she got to the steps, she glanced up. Her father stood waiting at the top of them, his hands clasped behind his back. Her breath seized in her throat.

"Back up," she said with false bravado. The cameras wouldn't pick him up there. He had to be center stage.

He only smiled in that knowing way of his. "I see you have something that belongs to me."

She forced herself to smile, even though she hated him, even though she was terrified. "It belongs to the people, actually."

His smile slipped, but just a little. "I thought that you wanted to trade the Enchiridion for a house of your own…away from everything. Is that not the case?"

"It's what I'll settle for," she said, lifting her chin, "but only if you tell me the truth for once."

He raised an eyebrow at that. "What truth is it you want to hear?"

Mira glimpsed someone along the far edge of the band shell, reaching up to adjust the camera. "I want to hear your plans for Pillar, why you want to destroy the Enchiridion, why you don't want anyone to have a choice."

He moved down the steps, his face marbled in a cruelty she'd never seen before – one that made her question if he had a LifeChip at all. "It's quite simple, really," he snarled. "People without passion can be controlled. Yet there are some like *you* who make things so much more difficult than they have to be." His hands curled, and for a second, she thought he might use them to strangle her. "But that ends tonight." He raised his hand and with a widening grin, circled his finger in the air. A loud oscillating sound announced an oncoming Sweeper that swooped in from the parking lot. Before she could even take a couple of steps, it had honed in on her face. Pillar immediately went from dark to dawn-like, her picture projected on the surfaces of all of its buildings. Beneath her picture was the flashing word *Captured!*

Mira swung the dictionary at the Sweeper, knocking it away. Dropping the book, she grabbed the handle of her knife. Just as she whipped it out of her pocket, her father smashed into her, hammering her into the ground. Pinned beneath him, she screamed and fought to get away. Only the scream was cut off by the hands that crushed against her windpipe.

"Vaughn!" She managed to croak. But no one came to help. All she heard was the sound of the fluttering pages of the dictionary and the buzz of the Sweeper that was headed back for more.

Her father squeezed harder and laughed. "You didn't think I'd actually come alone and let your group trap me, did you? You and your pathetic miscreant friends thought you could beat me – the Benefactor! Fools!" he bellowed.

Chapter 37

Nash's first plan had been to drive the Clavicar lookalike right up to the stage of the band shell, but now that he was close, he liked the idea of a surprise visit better. Parking on the south side of the COO, which was a half block behind the band shell, he flipped up his sweatshirt hood and grabbed his only weapon; a long handled metal bar he'd found in the FBI's garage. Jumping out of the car, he took off toward the curved structure, but then stopped short when he saw an image blink to life on every building's flat surface.

"Mira." Cold sweat glued the shirt to his back as Nash bolted around the southern edge of the stage. He froze when he saw them, his breaths shallow and painful, his veins filled with ice. He recognized the uniform. It was the Benefactor, their city's leader. He sat over Mira, both hands wrapped around her neck as she fought to pull them away.

Fear clenched a tight fist around Nash's chest as he edged closer. He raised his weapon in his sweaty hand. He had one chance.

"I've won, despite your stupid visions," the Benefactor jeered, the mocking sound echoing all around them.

The words sparked rage so powerful it overtook all Nash's thoughts and movements. He whipped the metal bar as hard as he could. It sailed along the stage, end over end as if in slow motion. *Thud!* The bar struck the man's broad back and he slumped to the ground, eking out nothing more than a quick, sharp cry.

Nash raced over to Mira, who lay there, gasping for breath between coughs as she rubbed her throat. He knelt beside her, his own throat swelling with an emotion he couldn't describe. "I'm here. You're okay," he rasped. Yet as he helped her to her feet, he caught a glimpse of several Elite Reformers stepping onto the edge of the hundred-yard-long lawn.

"You have to run, Mira," Nash said.

A quick glance to the side and her eyes widened. With a stifled cry, she stumbled toward the trees just north of where they stood. Nash followed a ways behind her, repeatedly turning to keep their enemy within his sights. There was no way he was going to let her do this alone – and there was no way he'd let anyone stop her.

Chapter 38

Her throat ached inside and out as Mira tried to draw breath through it. She ran westward toward the home and life she'd left many months ago. Repeated looks over her shoulder told her she'd lost the Elite Reformers, but she'd lost her friends too. Her stomach ached with guilt as she swiped at the wetness on her cheeks.

"I have to keep going," she whispered. The Enchiridion was the only thing she had left…and that meant she had to get to her childhood home before her father did. And if he'd died back there? The LAW would search his house for clues and they'd find the letter she'd sent him – which would be her death warrant.

With the edge of town now behind her and one giant hill left in front of her, she slowed up to rest against a tree. Leaning back, she put her hands on her knees and tried to catch her breath. She closed her eyes against the pain and the tears – neither of which would ease up.

But then a thought popped into her head. What if she could rescue her friends before the LAW took them to the Stint? Mira looked up the hill toward her house, and then toward Pillar. That's when she saw him - the man in the hooded sweatshirt who'd saved her. She gasped, pressing a hand against her bruised neck. "Wh… wh… what do you want? Who are you?"

"I want to make sure you don't go back there."

She recognized his voice. "Nash?"

He removed the hood. It was him alright, but who was Nash Montgomery really? And why had he saved her? There were so many things she didn't understand and her brain was too jumbled to make any clear decisions. She raised her trembling chin. "Leave me alone," she said.

"Not an option," he said, latching onto her wrist.

She struggled to get away, but he held tight, swinging her around so that her arm was twisted behind her back. "But I need to save my friends!" she cried out.

"Your friends are already on their way to the Stint. And *we* are going to your house to find the Enchiridion, or their suffering will be for nothing."

"*We* are not doing anything together." She lunged ahead, but he had a firm grip on her.

Pulling her back against him, his lips brushing against her ear, he said, "If you give me a chance to explain, maybe you'll change your mind." She could feel the rapid beat of his heart against her left shoulder blade and the warmth of his strong presence behind her. How she wished that she could trust him! But taking him to find the Enchiridion could be a trap – one that could lead to her capture and to the Enchiridion getting into the wrong hands.

"I won't believe what you tell me anyway," she said.

"You should." He swung her around to face him, his hands now cupping both of her upper arms. "Think about it, Mira," he said in a stern, low tone. "I already know where to look for the Enchiridion because you are the Benefactor's daughter and Elites know where their superiors live." He lowered his gaze, the grim look on his face affecting her almost as much as his words. "And yet I nailed, and quite possibly killed, the Benefactor with a metal bar to save you – and then I found you so that we could find the Enchiridion together. You can trust me."

The truth was staring her in the face, but could she except it? "I did paint you with me," she whispered, wanting to believe him, wanting to ignore that niggling in her brain that kept insisting it was all some sick trick.

"Are we in this together then?"

One thing she was sure about – he could get the Enchiridion on his own. He didn't need her for that. "Why *didn't* you just get it on your own?" she asked.

He reached up to caress the bruised skin along her neck. "I feel this strong connection to you – like doing anything without you is useless." His brows knitted tightly. "And then when I saw you." He paused to swallow. "I almost lost you, Mira, and I never want to go through that again."

His words eased the last tendrils of doubt. "We'll do it together then," she said, "if you promise to explain Freetown when we're done."

"I promise." He smiled tenderly, lowering his gaze and then his lips. Gently pressing them against hers, he paused there, the only movement a slight trembling. It was almost as if he was sealing the kiss into his memory. Then he pulled back and took her hand. Clearing his throat, he looked up the hill. "What's your plan once we're inside?"

"We'll go in through the front door," she said, starting up the hill toward her house. "It opens up to the stairs," she explained. "The first room on the right at the top of the steps is mine."

He followed close behind, never letting go of her hand. She couldn't get over how good it felt to trust that he was on her side. "Anyone in the house?"

"It's doubtful they'd be there to investigate yet. And my…the Benefactor is pretty confident in his own power, so he never had guards, but I suppose it wouldn't hurt to be quiet anyway."

They hiked the rest of the way in silence. Stopping at the plain metal gate, Mira punched in the code. The lock clicked open. "We'll grab the Enchiridion from my closet, then we'll get it back to The Compound and figure out what to do with it, okay?"

"Sounds like a plan," he said, opening the gate for her.

They went through it, and then wound around to the front of the house. After typing the word *perfection* into the code box, Mira opened the plain tall door. A barrage of feelings enclosed her as Nash shut it behind them. She glanced to her right, half expecting her dad to come stalking out of his office. But everything was stiflingly quiet.

"Are you okay?" Nash whispered.

She nodded, but as she looked into the dining room on her left and saw the window that overlooked Pillar, flashes of memory flooded her mind. Her mom had been with her when she'd had an episode, her last one in this house. And then her mom had taken her to Freetown, where Nash had been. She caught Nash's gaze.

"You can trust me," he said, as if he'd read her mind.

"I, ah…" She frowned, the consequence of trusting an Elite with the Enchiridion cementing her feet to the floor.

She had to turn away from the look of hurt in his eyes.

"I've been meaning to give you this," he said. Reaching into his pocket, he pulled out a key and handed it to her. "This is the key my mother had gotten from the woman who claimed it unlocked the Enchiridion."

His gesture doused the rekindled doubt. Tucking it into her pocket, Mira smiled at him. "Shall we?"

His relieved grin made her feel amazingly optimistic. "After you," he said, extending his arm toward the stairs.

She took them two at a time, anxious to get the Enchiridion in her hands and to start her life for real. Pushing aside the worry about her friends, she turned right when she got to the top of the stairs. Four steps down the wood-planked hallway, she stood in front of her bedroom. She hesitated only a second before going inside.

Not wanting to get trapped in any of her childhood memories, she ignored the empty coldness of the room and headed straight to the closet. She switched on the light and glanced over at her shelves. There was the purple elephant trunk poking out of the corner shelf, just like in her vision. Heart pounding, she looked up. Her shaky smile broadened when she saw the pillar of fire matching her tattoo painted on the ceiling tile. "It's here, Nash," she said in an excited whisper.

Nash shouldered his way into the tiny closet with her and looked up. A smile spread across his handsome face. "Ready for this?" he asked her.

"Way past ready," she said.

He reached up to push on the ceiling tile she would've needed a chair to reach. The two by four foot piece of composite slipped right out of the interlocking metal grid. As he tilted it to the side, an oversized envelope dropped right into Mira's hands, the corner of a painting peeking out of it.

For a moment, she stared at it, disappointment shoving her heart down to her toes. "It's not the Enchiridion," she said.

He squeezed her shoulder. "It might tell you right where it is, though." He flicked at the painted corner.

"You're right." Heart hammering, she pulled on the edge of the canvas. But Nash grabbed her hand before she could get it out. "What?"

He pressed a finger over his lips. That's when she heard it…footsteps, and they sounded like they were almost to her door. She grabbed the closet door and swung it shut at the same time the door to her room opened.

"Who's in here?" a man said. It didn't sound like her father. An Elite Reformer maybe?

Mira felt for her knife. It wasn't in her back pocket anymore. She searched for another weapon. All she had was a row of clothes, a purple elephant, and the envelope.

The footsteps drew closer and closer, then stopped. The knob to her closet began to turn, but Nash grabbed it, holding it still.

"I know you're in there," the man said, still working at the door.

With shaking hands, Mira stashed the painting against the wall behind her old clothes. As she turned to prepare for an attack, Nash shoved her down to the floor. She landed hard, half stunned as he flipped the clothes in front of her, making a curtain. Before she could extract herself from the web of clothes, Nash burst out of the closet, tackling their perpetrator. Through the sleeves, she glimpsed the patch on the man's sleeve. He *was* an Elite!

"Stop!" Another voice boomed across the room. A second Elite stood at the door, his gun aimed at Nash, who was on top of the first Elite with his fist raised.

Fear prickled her scalp as Mira clutched a shirt's sleeve and got into a crouch. Peeking around the fabric, she saw Nash's hand drop. He slowly got to his feet. The defeated Elite struggled to get up, spitting off to the side.

"You have caused me so much trouble," said the one from the doorway.

Mira recognized that voice! It was Nash's uncle Rand!

"Let's go," Rand said, and ushered Nash out the door, shutting it behind him.

Chapter 39

Nash trailed behind Rand down the steps. The assisting Elite Reformer followed them, the tip of his gun stabbing into Nash's back. What they had planned, Nash didn't know, but whatever it was, he hoped it would buy Mira enough time to escape.

They turned left, into an office. Flipping up a rug located on the floor behind the desk, Rand exposed a door, which squeaked when he opened it. "After you."

Nash peered down into what looked to be a storm shelter. The Elite nudged him forward with his gun. "Get moving, traitor."

"I'm not a traitor," Nash barked as he stepped sideways down the narrow wooden stairs, but his skin crawled, remembering the motionless body of the Benefactor who was the most important man in their city and quite possibly the world.

Rand entered the dank room right behind him and pulled the string of a single hanging bulb. It clicked to life, bobbling in the dense air, creating a pendulum of shadows all around them. Food-filled glass jars crowded the shelves on one side of the room. The other side held contraband, alcohol, and a variety of medication. Right next to where he stood was a wooden barrel. Inside were various items; a lantern, a rope, a double-sided fork, a vice of some sort, and two metal devices.

"Interesting torture tools, no?" Rand said.

"Why weren't these destroyed?" Nash asked, staring at the barrel, a sick feeling spreading through him.

Rand reached into the barrel and pulled out a lantern. "A guy named Burt Guyver recommended we keep them. He's a mastermind in how to use them to our advantage, too."

Nash recalled what Mira had said about him…that, combined with what he'd found out about the guy in Freetown, told him the guy wasn't someone to be trifled with. "Why would you listen to a 'Cord?"

"He's so much more than just a 'Cord – he's the brains behind the LAW, and he knows how to get things to go our way," Rand said as he lifted the lantern so Nash could see the lamp's open bottom. "Now take this for instance. During the war, Mr. Guyver strapped this against a shackled rebel's stomach." He flipped it back upright. "And see here at the top?" He pointed to a coiled filament. "This is a heating element. When a rat is trapped inside the lantern cage here, its natural instinct is to escape the heat so they burrow through the victim's body." His gaze zeroed in on Nash. "Mr. Guyver mentioned that Mira doesn't like rats."

Nash lunged, grabbing the heinous thing and smashing it onto the ground. The glass shattered, but he stomped on it too, bending the housing until it was unusable. Then he swung around, needing to unload the fury and fear pulsing through every fiber of his being, only to come face to face with a gun pointed right at his face.

"Now sit." Rand said, pointing to a chair beside the desk tucked into the far corner.

Seeing no other option, Nash did as he said. Rand looked up at the Elite who'd remained up top in the office. "He's ready to work with us," he said, "Check the house and report to me if you find anyone. Then, you can head back to Pillar and check into the Center."

"Yes, sir," the man said, closing the hatch. The room darkened, and so did Nash's hope. His uncle was crazy and with the Elite searching around the remainder of the house, Mira wasn't safe.

Rand crossed his arms over his chest. "So tell me, did you find the Enchiridion?"

Nash's nose flared as he fought for calm. "No."

"I want the truth," Rand said, strolling over to the desk.

"It's the truth."

Sitting down on the edge of the desk, he said, "Would you change your answer if I gave the order to torture Mira?"

The heartlessness of his uncle's threat sent shivers down his spine. His hands flexed, opened, then fisted. "A...a painting of the Enchiridion was supposedly hidden here. I came to find it."

"With the information I'd gathered, I figured that already. What I need to know is if you found it."

Nash didn't answer. Terror was trying to claw its way to the surface. How could he get them out of this mess? His mind scrambled for answers.

His uncle stared at him for so long, Nash began to sweat. "Is the painting actually here, or did someone do something with it?" Rand asked, standing, his left hand in his front pocket.

An idea popped into Nash's head. A diversion...he needed a diversion. "It's not here anymore."

Rand lifted an eyebrow. "Let's just say I believe that." He walked around the broken glass to the corner where a rack of wine bottles stood. He pulled one out. "Then I suspect you either ate the evidence or you had a partner that got away." He positioned the wine bottle on the edge of the desk, twisting the label to face Nash. "This is a good year. Good for the stomach and for the nerve."

Nash's stomach cinched up, knowing that the many ways this could end would not be something he'd be able to live with.

Taking a corkscrew out of the desk drawer, Rand twisted the curled metal into the wine bottle's cork. "So where is she now, hmm? At the 'Cord's base where you've been living since the accident?"

Nash sat up straighter. How did he know? "I don't know where she is."

Prying the cork from its glass prison, Rand flipped over two of the glasses sitting on a wooden plate atop the desk. "And if you *did* know her whereabouts," he said, his eyes narrowing, "I sense you wouldn't tell me. Am I right?"

He gritted his teeth, trying not to let the panic overtake him. "You're wrong," he lied. "I'll work with you on this, uncle. I only want what's best for Pillar." The last part was true at least.

Pouring the rich burgundy liquid into the goblets, he offered one to Nash. With a shaky hand, Nash took it.

"I *do* believe that, but I think you're very misguided on how to go about it. The signs we are taught to look for are all there." His uncle took a swig of the wine. "You've fallen in love with the girl, haven't you?"

Instead of answering, Nash took a giant gulp of the very berry-dense liquid. It burned all the way down his throat.

"Hmm. I guess that's answer enough." Rand swirled the drink in his hand. "You want to make a deal to keep her safe?"

He looked at his uncle. He knew way too much, and, if the torturous threats were any indication, he would do anything to get his way – or have Burt Guyver do it. "I'll make a deal," Nash growled.

"I kind of thought you'd say that." Rand put the goblet down and went again into the desk drawer. He pulled out a piece of paper and began to write. "This is a contract between you and me. One that, if you sign it, I will personally guarantee that," he paused to stab a period at the end of a sentence, "I will not harm Mira."

With each scratch of pen against paper, Nash's chest grew heavier and heavier. And when his uncle finally handed the contract to him and he started to read it, the air swept from his lungs.

I, Nash Montgomery, agree to wear a LifeChip as I infiltrate the Accordance. Any information about the Enchiridion of Emmanuel, the location of the Accordance, or any other pertinent information the LAW requests, I will relay willingly to them. I will marry Reba, my Compatimate, and my first child will be given to Rand Montgomery to raise as he sees fit.

Signed:_____ Date:_____

The paper trembled in Nash's hands as he fought to hold himself together. "I understand that marrying Reba to me, your nephew, will give you the political advantage you need." Reba was the only child of the leader of another surviving settlement, a leader who was in negotiations with Pillar to form an alliance called Unified World Organization. Nash cleared his throat, but he still had trouble getting the words out. "But why would you want my first child?"

Rand handed him a pen. "Insurance." He shrugged. "And because this would give me the child I'd never had – one of my own design."

Nash stared at the tear-blurred words on the contract. "If I don't sign?"

"A while back," his uncle said, "the Benefactor talked to Mr. Guyver about his frustration with Mira. His suggestion?" He paused. "Use this wooden tub here to get her to bend to his will." Rand looked down at the barrel. "She'd be painted with honey and tossed inside it with only her head sticking out. Flies would feed on her, and after days of swimming in her own excrement, maggots and worms would have their turn, devouring her body as she's decayed alive." He looked back at Nash, his face devoid of emotion…no revulsion, no pity, no guilt or delight even. There was nothing. "This contract is the only way you can help prevent the torture that would surely await her," he said.

Closing his eyes, Nash fought the nausea as he dug deep into his mind for solutions. He couldn't come up with anything that ended with him and Mira together. The hurt that slashed at his heart was almost unbearable, but he reminded himself, the main issue here was her safety. Slowly, he put the tip of the pen up to the line. Tears swelled and hovered on the edges of his lower lids as he scribbled his signature across the page. He felt like he was dying.

Rand took the paper from him and laid it on the desk. "Tell me, what's it like to have your heart influence a decision?"

Nash said nothing, but what he felt was worse than anything he'd ever experienced.

Rand pulled a plastic wrapped nano-chip from his pocket and grabbed Nash's limp hand. "You sure you aren't going to miss all those," flat eyes zeroed in on his face, "feelings?"

Nash watched him shoot the LifeChip beneath his skin, knowing that it would change his life forever. He closed his eyes, trying to say good-bye to that world, but it hurt too much. He wanted that life back, but most of all, he wanted Mira.

"We can't wipe your memory just yet, which will be," Rand shook his head, "heartbreaking I'm sure. I wonder how hard it's going to be to play boyfriend, knowing that you're destroying all her dreams and her entire world."

"Stop," Nash said under his breath.

He patted Nash's throbbing hand. "I think this low dose LifeChip will be perfect for now. We'll worry about a better fit and your memory cell extraction after you lead us to their hideout…and the Enchiridion." Rand tucked the contract in his pocket and yelled up to the Elite.

Chapter 40

Safely back at The Compound, Mira dropped the pictures, painted side down, onto her pillow, and then wiped at the tears that kept falling. These paintings could give her the answers she'd been waiting and working for, yet now that they were right in front of her, she was too overwhelmed with grief to even dredge up a blip of enthusiasm. The frantic fingers of loss crawled up to her soul and grabbed hold as she remembered hiding beneath the dining room table. She'd been frozen in fear, wondering where they'd taken Nash and if she'd be caught too. She'd watched as one Elite had left the office and had marched out the front door. And she'd chanced a look through the dining room window, seeing his shadowy form as it had headed down the hill toward Pillar. The quietness of the house had prompted her to take a look around – maybe they'd left Nash injured or dead! But every room had come up empty. Not knowing where or how to find Nash, she'd gone back to The Compound.

The deserted compound hid her, but it did nothing to ease her agonizing regret, nor did it give her hope that she was anything but alone. Only one thing could salvage what she'd worked for – a guarantee that the Benefactor and the LAW wouldn't win.

She reached for the topmost painting. With the canvas in her grasp, though, she hesitated, uneasiness twisting alongside her pain. What if the pictures didn't tell her anything? She felt for the key Nash had given her. It was still in her pocket, still affording her opportunities – and a tiny bit of hope.

She breathed in and out, in and out, then hooked her finger behind the edge and flipped the stack over. The top picture was of a guy on a bench, playing a guitar in the moonlight as he stared out over a flower garden. Pressing her fingertips against it, she could feel his loneliness as if it was her own. In fact, it was so real to her that she could hear the poignant tune from his guitar strings in her mind.

She flipped to the next picture – one she recognized. "It's here," she said, a slow grin spreading across her face. She rubbed her eyes and looked again. "The Enchiridion is really here...at The Compound," she squealed. As she bolted for the door, she caught a glimpse of movement out her window. A closer glance revealed something she'd never thought she'd see again. "Nash!"

She dashed out of the room, half running, half tripping down the hallway. She rushed through the doorway and ran around the theater to the back side of the dorms where the garden was. "Nash!" she yelled, waving her arms like two streamers tied to a fan.

The music stopped and he stood, stepping from behind the bench to face her with open arms. Nothing could keep her from running into them. The moment they connected, it was like coming home. He rained kisses on her head as she squeezed him tightly against her. "The house was empty. I couldn't find you," she said through a throat clogged with emotion. "I thought I'd never see you again!"

"Well, I'm here now," he said softly.

"How? How did you get away?"

He searched her eyes in the dimness of approaching dusk, a tiny frown creasing his own. "The details don't matter, but there are a few things that do. Can we talk?"

She'd wanted to tell him about the Enchiridion, but when she looked into his somber face, she decided it could wait a few minutes. "If you need to explain about Freetown and get it off your chest, go ahead. But I trust you, Nash." And she was so, so glad he was alive and well and in her arms where he belonged.

"It's more than Freetown," he said, taking a deep breath and releasing it through tight lips, "But I'll start with that."

Dread crept up her throat and settled there. "I'm listening."

"I *had* been sent there to spy on you. It was part of one of my Elite exams." He cleared his throat. "When Logan went after you…"

She frowned. "Logan was there?"

"He was blond at that time." He brushed his hand down her cheek. "You don't remember?"

She shook her head.

"Well, I stopped him, and not because it was my duty, but because of the strong feeling I got when you smiled at me." He snugged her in closer, but kept his gaze on her face. "I didn't know what it meant, but I decided not to follow you and reported that you'd slipped away while I was dealing with Logan."

"I wish I could remember more of what happened, how I ended up at the Stint, how my mom disappeared." She shrugged. "But I guess it doesn't matter as much now," she said with a smile. "Because I know where the Enchiridion is."

Nash pressed a finger over her lips. "Don't tell me," he whispered. "You just make sure to get it into the right hands. To Pastor Ettreim specifically."

"You're not going with me?" she asked, confused.

He smiled slightly. "It's been your vision. You should get the credit."

"But I don't…" Again, he stopped her words with a gentle touch to her lips.

"There's one more thing I have to tell you before…" He frowned, rubbing his hand up and down her back.

"Just spit it out."

"Um, I know that I'm fairly new to this emotion thing," he said, looking toward the chapel, "but I've also had to go through the agony of almost losing you – several times." He gazed down into her eyes – and she could see passion there, passion for her. "I love you, Mira," he said, "and I'd do anything to protect you." He lowered his mouth to hers, tenderly pressing a kiss to her trembling lips. "Say you believe me," he whispered against them.

She smiled. "I believe you," she said.

"Then let's celebrate by watching the sunrise," he closed his eyes, "before I go."

Mira's heart stopped beating.

Chapter 41

Nash led a quiet Mira to the bank where she'd first told him about her visions. He sat on the dewy grass and gently pulled her down so she was nestled in front of him. With his legs on either side of her, he wrapped his arms loosely around her stomach. She allowed the closeness, one he thought he'd never be able to experience again.

"Why are you leaving?"

He could hear the confusion and hurt in her tone and felt horrible about it. But what else could he do? Even though he'd dug out his LifeChip, his uncle wouldn't give up until he'd found him. "I've decided to go away for a while."

"But...you just said you loved me." She clutched his thighs, her back stiff as she looked out over the rushing water.

"I do love you. And I'm only leaving for a little while," he said, hoping she'd leave it at that.

She didn't. "I'll come with you."

"Not this time," he said, fighting the yes that wanted to come out. "It's just something I need to do."

"I don't get it," she growled, leaning her head back against his chest. She relaxed a little. "But don't think I won't try to change your mind."

His heart ached more than he thought was possible. Was all this pain worth it? "I'm hearing birds again," he said softly. A slight breeze seemed to brush the sky with colors he hadn't before even realized existed.

"They don't seem to have a care in the world, do they?" She glanced up at him. "Lucky birds."

"More like lucky us." He pointed upward. "Before I met you, the idea of a Creator never even crossed my mind. Now, everything seems to point to one…like this sunrise. It's like we're watching the painter as he paints his masterpiece."

She said nothing for a while as they observed the sun's curve of gold dial the sky's color up a notch. Then she asked, "Do you think he paints the future, too? That it was the Creator driving my visions and my painting?"

He thought about that. Since coming here, he could see so much more - and believe so much more. "I wouldn't doubt it. Obviously he's quite talented."

"I don't know if I'll ever have another vision, though," she admitted.

The pinks and oranges were starting to turn blue. "Why do you think that?"

She twisted to look up at him. "I refused to believe the one that painted you beside me in my closet. I thought you'd convince me that you were trustworthy, even if you weren't, and that you'd ruin everything."

He held very still, hoping she wouldn't find out the entire truth…ever.

She frowned and looked back out over the water. "I was actually having another episode and yelled for it to stop, that I didn't want it." Circling her finger on his knee, she whispered, "It disappeared."

"Maybe it's for the best," he said, not wanting his secrets to be revealed to her that way. They sat there together for several minutes not saying anything. But then he remembered this was the last time he'd ever talk to her. "That first day, when you brought me here, you really opened my eyes to a whole new world. Thank you for that," he said softly.

She found his hand and squeezed it. "I made you close them, actually. And not having a LifeChip does that to a person anyway."

"I keep thinking, if I'd stayed in the hospital that day, I would've gotten a new LifeChip." He waved his hand toward the sky that was now dialed to brilliant because of the sun. "And I would've missed out on all this." He leaned down so that he could whisper in her ear. "I would've missed out on you." He couldn't help the tremor in his voice or the tears in his eyes. LifeChip or not, the way he felt, right here, right now, was more overwhelming than any feelings he'd had thus far. "I'd love to hold onto this forever."

At his confession, she turned to him, his name on her lips. It was the most beautiful sound he'd ever heard. Kneeling in front of him, she captured his mouth with her own. The feeling of their perfect connection consumed him…made him believe for a moment that things could be different. But then someone said his name.

Uncle Rand.

Chapter 42

Mira gasped and scrambled to her feet. Rand Montgomery stood not more than three feet away, two Elite Reformers making bookends on either side of him. A woman in a bridal gown hovered right behind the group…Nash's Compatimate. Mira's heart dropped to her toes.

"Well, well, well. Isn't this just a lovely scene?" Rand's hand was on the X4 hanging from his belt.

Nash edged in front of Mira and she was too stunned to do anything but stand there and stare at his broad back. "What are you doing here?" he asked.

"You know why I'm here, nephew. Or did you forget about the contract you signed."

Nash turned to look at her over his shoulder. "It's not how it looks."

She wanted to believe him, but one Elite was inching closer and she couldn't help but feel she'd walked right into a trap. Her heartbeat swooshed in her head like the rushing water behind her. She let go of Nash's shirt and took a step back.

"Let her go, uncle," Nash said, still looking at her, begging her with his eyes.

Think, Mira, think! Only her mind was numb, her body shocked into stillness.

Rand waved at the second Elite. "Get her and let's get this over with."

Nash wedged himself between her and them. "You promised you wouldn't harm her."

"It won't be *me* doing the harming," his uncle said. "Besides, I don't remember anything written about that on the agreement you signed."

Nash's fists clenched, the action confusing Mira even more. What agreement had he signed?

"You had to realize it would be like this," Rand said with a shake of his head.

"No!"

Mira didn't know if the anguished look on Nash's face was feigned or not, but her hopes were fading fast.

"And you, young woman, had to know that Nash's loyalty is with us," Rand said. "Did you know he agreed to marry Reba *and* to lead us to you and the Enchiridion?"

Mira whimpered, her heart and dreams shredded completely in an instant. And she knew that no matter how hard she tried, they'd never find their way back together. The only hope she had left was the Enchiridion. She was so glad she hadn't told Nash where it was. But how could she escape? Five against one weren't good odds. After a quick look, she realized she only had one chance. The water.

Swinging around, she paused to look up to beg the mysterious Creator for protection, then dove in.

The cold liquid smacked against her face and embalmed her body with liquid ice. Shock held her motionless, but the current wasn't waiting for her to move. It sucked her under and swept her along its winding path. If she could get to shore and to the chapel, she could finish this. Kicking her legs as hard as she could, she fought to reach the surface. If only she'd looked at all the paintings…then she'd know how this all would end.

Chapter 43

Nash lunged toward the water to go after Mira, but one of the Elite Reformers tackled him to the ground. The point of a gun pressed against his temple. "Sit up and put your hands out in front of you," the Elite ordered. Nash couldn't die until he knew Mira was safe. He obeyed. After the cuffs were slapped on his wrists, Rand said, "We made a deal and you aren't going back on it."

Nash stared down the rushing river, his insides screaming with a sickening terror. Could Mira even survive the current? And if she did, would he ever get a chance to explain? "Written or not, the deal included Mira's safety," he shouted. "I won't work with you otherwise."

Rand grunted. "Go after her," he ordered the Elite beside him.

"Yes sir," the guy moved along the riverbank, in the direction of the current.

Storm clouds built around them like multiplying cells, reminding Nash that there were things he couldn't control. But there were some things he could. His silent tears whispered his good-byes even as his mind shifted back to what needed to be done. He loathed his uncle – hated everything he stood for. And he was going to make sure the Enchiridion wasn't destroyed if it was the last thing he did.

Rand yanked Nash to his feet. "We'll get you fixed up and back to normal – after the wedding."

But Nash didn't want Pillar's normal any more. And he was *not* going to marry someone he didn't love. He ground in his feet, his mind scrambling for a plan.

"Come on." Grabbing the crook of Nash's arm, Rand dragged him toward Reba, who clutched the corner post of the bridge's railing. Her wedding dress flapped in the wind, but *she* seemed unflappable. How had he ever thought that a Compatimate was a good thing?

"I won't marry Reba. And you'll never find the Enchiridion."

His uncle's laugh was forced. "Ah. That's where you're wrong." Rand looked down the raging river where Mira had disappeared. "Your lover-girl left her paintings in her room, so we know where the Enchiridion is. And as far as the marriage?" He yanked Nash onto the swaying bridge. "I have my ways of making things happen – and that includes ridding myself of any obstacle." Rand grabbed the railing, trying to keep his own balance.

Nash understood the threat. And talking his uncle out of the forced marriage was impossible. Yet Nash *could* use the undulating bridge to his advantage. He waited for his opening.

"You," his uncle said to the Elite, "get the paperwork out of the jeep."

One less body to worry about, Nash thought as the young man strode to where the vehicles were parked beside the Daly Theater.

His uncle spoke up again, his voice raised over the sound of the rushing water. "Do you, Reba, take this man in marriage, according to, and abiding by the laws of Pillar?"

"I do," she said.

This couldn't be happening! Nash felt like he was going to vomit.

"Do you, Nash, take this woman in marriage, according to, and abiding by the laws of Pillar?"

Nash couldn't say it. He stared down at his hands, cuffed in front of him. There had to be another way.

His uncle's eyes narrowed. "There's a chance Mira's still alive, you know. If you don't follow through with your agreement, there will be *no* chance she'll stay that way."

Nash looked over his shoulder toward the Elite who had just closed the jeep's door, papers in hand. Shifting his gaze down the river, Nash glimpsed the top of Mira's head break through turbulent surface, then dip below once again. His hope flared. "I do," he said, though it was barely a whisper.

"I didn't hear you, nephew."

"I do," he said more loudly.

Rand smiled. "I knew you'd see it my way. Let's go to the chapel for the...wedding reception. You can sign the papers there, and watch me retrieve the coveted Enchiridion. Then we'll take care of all of the loose ends."

He should've known! Pain and anger became Nash's only friends and he wouldn't let his uncle win without a fight. "Aaaah!" he yelled, swinging his cuffed hands at the side of Rand's head. The metal edge split the older man's flesh, the slice exposing glowing white skull and gushing blood as he fell back against the roped-railing. Nash's own momentum tossed him forward. He landed on his right side and slid across the water-doused planks. Getting up onto his elbow, he looked back to see his uncle's feet skid beneath the rail as his bloodied hands grabbed for the rope. Rand managed to snag it and hung, one-handed, with his feet dragging in the turbulent water. Reba clung to the opposite rail as she tripped along, thankfully moving back in the direction of the jeep.

Nash staggered to his feet and barreled ahead, intent on getting to the chapel. Halfway up the bank, his foot slipped and he landed face first on the grass, his cuffed hands twisted painfully beneath him. With a growl, he got to his feet again. A quick look behind him spelled trouble. The Elite was racing toward the bridge, papers waving in one hand, a gun drawn in the other.

Surging ahead, Nash's gait turned awkward. His cuffed hands swung oddly, and his right knee felt like his side had after he had been shot. "The chapel is only twenty steps away...ten...five...," he croaked. Hope surged as his hands connected with the door handles. He managed to open one, and dashed inside, slamming the door behind him. He looked around for something to create a barricade and spotted a narrow cross that hung on the wall between the first two stained glass windows. Racing over to it, he used his head to knock it from the wall. He knelt to pick it up and hurried back to the entrance. He shoved the longest part of the cross through the two wooden handles, effectively barring it.

"Now the Enchiridion." He jogged up and down the aisles, looking for something that would need a key. He charged toward the pulpit, running his hands along the top, the sides, the back. And there it was - a locked panel fronting its base. On it was an inscription; *"I am the way, the truth, and the life."*

He dug his fingertips into the crease of the panel and pulled. He tried again and again. It wasn't going to work. He needed something to pry it open. As he stood up to look, lightning flashed through the window, followed by the rumble and crackle of thunder. In his mind's eye, Nash could see Mira struggling to get to the surface of the water. His senses said she was still alive. He had to save her. But as he ran toward the back door, it swung open.

"Funny how I keep showing up, huh?" his uncle said, wiping blood and water from his face.

Reba poked her head around him. "Hello, husband."

Chapter 44

Mira struggled to the surface and gulped at the air. It was so hard to keep her head up and the strong current kept dragging her back under. Her lungs felt like they'd burst any second. She pushed toward the surface again and caught a glimpse of where she was. The boundary fence crossed over the river not far ahead, and it wouldn't be long before she'd be swept beneath it and carried out to sea. If she could reach the bottom of the fence…hold onto the rungs…maybe she'd have a chance of surviving.

The water swallowed her again just as lightning flashed over her head. *Please help me, God,* her mind cried as she swirled closer to the fence. She shoved her hand upward and trembling, kept it held above the water. Within moments, her fingers connected with the metal and curled around the crossed wire. The barbs at the base of the fence scraped at her face as the current banged her rag-doll style beneath it. She could barely hold on.

Then she heard a voice carry across the water. "She's probably drowned by now," he said. "But we need to be sure. Boss' orders. You check out the fence. I have to gather up the papers that I dropped and then help pick the lock in the chapel."

They knew where the Enchiridion was hidden! The fight inside Mira drained and her angst sat like a tumor inside her chest. Yet for some reason, her fingers stayed locked into place. Not even when the Elite reached the fence did she let go.

"Don't make me come and get you," he said, staring at her from the bank.

When she didn't respond, he grunted then inched down the sloping embankment, holding onto the fence as he moved toward her. "Leave it to a 'Cord to make things more difficult than they have to be."

Now right beside her, a death grip of his own on the fence, he tried to pry her fingers loose one-handed. When that didn't work, he grabbed his weapon.

Mira squeezed her eyes shut just as his gun crashed down onto her knuckles. She cried out in pain and let go. The current dragged her under before the Elite could grab her. She tumbled along to the opposite side of the fence where again, the flow of rushing water swept her away.

One hundred yards further, the current thrust her into a rotting post jutting above the surface and her shirt caught on a barbed twist of wire that was wrapped around it. She latched onto the water drenched wood and tried to rip her shirt off the barb. The sharp metal point sliced the skin on her finger, but she managed to work herself free. With quick shallow breaths, she looked back toward her pursuer. The Elite, still holding onto the fence, was working his way back to the bank.

Mira scooted up higher on the post, the motion tilting it toward the bank. "Please, please, please," she rasped, swinging her foot out in a wide arch just barely touching the shore with her toes. She rocked back hard again and again, praying the extra boost would get her to land. On her third try, it did.

She crumpled on the muddy ground, trying to calm her shaking limbs and catch her breath. Out of the corner of her eye, she noticed the Elite. He had started his methodical climb over the fence to come and get her. She needed to run! But then she saw something weird. The fence…it was buzzing with an eerie soft blue-green glow. *Crack!*

Mira jumped at the ear-splitting sound and slammed her arm across her face because the flash was so bright and hot. After a moment, the buzz drifted away, leaving a dead silence. She chanced a peek through the crux of her bent arm. The Elite had dropped to the ground, unmoving.

Stumbling along the shoreline toward him, she finally made it to the fence. Peering through it, she observed that his hands were burned and blistered, as were his feet - which no longer wore shoes. His shredded shirt gave her a view of his back where the lightning bolt had left faint raised red marks that feathered out in a whispery fern-leaf pattern.

After tapping the fence to see if it was hot and finding it cool to the touch, she climbed over it and dropped down beside the man. As she reached toward his neck to feel for a pulse, his eyes popped open. With a yelp, she scrambled backwards. Frantically, she scoured the area for some kind of weapon and spotted a stone with jagged edges wedged in front of one of the leaning fence posts. She lunged toward it, gouging at the dirt-packed boulder to work it free. With the skull-sized rock in hand, she rushed over to the Reformer, who was fumbling for his gun. She swung her weapon up over her shoulder.

Chapter 45

Rand frowned at the Elite who had just come in a few moments ago with the papers, but without Mira. Nash was relieved, but not when he heard the guy's next words.

"Larry spotted her hanging onto the fence at the edge of the property. He should be back with her shortly."

Rand grabbed his own shoulder where the fabric was seamed. He yanked down hard, tearing the threads. "Don't just stand there. Make yourself useful," he said to the Elite.

"What do you want me to do?"

Rand pursed his lips as he wriggled the sleeve off his arm. "Why don't you sit Nash down and give Reba the X4." After tying the sleeve around his head to stop the bleeding, he added, "Then you can help me get the lock open."

The Elite ushered Nash to a nearby pew and shoved him backwards. Nash dropped onto the wooden bench. Reba, his new "bride", sat down on his left. The Elite Reformer handed the projection pistol to her. She waved it at Nash. "Got him covered," she said.

The guy grunted then left them to help Rand with the lock.

The gun Reba held seemed like it was too heavy for her. It kept bobbing up and down in her loose grip. Reba was drenched and her dress was full of grass stains, but she didn't look angry. She didn't look happy, or anxious, either. She didn't look…anything. How could he ever have thought that was a good thing? Nash imagined Mira, how different it would be if she was the one wearing the gown, sitting beside him. He pressed his cuffed hands against his aching chest, wanting more than anything to go after her.

"It doesn't have to be like this, you know," he whispered to his new wife.

"It's better this way," she said. She poked the barrel in his direction. "You do dumb things without a LifeChip."

He sat up straighter, but tried to relax his shackled hands between his knees. Maybe she knew more than he'd thought. "So how did you know where to find us?"

Bending over her right knee, she gathered up the hem of her dress with one hand. Her other hand swayed a little, but the gun it held remained trained on Nash. "Doesn't matter how we found you. The only thing that matters is that this will be over soon and our Unified World Organization will be underway." She squeezed the soggy fabric, letting the water drip onto the floor. The pistol twisted sideways as she worked.

Nash leaned back against the pew to get out of the line of fire, should it go off – either on purpose or by accident. "You want that to happen?"

"Of course. I've been promised a lot of things when it does," she said, putting the dart gun down so she could wring out the material with both hands.

Nash stared at the pistol sitting a little over an arms-length away. "What have you been promised? I should know since we're married."

As Reba sat back up, Nash latched onto the gun. Before her mistake even registered, he jumped in front of her, smacking the heel of his palm against the flat of her forehead. Her head snapped backward, her short thick hair deadening the thump against the pew. She was unconscious and his uncle and the Elite were so involved in their task, they hadn't noticed.

It was time to move, and yet as he looked at Reba's lifeless form, he felt sick. *You practiced this move many times in Elite training, Nash,* he reminded himself. *And you also know how to, and did, use just the right amount of pressure to knock her out. Her brain won't hemorrhage.* Still, he had to be sure. He felt for a pulse, somewhat reassured when it, and her breathing, continued on at normal rates. Clutching the gun, he made a quick decision and charged toward the platform.

Chapter 46

Mira's throat squeezed painfully as she stared into wide-eyes that were already glazed with pain. Her arms trembled with fatigue and her fingers ached as she clutched the rock over her right shoulder. *It's him or me,* she told herself. She cried out, raising the stone higher like a lumberjack with his axe. Yet as it swung downward, she angled the thrust. The rock missed the guy's head, but just barely.

She didn't wait around to see his reaction, but sprinted across the lawn toward the chapel, hoping the group was too busy to be looking out the windows. After slipping more times than she could count, she tried to convince herself that she wasn't exhausted and alone, and that she hadn't been betrayed by someone she thought she loved. She didn't buy her own words, but they helped urge her on and she finally made it to the windowless northern side of the chapel.

She paused a moment to catch her breath and jammed her hands into the pockets of her sopping wet jeans. Her fingertips grazed the key Nash had given her, and a spark of hope flared to life. Mira smiled, even though her heart and body felt like they couldn't go on.

"You can do this," she whispered, "You have to do this." What else did she have? Nothing...not one thing. Hugging along the chapel's outer stone walls, she wound around the structure to the side that faced the ocean. Standing on her tiptoes, she dared a peek into the one clear window.

Mira's breath caught, watching Nash's broad back as he walked toward the pulpit. She ached with a longing that she knew she shouldn't be feeling. She tore her gaze away from him to survey the rest of the sanctuary. She couldn't see his uncle or the other Elite, but she did spot Nash's bride sitting, relaxed, in one of the pews. Mira's mini-burst of strength and resolve fled, her forehead dropping down to rest against the cold stone wall. Small breaths, she told herself. In, out...*one*, in, out...*two*, in, out...*thr*...A hand clamped across her mouth and an arm swept around her waist. She clawed at them both, kicking her legs as she thrashed and twisted.

"Shh. It's me. Logan."

She stopped fighting. He let her go.

She turned around and stared at him, wondering if Nash's words were true about him being in Freetown. She guessed it didn't matter. Many from the Accordance were known to have visited Freetown. She leaned against Logan, hugging her friend tightly, unable to hold back the sob that had been sitting in her throat since Nash's uncle had shown up.

Logan ran his hand over her wet hair. "It's okay. I've got you now."

She calmed down a little. "How did you find me?"

"It's a long story that I'll have to tell later. In case you haven't noticed, it's not safe here anymore." He glanced at the window. "I've got a car waiting for us right outside the gate."

"But the Enchiridion," she whispered.

"We'll come back for it – with backup. Vaughn and Kya are meeting us at our new hideout."

The air seemed easier for her to breathe in. And she did still have the key. "How did they escape? Were they hurt?"

"They're okay, but we need to move!"

Mira wasn't about to try saving the world on her own again. She just didn't have it in her anymore. "Lead the way," she said.

Logan took off in the direction she'd come. As they neared the fence line they'd follow to the entrance, her legs felt as heavy as her heart. Was she doing the right thing, leaving the chapel? Her stomach roiled with indecision, and apprehension. Because her alternatives were few, Mira forced herself to keep going. A couple of minutes later, they stood on the bank where the fence crossed the river. She stopped to stare at the rock she'd thrown…and the slight depression in the ground where the Elite had been.

"Something wrong?"

She frowned, scanning the area for the guy. Nothing. "I'll explain later."

"You've been through a lot, haven't you?" Logan said, giving her a pitying look.

"That's an understatement," she grumbled, reaching for the fence.

"But you're resilient," Logan said, tugging at the chain around her neck. "Just like the necklace I gave you."

She didn't want to talk about necklaces, or anything else. "Let's get out of here."

"As you wish," Logan said, and followed her over the rushing water to the opposite bank. "Besides. It'll all be worth it in the end, Mira," he said with a smile. "Trust me."

Chapter 47

With the dart projector pistol squashed between his palms and resting just in front of the metal cuff, Nash approached the pulpit from the far right, close to the back door. "Back away from there, or I'll kill you both," he ordered.

Rand and the Elite froze in their crouched positions behind the pulpit.

"Now."

The men got to their feet. "We got it open and we have the Enchiridion. Think about what that means," Rand said.

"It means nothing until I find out the truth."

"I'll tell you the truth – and it won't be some made up nonsense about a stupid book that teaches you about a Savior that will fill you with hope, joy, peace, and love."

"You've read it then?" Nash asked, surprised.

"Parts of it…and it's for gullible people, people who are easily misled." He took a step closer. "Now hand over the gun."

"No. You hand over the Enchiridion."

"Okay. Okay." He glanced at the Elite. "Get the book."

As the man knelt back down to get it, Rand hurtled across the platform. Nash squeezed the trigger. *Thwack*! The dart sank into his uncle's bare shoulder. Rand cried out as he fell to the ground. "You're making a mistake," he yelled. "And you'll regret it!"

The Elite stood up, the Enchiridion in his hands, his eyes on Nash. "Don't shoot me."

A glance at the rotating rear barrel of the pistol assured Nash that he had a few darts left. He lifted it so that it was aimed at the man's shoulder. "Lay the key for the handcuffs on the floor, along with the Enchiridion."

Squatting down, the young man laid the key on top of the Enchiridion and he slid them both toward Nash.

"Now take the cuffs you have on your belt and put them on yourself."

He reached for them, but grabbed his gun instead. As he shifted the barrel toward Nash, the back door swung open with a loud bang. The Elite, that had been tasked to retrieve Mira, stormed in. His hands were covered with blisters, and bright red singe marks oozed on his exposed chest.

"Larry?" The other Elite dropped his gun to waist height, a slight frown on his face.

Larry's hands flexed as he aimed his own gun at his partner. "Take the book and run," he said to Nash. "I'll cover you."

"What are you doing?" the Elite spat. "Your LifeChip must have shorted out."

"Doesn't matter." Larry had swept in closer, cornering the guy. "I owe her."

Nash didn't understand, but hope flickered in his chest. He grabbed the key off the Enchiridion and worked it into the keyhole on his left cuff. "What does that mean – you owe her?"

"Just get out of here. Now," he said.

Free from his cuffs, Nash grabbed the Enchiridion. The cornered Elite lunged, trying to get past Larry. Nash scrambled for the back door, the book clutched against his chest. As he slipped outside, he glanced back at the skirmishing pair. Larry now sat atop the downed Elite, frothing at the mouth as his hands shook him with forceful relentlessness.

Not wanting to waste the opportunity he'd been given, Nash ran. The humid air was stifling as he raced toward the bridge, his eyes and heart desperate for signs of Mira. There were none. His small spark of hope withered, his pain resurging tenfold. Crying out, he let all the anguish from the depths of his soul echo around the grounds of The Compound. He wanted her back! "I'll get this where it belongs, Mira," he promised, wishing she could see that he wasn't the traitorous guy she'd thought him to be. Nash crossed the bridge, carefully shutting out the memories and bolted down the road toward the dorms where his uncle had claimed he'd found her paintings.

Once inside, he ran directly to the only room that had its door open. He knew it was Mira's once he stepped inside. He half expected her to be sitting at her desk, but of course she wasn't. And it felt hauntingly empty and cold without her. The paintings were scattered across the bed. Nash gathered them up, trying to get a glimpse of each one as he did. The one stuck to the bottom of another, he peeled away and put it on top of the pile. It was a painting of him – and in it he was rifling through Mira's desk drawer.

Nash went to the desk and opened the drawer. There, inside, was a small box containing three vials. The box was labeled Alpha-Kinase. He shoved the box into his pocket and tucked the paintings into the Enchiridion. Then he headed out to the jeep, hoping they'd left the keys in it. They had.

Nash glanced at the book so many had risked their lives for. Beneath the words Enchiridion of Emmanuel was another title. It said *Holy Bible*. Carefully, he slipped it under the passenger seat. Getting into the driver's seat, he reached for the door handle. That's when he heard a curdling scream.

He bolted out of the vehicle yelling. "Mira!" He ran in the direction the sound had come from. The scream came again. It was coming from the chapel. "I won't let them hurt you," he cried out, envisioning Mira taking on whatever was in between her and where the Enchiridion had been hidden.

He vaulted across the bridge in two leaps, his lungs burning as he sprinted to the chapel. He whipped the doors open, his gun raised, prepared to save Mira no matter what it took. Only the scene wasn't the one he'd hoped or expected to see. Larry was laughing madly as he chased a squealing Reba around the pulpit.

"Stop right there," Nash said, his heart pounding with disappointment.

Larry paused to look at him. Nash could see the mix of overpowering emotions that came with withdrawal from the LifeChip – lust, fear, confusion. The Elite had been right. Whatever had burned the guy had destroyed his

LifeChip. "What do you want?" he barked. "I let you go…and with that stupid book, no less."

"You said earlier that you owe her. What did you mean? Who were you talking about?" Nash asked, hoping to get some information out of him, something that might lead him to Mira, if she was even alive.

But Reba's whimper lured Larry back into his emotion-filled haze before he answered. The guy lunged for the dress-hindered woman, who'd have no chance against him.

Nash pulled the trigger. The man squealed with pain, clutching his leg as he dropped to the floor. "Why did you do that? I helped you!"

"And I helped you. You're going through drug withdrawal and emotional over-load. I know. I've been there myself. When the dart drug wears off, you'll have a little more control of yourself," Nash said. He approached the downed man, who was already fading out of consciousness. "Who were you talking about? The girl you owe?" he asked again as he knelt down beside him. Larry opened his mouth to answer, but then his jaw went slack, his eyes glazing over.

Nash rolled the vial of the Alpha-Kinase between his palms. He didn't want Larry to remember where the Enchiridion ended up, and yet, he wanted to find out what he knew – if it had been Mira he'd been talking about. Protecting the Enchiridion would be what Mira would want, but even thinking about losing the chance to get valuable information that could reunite them was something he longed for more than anything.

"Where did you put the Enchiridion, Nash?" Reba asked.

He didn't answer her. She already knew too much. All of them did. Holding the vial in Larry's nostril, Nash squeezed it lightly, waiting until the man breathed it all in. Then, trying not to think about what he was giving up, he walked over to where Rand lay sprawled on the floor and used the second vial on him.

"What are you doing?" Reba asked.

"Making them forget." He went to the Elite Larry had attacked. The marks on the guy's neck were clear signs he'd been strangled, but he felt for a pulse anyway. There was no heartbeat beneath his fingertips. That left Reba.

"This is going to turn out well after all," Reba said, smiling at him as he approached. "Now we can both take credit for finding the Enchiridion, husband."

Hearing the word on her lips disgusted him, but, he realized, she was really a pawn in all this too. "Oh, you won't be taking credit for anything. And I won't be your husband." He pulled the last vial out of his pocket and snagged both her hands in a viselike grip.

"Don't do this, Nash," she said, shaking her head wildly as he brought the vial to her nose. He managed to keep it in her nostril, only she kept breathing through her mouth. She had spirit, even with her Lifechip. "You should consider getting rid of your Lifechip," he said, forcing her to the floor. She screamed and fought as he sat on top of her, but no one was around to hear. He pinned her arms to the ground with his knees, but could do nothing about her vicious kicks against his back but ignore them.

"You're a traitor," she growled right before he covered her mouth with the palm of one hand.

With the other, he shoved the vial back into her nose. "And you won't even remember it," he said, counting the seconds as she breathed it in.

She struggled still, but this time, his efforts succeeded. She was out.

Chapter 48

Mira wanted to get as far away from town as possible, but as they drove into Pillar from the north and worked their way toward the city center, she began to feel uneasy. "So where are we going?"

"Actually, we're already here." Logan whipped into the parking lot of the Reformer housing unit located across from the COO. "It's the perfect place to hide when you think about it – and it's part of our new plan."

There was no way Vaughn and Kya agreed with this hair-brained idea. "You're joking, right?"

Logan chuckled as he pressed a LifeChip against his skin so that it stuck. "Nope. Let's go," he said, and got out of the car.

He's crazy, Mira thought, watching him as he came to her side. He looked confident, but as he opened her door, whispers of doubt taunted her. Logan hadn't always made the best decisions. Of course, neither had she. "There's no way I'll pass any inspection," she said.

He grabbed her hand and yanked her to her feet. "You're my new recruit," he said, dragging her along toward the stairwell.

She stumbled along behind him. "But my picture...the Sweeper captured me on camera." She dug in her heels. "There's got to be a better place."

Logan sighed. "Wait a sec." He went to the Renovatron Custodial open-door closet and wheeled out a three by three bin that held a few dirty towels. "Hide under these and I'll wheel you inside."

"Isn't there a check-in crew? And the Renovatrons take care of all laundering needs. You're hardly a Renovatron. It's not going to work."

He shrugged. "I'll just say it's a special case. We need to diagnose the towels for bacteria. They won't really care, Mira."

He was probably right. Swinging her leg over the edge, Mira lowered herself inside. After curling into a ball, Logan adjusted the towels over her.

"This is going to be a bit bumpy. I don't have the key to the elevator," Logan said.

Thump, thump, thump. The wheels clunked against each concrete step as Logan yanked the cart up them. "Lucky we only have one more flight to go," he said.

"You're telling me," she grumbled, each jarring step jamming her teeth together.

"Just keep thinking about how they'll never guess to look for you here. And once Vaughn and Kya get here, we'll be one big happy family again."

"I guess," she said.

Logan rammed the cart through a door. Mira could hear the check-in crew, but the sound was muffled so she couldn't tell exactly how they'd responded to Logan's lies. They must have believed him, and must have checked him through because they were on the move again.

"Here we are," he said, thrusting the cart into one of the Reformer apartments. "Sorry we had to take the long route past the lab." He flipped the towel off her head.

As Mira climbed out of the cart, she frowned. "How did you know where the lab was?"

"I make it a point to know details like that." He walked into the living room.

She trailed behind him, staring out the window he was exposing by opening the room-darkening curtain. The COO was right across from them.

Logan pointed out the window as she approached. "That system is the heart of Pillar."

She frowned. "What do you mean?"

"I mean…" He curved his hands around both her forearms and turned her to face the kitchen area. Between her and the bar was a chair – identical to the one at the Stint. "I am a spy."

Mira squeaked as Logan's grip tightened painfully on her arms. She kicked at him, but he spun her around, cross-linking her arms behind her as he leaned her back against his chest to drag her. "Let me go, Logan. I thought we were friends."

"We could've been more than that," he said, and dumped her into the chair.

Large clamps smacked onto her wrists and ankles. She barely managed to hold back the scream pushing at the base of her throat. Alerting an apartment building full of Reformers was suicide. She tried not to freak out, but her breathing was hard and fast.

"You had a chance to be on the winning side," he said. "I asked you to marry me, remember?"

"But I thought..." she frowned. "Why are you doing this?"

"For this." Logan pulled a piece of paper out of his pocket and held it in front of her face. "And for the Enchiridion of Emmanuel that it talks about."

It was the journal entry that Gabe had given her...the one she'd left at Necropolis. "Where did you get that?"

"Not that it matters much, but Nash had it tucked in his pocket on the ride to the hospital." He laid the page on the desk. "You really shouldn't trust him, you know."

She knew...oh, she knew. Tears filled her eyes even as pain filled her heart.

Logan turned on a small lamp and the computer next to it. "I've been working with the LAW the entire time. Deidre too." He scooted up onto the desk, his legs swinging. The computer hummed to life, its screen flickering.

"We figured out that you were the key to finding the Enchiridion when the Benefactor found you - and your painting of the book - in Pillar Media. We couldn't get rid of you until you led us to it." He shook his head. "Gabe almost ruined everything, by sacrificing his life to help you and Vaughn escape, but I'm *so* smart. Not only was I able to track you and your little group, I was also able to plant myself on the inside." He grinned, only as he stared at her a few moments, his smile turned to a sneer and his eyes hardened. "If you'd have said yes to my proposal, none of this would be happening." He rolled his head as if to stretch his neck…like none of it was a big deal. "But you didn't. And thanks to your lovely necklace, we were able to trace you, your paintings, and the Enchiridion so I, at least, get some of what I want."

The unlocked heart necklace! She wanted to rip it off her neck, but her hands were secured. "So why am I here now? Why haven't you killed me?"

"Insurance," he said, and tapped the computer's mouse.

The Benefactor appeared on the screen. "Got her, boss," Logan said.

"Good to hear, but we have a problem," the Benefactor said, a bandage strapped around his chest area.

She smiled, knowing her hate would show through. "Now *that's* good to hear," she said.

Logan shot her a dark look. "You are really a pain in the butt." Then to the screen, he said, "What's the problem?"

"One man of ours was found dead by strangulation because another Elite's LifeChip had short-circuited from a lightning strike."

Mira's jaw dropped.

"And?" Logan said, jumping off the desk to pace in front of it.

What a heartless monster, Mira thought, amazed that she'd never sensed it.

Her father continued. "And Rand came up empty-handed. No Enchiridion, no Nash Montgomery."

The sunshine seemed to brighten. Again, she smiled, the warmth of hope filling her.

Logan stopped and slammed his hands on the desk. "But they were there, at the chapel. I saw them."

"Doesn't matter," the Benefactor said. "What matters is that they failed."

Hands on his hips, Logan asked, "So what do you want me to do?"

It was the Benefactor's turn to smile. "Make sure Mira's facing the screen."

Logan scooted her closer. "Done."

The camera turned away from the Benefactor to the man beside him.

Mira gasped. Vaughn was strapped to a metal post, his hand between spiked metal plates. The Benefactor grasped a handle directly above it.

"Mira...meet your real dad, one who will be dead if you don't tell me where to find the Enchiridion!"

He paused to let the truth sink in. Vaughn was her dad?

"Tell me where it is!" When she didn't answer, the Benefactor twisted the handle of the device. Vaughn howled and squeezed his eyes shut as the spike pierced his skin.

"Nooooo!" Mira screamed.

Vaughn yelled, "Don't listen to him!" The Benefactor turned the handle again. And again, Vaughn howled out in pain, dark blood oozing down his wrist.

Tears hovered on the edge of Mira's eyelids. "But he'll kill you!"

"Your mom sacrificed her life to save you – and to protect the Enchiridion," Vaughn said, struggling to catch his breath. "I am willing to do the same."

Mira didn't want things to be this way. This was her real father!

Logan stepped beside her and leaned over so that his lips were close to her ear. He twisted his head slightly so that he looked toward the screen. "I'm sorry, dear old dad. Mira's got me to answer to, so your sacrifice won't mean anything."

"Get out of there, Mira. Find Kya, Hayes and Mel. They'll help you," Vaughn shouted.

Logan laughed. "Deidre actually led them all from the band shell to an escape vehicle...which happened to be an actual transport van, so don't count on getting any help from them."

"Enough talk," the Benefactor said, and smacked Vaughn with the butt of a gun. Vaughn cried out, but then was silent, his head hanging.

Stunned, Mira stared at the screen. The leafless tree symbol on the wall above her dad's head taunted her. Her mission...dead. Her friends...taken out, just like she now seemed destined to be.

"Logan," she whispered.

"Yeah."

"I want to save Vaughn...my father." She let the tears fall. "Can you guarantee he'll be safe if I tell you where to find the Enchiridion?"

Logan glanced at the screen. The Benefactor nodded.

"And you'll let me go free?" she asked.

Again the Benefactor nodded. "I can even throw in an island hut for your nice little family."

"Tell me, Mira. Tell me now," Logan said. Rubbing his hands together, he smiled. "I've waited so long for this."

Mira lifted her chin. "The Enchiridion is in the base of the pulpit. And the key to unlock it is..." She paused. Could she really do this? She closed her eyes. More tears escaped down her cheek.

Logan pressed his hands over hers, and when she opened her eyes, his eyes were an inch from hers. And she didn't like what she saw in them. Evil...hate...and death. Hers.

"Turn off the computer. I can't tell," her eyes narrowed, "him."

For a moment, the Benefactor stared at her. Then he said, "I need to take some more pain pills anyway. My chest is killing me," he said. "I'll give you twenty minutes at the most. If I don't hear anything back from Logan, Vaughn is dead."

Wandering over to the desk, Logan shut off the computer. He turned around, looking so smug that she wanted to slap him and worse.

"You know you're doing me a favor," he said, tilting his head toward the screen. "I'm going to get all the credit now." He chuckled. "You sure you don't want to switch to the winning side? We'd make great partners."

She yanked against her bindings. "I'd die first," she said.

He cracked his knuckles. "You'll get that wish if you don't tell me where the key is ASAP."

"The key is..." The rest of the sentence she whispered so quietly, he took a step closer, and then another.

"Quit playing games, Mira."

"It's…" She couldn't do it. She couldn't let the Enchiridion get into the enemy's hands. In her heart, she knew it.

Logan shook her chair. "The key is where, bitch?"

She closed her eyes. "It's in my front right pocket."

With a grin, Logan jammed his fingers into her damp jeans. He wiggled and shoved for several moments, then finally pulled his hand back out. "There's nothing in there," he growled, and slapped her hard across the cheek.

The sting was followed by a throbbing heat and a realization that she had nothing to bargain with. "The key was there. I swear."

Seething, Logan lifted his hand again to strike. She squeezed her eyes shut, bracing for the blow, but it didn't come. A click of the apartment door did…and so did Nash's voice. "Touch her again and I'll kill you."

Chapter 49

Nash buzzed with energy at the realization that Mira was truly alive, but he had to deal with Logan before he could go to her and explain.

"How did you find us? How did you get in here?" Logan stuttered, clearly taken aback.

Nash kept the X4 trained on Logan. He had one dart left. "Your computer was running back at The Compound – the one tracking Mira and her necklace. And I know where the Reformers keep their spare keys. I *was* one, you know."

Logan's hands clenched. He was too close to Mira, which made Nash extremely uncomfortable.

"The Benefactor has Vaughn," Mira said in a rush. "Tell us where they are, Logan."

"Not until you cough up that key." He glanced at Nash. "Shoot me, and her daddy's dead."

"Alright by me. Pillar needs a new leader."

"Not the Benefactor…Vaughn," Logan said with a sneer. "Vaughn's her real dad, idiot, and without the key, she'll have no heartwarming reunion with him."

Whoa! Vaughn was her dad? That upped the stakes considerably. "I'll make a better deal with you," Nash said.

"Stop playing games. I NEED THAT KEY!"

Mira clutched the armrests beneath her hands. "The key was in my pocket after I escaped the river." Her voice shook. "I swear I don't know where it is. Please don't do this, Logan."

Logan's eyes narrowed as he stared at her. "You're telling the truth." For a moment, he seemed lost in thought, forgetting that anyone else was there. "Maybe it's in the car," he muttered.

Nash edged closer to him, his leg bumping…a laundry cart? He glanced down and smiled. "I know where it is."

Logan's eyes snapped up. "Tell me."

Head tilting toward the cart, he said, "In there."

Logan smirked, sending Nash's trigger finger into twitching fits. "Hand it to me."

"Don't, Nash. We can find another way." Mira's nose was running, her eyes black from smeared makeup and she had a welt on her cheek.

Nash was done dealing with this loser. He shoved the cart across the room with his foot. It smacked into Logan, who dove in for the key. When he popped back up, it was clutched in his fist and raised in victory.

"Get out. You got what you wanted," Nash said, stepping back against the wall so that Logan could get past him to leave.

"No can do, brother," Logan said, "I don't want to have to worry about you two anymore." Snatching something off the desk behind him, Logan whipped it at Nash, who feigned right, pulling the X4's trigger just as the silver bladed star whizzed past his cheek and sank into the wall behind him.

As Nash straightened, he saw the priceless look on Logan's shocked face as he toppled head first into the bin.

"Get me out of here," Mira said. "We don't have much time to find my dad before the Benefactor kills him." She yanked against the straps that imprisoned her. "But I don't even know where to start looking."

Nash turned the switch on the side of the chair to release Mira.

"They're in the broadcast room in the COO," he said, and pulled out the folded painting he had tucked into his back pocket.

Mira stood up, rubbing her wrists as she took the painting from him. Her nearness made him want to hold her, but a rescue wasn't enough to forgive the things she'd thought he'd done – that he *had* done.

Her trembling hands unfolded the picture. "You recognized it," she said, staring at it. "Another perk to being an Elite I guess?" She walked past him to drag Logan out of the bin. "Help me get him in the chair."

He did as she wished, wanting more than anything to explain everything, to beg her forgiveness, but now wasn't the time.

"It was a dart, right?" she asked, strapping Logan into the chair then going to the kitchen.

"It was," Nash said, watching her as she splashed her face with water and reached into the drawer beside her for a cloth to dab it dry. She was so pretty, he thought, his heart aching.

She hurried back into the living room and stuffed the washcloth into Logan's slack mouth. "That should work." She went to the desk and shoved a folded piece of paper into her pocket. Then she looked at Nash and smiled. "Thanks for rescuing me, by the way."

The smile was the best gift he ever remembered getting. "My pleasure," he said, reaching for her. Only she backed away from his touch. His heart squeezed painfully.

"I don't get involved with married men," she said and brushed past him. "Let's go save my dad." She grabbed a Reformer's hooded sweatshirt off the coat hooks, and slipping it over her head, bolted out the door.

Chapter 50

Mira stood behind Nash at the back of the COO building. A parking lot sprawled between them and the band shell where she'd been just last night. She didn't know what had all happened with Nash, but she was glad he was here. "The Benefactor admitted he was in pain," she whispered. "At least we have that going for us."

"That's not all," Nash said, swiping the card - the one with his Compatimate's picture - in front of a scanner bolted on the wall next to the door. "Good. This still works."

Her stomach balled up when he slid his *wife's* cameo into his pocket.

He slipped inside the building, pulling Mira along with him. His hand felt warm and sure.

"This stairwell is used only in an emergency evacuation and leads to all the floors," he said, "another thing we have going for us."

She looked up at the flights of concrete steps. "And the broadcast room is on what floor?"

"The top one." He paused on the bottom step, but didn't turn around. "I know you're probably exhausted," he began.

That was putting it lightly. "I'm fine."

His shoulders slumped. "Just let me know if you need to rest – or if I can carry you or whatever."

That he didn't say leave her behind boosted her energy...a little. "Thanks."

She climbed the stairs behind him, pulling herself ahead with the metal rail. Their feet made little sound against the steps, but her breathing was ridiculously loud to her ears.

Nash must have noticed, too, because he stopped to lean against the rail. "Give me a minute," he said, but she knew it was for her sake because he was breathing easily.

She accepted the gesture, knowing that she'd need her strength and wits once they confronted the Benefactor. Sucking in a deep breath through her nose, the stale air layered with the smell of metal filled her lungs.

Nash's gaze travelled over her face. She shifted uncomfortably. He looked like he was about to unload something heavy, so she said, "I'm ready to go again," she said.

He nodded and continued up the steps. Two flights from the top, he paused to look over his shoulder. "I don't have time to tell you everything, but," he whispered, "I want you to know that I made my decisions based on the fact that I love you. That love hasn't changed, nor will it ever."

Her lips parted, her eyes moist with tears. "We'll talk later," she said. But it wouldn't change anything.

He brushed her hair from her face before planting a quick kiss against her cheek. The connection tingled.

"Ready?" he asked.

She nodded, not able to speak past the yearning that constricted her vocal cords.

They hurried up the last flights of stairs and snuck into a hallway. It was dimly lit, clean, but its drab walls seemed to close in on her.

"She has five minutes, dear old dad." The Benefactor's voice floated through a door that was ajar, halfway down the hall.

Mira's fists clenched as she pushed ahead, slinking toward them. She peeked inside the room. The Benefactor stood in front of an open window just to the right of her father, who was still tied to the metal post. Vaughn's bloody hand remained clamped in the spiked vice. His face was pale, and he groaned often between head bobs. Mira clutched the door jamb to keep herself still.

"Think she'll come through for you – or that she'll leave you like her mother did?"

Vaughn straightened his head and spat. The wet blob hit the Benefactor right on the side of the face, resulting in a look of revulsion as he quietly wiped his cheek. "I'm going to get the Enchiridion that your dear Addie's mother hid from me – and I'm going to burn it…in front of you, in front of the cameras. I will control Pillar completely, and then I'll leave your pretty daughter to Burt Guyver." He smiled, his eyes blazing an inferno gold. "For some reason he's taken with her."

Nash pushed her to the side and barged into the room, his 4X raised. "Step away from Vaughn," Nash said.

The Benefactor stared at him then held up what looked to be a scepter dotted with various sized holes, steam pouring from them. "That gun won't do you much good without darts," he laughed, "but this…" He swung the scepter toward Vaughn and laughed. Glowing liquid shot out, landing on Vaughn's bare chest.

Vaughn yelped, his skin sizzling as it started to melt.

Mira shoved past Nash to get to Vaughn, who was imprisoned in his scalding pain. "Stop!" she yelled, swiping at the boiling, sticky liquid even as she tried to untie him.

Vaughn screamed again, thrashing his head back and forth as he struggled frantically against his bindings.

"Logan has the key. Logan has the key," Mira wailed, still brushing at the molten liquid, her fingers blistering. Vaughn's piercing cries broke off into muteness. His head lolled to the side, his face deathly pale.

"I don't believe you," the Benefactor said, aiming the scepter at her face.

Nash dropped his gun on the floor. The clatter drew the Benefactor's attention. "I have the key. I grabbed it out of Logan's hand before we escaped." Nash held it up. "Let Mira and Vaughn go – and the key is yours – along with the Enchiridion's new location, which I scratched onto the surface of the key."

"No," Mira cried. There had to be another way, she thought, working to release Vaughn's hand from the vice. Vomit worked its way into the back of her throat. This was because of her!

Nash stalked toward the Benefactor, stopping about three feet in front of him. "If we have a deal, put the scepter down." The key dangled as he held it by a slim ring between his thumb and forefinger.

After a moment, the Benefactor laid the apparatus against the wall behind him. It blistered the paint beneath its smoking orb. He turned back to Nash, confidence smearing into his heinous smile. "Give it over," he said, holding out his hand again.

Nash stepped forward, lowering the key toward the outstretched hand with aching slowness.

"Don't do it!" Mira pleaded, judging the distance to the scepter. The Benefactor was closer. Helplessness squandered her innovation, her emotions raging at the injustice all the while crying for a chance to get Vaughn the medical attention he needed.

The Benefactor licked his lips, watching the descent of the key. Then he swept his hand upwards, knocking it from Nash's hand. It clanked, bouncing across the floor and landed near the window. Mira, Nash, and the Benefactor all scrambled for it, but Nash snatched it up first. Using the sill, he got to his feet. Dangling the key between his thumb and forefinger, he said, "Come and get it."

Boiling with rage, the Benefactor lowered his head and charged. The force of his body thrust Nash into the wall, but Nash managed to grab onto the sill and extend the key out the window. Looking like he was about to drop it, Pillar's leader lunged, snagging the end of the key. "I win," he roared. But Nash let go of the key and moved over. The Benefactor tottered, then flipped out of the screen-less window. His curdling scream ended with a thud of finality.

Mira slapped a hand over her mouth as the reality of what just happened hit her. "Is he dead?" she whispered. Vaughn stirred.

"No doubt, but…" Nash poked his head out the window. "Hey! You," he shouted. "Stop right there!"

Mira rushed to the window. With a sick twist of her stomach, she stared at the motionless man that, until today, she'd thought was her father. Another man stood just beyond him and smiled when she caught his gaze. "Burt Guyver." She shuddered and took a big step back.

"Thanks for the key!" he called out as he walked away.

Nash grabbed the phone sitting on the desk and called the ambulance.

"Aren't you going after…the key?" Mira's breathless voice sounded weak and pathetic as she stared at the retreating Burt Guyver.

"No. We're going to get Vaughn the medical attention he needs, then we're going to visit Pastor Ettreim."

"I don't understand," she said, holding Vaughn's hand as his dull eyes stared up at her.

"The Enchiridion isn't in the chapel anymore," Nash said.

"*What?*"

"I brought it to the pastor."

"How did you…" her voice died away. She was thrilled and yet she felt like she'd just stopped spinning around in circles and had landed on her butt. It was over? It was really over?

Nash shrugged. "The Elite picked the lock and I took the book off his hands." He went on to explain what had happened in the chapel, how Larry had showed up out of nowhere to help.

"He was struck by lightning," she said. "I was going to finish him off with a rock," she admitted, "but I couldn't do it."

"Well, he was grateful." Nash smiled at her. "Only he won't remember it – and neither will Rand or Reba, thanks to the Alpha-Kinase you had in your desk." The phone rang. Nash answered it. "Yes…okay," he said, then leaned toward Vaughn. "Your ambulance is parked outside. They're on their way up," he said softly.

Vaughn reached up with his good hand and rested it on Nash's shoulder. "Thank you," he said. "Thank you."

A few moments later, the door swung open, and Kya, Mel, and Hayes burst through it, all wearing scrubs. When Kya saw Vaughn, she started to cry. As Mel and Hayes worked to get him on the stretcher, Vaughn rasped, "I don't know how you managed, but I'm really glad to see you."

Hayes strapped his brother into place while Mel smeared ointment on his blisters. "Turns out Deidre likes being chipless," Hayes said, moving to the front of the stretcher. "It wasn't hard to strike a deal with her."

Mel moved to grab Vaughn's feet and after a nod from Hayes, they lifted their patient between them and moved out the door toward the elevator at the end of the hall. "He'll be back to normal in no time," Mel said over her shoulder to a still crying Kya.

Kya worked up a watery smile. "Vaughn's normal, or actual normal?"

Hayes laughed. "Who's riding in the ambulance with us?"

"I am," Kya called out, racing after them.

"We'll take our own vehicle," Nash said, moving closer to Mira.

She ducked beneath his keen gaze. "Reba will probably want to see you, too." She crossed her arms over her stomach to hold herself together. "And I bet she'll be deliriously happy that you're the hero...once she gets rid of her LifeChip."

"I'm not married, not officially and not otherwise." He took a step closer so that if she reached out she could touch him. "Most certainly not in my heart," he said and took another step. The tips of their toes were touching. "And if you recall the Alpha-Kinase? The fake ceremony of the forced marriage won't even be a blip in anyone's memory."

She wanted to believe him. Her heart thudded a resounding *yes*, but so much had happened she didn't know if she could trust it.

Nash lifted her chin to look at him. His eyes were glazed with an intensity that spoke volumes. "I thought I'd lost you," he said as he reached out to caress her cheek. "I never want to go through that again." Brows pinched together, he added, "And I'm not the one who betrayed you."

Her constricted throat held her speechless.

"I love you, Mira. And I'm asking you for a second chance."

Tears welled in her eyes as trembling hands grasped his shirt to pull him closer. "Yes."

He whooped and scooped her up so they were face to face. With a grin, she ran her hand along his scruffy jaw - and then she kissed him soundly on the lips.

After a moment, his hold loosened, and he lowered her to the floor. "Before we go see Vaughn at the Accordance Hospital Unit, I want you to see this." He reached into his back pocket and handed her two folded pieces of paper. "Take a look."

Frowning, she unfolded them.

"It's the last of the paintings I took from your room."

In the first picture, Nash was holding her in front of him, his arms around her waist. They were looking toward a stage where musicians performed in front of a banner of the Enchiridion of Emmanuel. She was smiling. He looked like he was singing in her ear.

"I can almost feel the energy of the crowd," he said.

"And from us," she said.

He took her hand. "Look at the next one."

She flipped to the second painting. In it, she and Nash were sitting together on a blanket with a picnic basket on the grass beside them. Their hands were clasped as they read the Enchiridion together. John 3:16 to be exact. "For this is how God loved the world: He gave his one and only Son, so that everyone who believes in him will not perish but have eternal life." And behind them was the city of Pillar. And it was ablaze with color and life.

Epilogue

Several boats pulled up to Enab's docks beside theirs, but Mira only had eyes for the group of people who had gathered on the shore. Was her mom there among them? She could only hope and pray that she was.

Out of the corner of her eye, Mira saw Nash jump from the boat onto the sand. She could feel his eyes on her, so she tore her gaze away from the crowd to look at him. What she saw in his eyes was love…love for her…and a confidence she didn't feel. He held out his hands. Mira made her way to the front of the boat. Her legs shook – from the rough ride, she told herself – but she managed to jump from the bow to the shifting beach sand. Nash gathered her in his arms, only she squirmed to get away. "I need to go look for my mom now."

"I know sweetheart, but just let me hold you a minute."

"But…"

"I want you to believe that whatever we find here, or don't find, everything is going to be okay."

Could she believe that?

Nash kissed the top of her head. "Know it and believe it, Mira. Remember what we read this morning?"

She did. It was from the Enchiridion of Emmanuel. "Don't worry about anything; instead, pray about everything. Tell God what you need, and thank him for all he has done. Then you will experience God's peace, which exceeds anything we can understand. His peace will guard your hearts and minds as you live in Christ Jesus." She let the words of Philippians 4:6-7 wash over her and after a moment, she relaxed against Nash. A sense of peace came over her.

She squared her shoulders and glanced up at his handsome face. "Everything *will* be okay."

He smiled, and grabbed her hand to lead her down the shore along the throng of curious people.

They walked for what seemed like a mile. "I don't see her, Nash." The anxiety was building up again.

"There's a lot of island to cover," he said, his own gaze scouring the crowd.

"I know…but it's not quite the way I pictured it would be." Of course, the reunion with her mom was only in her imagination. Her visions had not returned.

"Maybe it will be better than expected."

"Maybe." It would be hard to beat the spectacular one she had in mind, but who knew?

As they neared the enormous rock that marked the end of the shoreline, Mira's heart sank. "Where next?" she asked, trying to remain hopeful.

Nash tilted his head to the right, toward a thick line of palm trees.

She nodded. Hand in hand, they took the path that Mira assumed would lead them to one of the island villages. But before they got far, a high-pitched cry pierced the air. They paused. The wail came again, pain-filled, as if a woman was being tortured to death.

"Over there." Nash pointed to an area shrouded by thick brush and took off at a run.

Mira scrambled after him, her heart racing faster than her legs. "I hope we're not too late," she rasped.

Nash burst through the wall of foliage, only to stop short. Mira pushed in front of him and gasped. "A baby?"

It was the most beautiful thing she'd ever seen! There, shrouded in beautiful fauna, was a natural spring pool that looked like paradise. Across the water, on the edge, sat two women – one, holding a newborn infant against her skin, the other hovering over her as she rubbed the baby's tiny body with a square of fabric. After resting another piece of fabric over the baby, the woman turned.

Mira couldn't believe her eyes. "Mom?"

"Mira?"

It was really her! Mira squealed as she raced along the water's edge to where her mom stood. "I never thought I'd see you again!"

"I never doubted...but I'm glad to see you!" Her mom hugged her, laughing.

Nash joined her and her mom, and as they stood there together, Mira felt that her heart had truly found its answers. Everything had fallen into place and she was just where she needed to be.

Afterward

Thank you for reading *Pillar's Fire!* I hope you enjoyed getting to know Mira and Nash and that you are curious about the true and transformational power of the Enchiridion of Emmanuel. The Enchiridion (pronounced \, en-, kī-' ri-dē-ə n\ ) is defined as a book containing essential information on a subject. Emmanuel means God is with us. Although the Enchiridion of Emmanuel is a fictitious name for the Bible - the Word of God - it emphasizes two facets of its beauty: God's Word as a guide and God's Word being His Son who came to this earth to show us who God is and to sacrifice Himself to save us from the evil that keeps drawing us closer to the abyss.

Bible verse favorites for this book:

Psalm 119:105 - "Your word is a lamp to guide my feet and a light for my path."

John 14: 5-7 - "No, we don't know, Lord," Thomas said. "We have no idea where you are going, so how can we know the way?" Jesus told him, "I am the way, the truth, and the life. No one can come to the Father except through me. If you had really known me, you would know who my Father is. From now on, you do know him and have seen him!"

2 Samuel 6:14 – "And David danced before the Lord with all his might, wearing a priestly garment."

Song favorites for this book:

Come Alive – Lauren Daigle

This Is Living - Hillsong Young & Free

God's Not Dead – Newsboys

A Personal Journey of Discovery:

The Bible is God's gift to us…it's the way we can uncover who we really are and how we fit into this thing we call life. It is rational, experiential, relational, and relatable too! And it's filled with powerful stories of God's love and grace, and His work in and through even the worst of us. We can trust that the Bible is true for many reasons – historical accuracy and reliability, archeological proof, scientific observations, and prophesies, to name a few. Dig deeply for the truth with all your heart and the truth will be revealed to you.

Jesus is the most awesome, fascinating, loving, and brilliant person to have walked the earth. It shouldn't be surprising, because, as Jesus Himself claimed, He was God in the flesh. What's just as amazing is that His perfectness and His perfect love (shown by sacrificing His life for ours) keeps all of us who trust in Him from life-ending destruction as He scoops us up into His arms of saving grace.

Michelle Heisel

is the author of The Heart of it All series. Her passion to bring heart into a dark world inspired the ideas for Pillar's Fire, the first book in the series. Her love for people begged her to write the story. And her desire to use her talents to revive and restore our world for the good of all, drove her to share this novel with the world. The mother of three sons, Michelle lives with her husband in SD.

Go to **michelleheisel.com** to find out more about the author and to read an excerpt from Wormwood's Water, the next book in The Heart of it All series.